For :

Best wishes,

Dick Stoudevig

9/5/03

Dangerous Encounters

A novel
By Richard Standring

Copyright © 2003 by Richard Standring

ISBN 0-7414-1574-7

Published by:

PUBLISHING.COM

519 West Lancaster Avenue
Haverford, PA 19041-1413
Info@buybooksontheweb.com
www.buybooksontheweb.com
Toll-free (877) BUY BOOK
Local Phone (610) 520-2500
Fax (610) 519-0261

Printed in the United States of America

Printed on Recycled Paper

Published July 2003

Other Published Work:

Hustle (1989)

Dangerous Dancing (2000)

Dangerous Relationships (2001)

This novel is dedicated to all those readers who read **Dangerous Dancing** *and* **Dangerous Relationships** *and have asked for more. This is the third Nick Alexander novel in the Dangerous trilogy.*

Special thanks to Sharon Templeton for her editorial help, suggestions and continued encouragement.

A word of caution -- This novel, like the other two novels in this Dangerous trilogy contains some adult situations and language that might be offensive to some readers. Fiction mirrors real life in almost every aspect, good and bad. However, it is not my intention to deliberately offend anyone. I apologize to anyone whose sensitivity has been tested.

RAS

Going to a Party

Zipping down the highway,
Better use the by-way.
Top down, go around,
Turn it up, hear the sound.
… Going to a party!

She's a fox,
Big boom box,
Really rocks,
Knocks your socks,
… Really likes to party!

Music blaring,
Really tearing,
People staring.
She's not caring.
… Going to a party!

Comes the Fuzz,
Needs a buzz,
Likes her style, gets a smile.
Makes her stay, for a while.
… So they can party!

By Richard Standring

Prologue

"Hey, Terry, d'ya know what day it is?" The sheriff asked.

"Yes, Sir, it's Friday," the deputy replied.

"And d'ya remember what I like on Friday nights?"

"Yes, Sir, I need to find an occupant for the Honey Hole." It was a ritual between them lately, each knowing what the other would say, yet they said it any way as if it were some sort of law to be enforced, or code to be honored.

"You got it! So get your sad ass out there and find me a cute one. The younger she is, the better. Last one had a face that'd stop a watch. She was a real three-bagger! No more like that, understand?"

"I'm on my way. I'll call you if I find anything inter-esting out there." There was no way of telling what he'd find when he stopped someone for speeding. Every once in a while he got lucky and stopped a naïve young lady in a hurry to get somewhere, who didn't know much about the law, wasn't carrying much cash and wasn't from Harmon County. Most of the 9,320 residents of Harmon County knew about the speed trap on the by-pass, even those who didn't drive.

"You do that," the sheriff said leaning back, putting his size 8-C shiny black cowboy boots up on his gray metal desk.

1

It was a routine that had been going on for the last four years. The sheriff knew he could trust Deputy Terry Wolfe to keep his mouth shut and his eyes open. Consequently Deputy Wolfe was always tagged for working the speed trap on Friday afternoons. In return, he got extra time off whenever he wanted it. He also collected overtime for special assignments, like escorting a funeral or directing the parking and departures at the special Saturday night auction at Bovis Tinch's barn.

The Honey Hole was a special cell behind the office. The fold down bunk had a newer, thicker mattress, a toilet seat on the commode and a small hole drilled in the wall so that the sheriff, or one of his deputies, could peek at the occupant without being seen. A religious plaque mounted on the wall in the cell camouflaged the hole.

This particular cell was around the corner from the other two holding cells and isolated from the entrance. A high window in the hallway outside the cell provided natural light; however, the glass was double insulated to keep inside yelling from reaching anyone outside. It was just one of many small considerations Sheriff Billy Hargis had installed to insulate the citizens of Paradise Valley from undesirable elements that occasionally discovered this quaint little town in Harmon County, located in rural Southeast Tennessee.

To Serve and Protect was the motto on the side of Sheriff Billy's white four-wheel drive Ford Bronco. It remained anyone's guess just who Sheriff Billy Hargis served, or what it was he was protecting, other than his reputation and a few selected friends and one very important county commissioner. At five feet seven inches, he was just below average height. With cowboy boots, he gained another inch and a half. His secret wish was to be taller. He had the juice and big ego to make demands of others, without any thought or regard for the consequences. He ruled Harmon County, and Paradise Valley since there wasn't a separate police force.

The town wasn't large enough to support that many law enforcement officers.

Most of the tax-paying citizens who voted remained comfortable knowing the sheriff was looking out for them... and himself, of course. They understood there had to be a few extra privileges so he could make ends meet every month. The sheriff's position didn't pay much in wages, but the perks were good.

Most of all, Sheriff Billy enjoyed the respect, and sometimes fear, that others had of him. In many ways he was a *big* man in a small town. It was rare that anyone would challenge him to his face. On those few occasions when it happened, pain in one form or another, and public embarrassment usually was the consequence to the offender.

* * *

The new Going to a Party rap piece had Cindy's head nodding to the cadence. Her left hand on the wheel while her right hand was tapping her bare right thigh. It was a perfect Friday afternoon for driving through one of Tennessee's more scenic valleys. Cindy Mae Stevens was on her way to spend the weekend with a girlfriend in nearby Chattanooga while her mother was on her way to Las Vegas, hoping to get lucky. Cindy's friend was also alone for the weekend. Her parents were spending a few days somewhere in the Smoky Mountains playing golf.

Because Cindy had the top down on her 11-year old Mustang GT convertible, it was necessary to crank up the radio to hear it above all the wind and road noise. An ex-boyfriend had installed resonators on her dual exhausts, producing a noticeable roar guaranteed to turn a few teenage heads in her direction. The over-amplified radio with extra speakers also got a lot of attention.

Being 17, having just a year left in high school, and having her own wheels, plus an understanding mother, for Cindy, life just didn't get much better than that. Cindy named her '91 Mustang, "Charlie" so she wouldn't feel foolish when she talked to it. At 4:15 on a sunny Friday afternoon, Charlie was carrying her down Highway 67 at about the same speed... 67 mph.

The by-pass around Paradise Valley becomes a divided four-lane highway, beckoning motorists who are in a hurry, and who don't want to wait at the town's three stoplights along Main Street. Mountain ridges to the east and west protect the valley area, providing an awesome view on a clear day. The Pine Fork River runs a zigzag course parallel to Highway 67, both running on a Northeast to Southwest line from Rockwood to Chattanooga. From the air, one can see another parallel line of railroad tracks. The tracks swell out to become a storage and switching yard at the southern edge of town before continuing on to Chattanooga.

Just about anyone who drives through this area regularly knows that Paradise Valley is notorious for its radar traps along the by-pass. Because of the nearby river, fog can quickly develop, providing a good excuse for lowering the speed limit to 55 mph, even though the four-lane highway looks similar to most Interstates. This false appearance can lull strangers into driving faster, thus contributing to the economic welfare of Harmon County and Paradise Valley. Just before the by-pass begins, a half-hidden sign warns motorists to reduce speed. Farther down the road in clear view is another sign:

Welcome to Paradise Valley, population 4,116.

A few bullet holes in the sign are a subtle clue that there's more going on here than just a quaint village atmosphere with a few antique shops and an old courthouse on the square.

4

Chapter 1

As soon as Cindy saw the flashing lights behind her she slowed down, hoping the police car would pass her. When she realized it was following her, she pulled over, turned down the radio, still tapping the wheel in sync with the music. She was hoping a nice smile might get her out of whatever jamb she was in. It usually worked, if the cop was young enough. What she didn't need was another speeding ticket. Because it was summer, she was wearing shorts and with the top down, the officer would get a good look at her tanned shapely legs.

"I guess you didn't realize you were in a fifty-five zone. I clocked you doing sixty-seven." Deputy Terry Wolfe was enjoying the shapely legs along with the rest of the young lady's well-defined body. He gave her a big disarming grin. The sunglasses helped hide his stare.

"Is it really only fifty-five? I don't think I saw the sign." Cindy was trying to act nervous and shy. "I'm really sorry, Officer, I'll be more careful, I promise."

"Well we need to do the license and registration thing, so get 'em out so I can see 'em." One time when Deputy Wolfe said those exact words, to an attractive lady he'd stopped, she un-buttoned her blouse and revealed a fantastic bosom that left him short of breath. Ever since that exciting day, he used the exact same phrase whenever he stopped a younger woman, hoping for a repeat performance. This young lady was from a different county, making her a good candidate for the Honey Hole. "And turn off that damned

5

music!" He hated the loud boom boxes the kids played. Sometimes the noise would rattle his windows.

Additional questioning revealed that Cindy's destination was Chattanooga. Deputy Wolfe made her wait while he ran her plate and license. He learned she had two prior arrests for speeding, which meant she wasn't getting off with just a warning. Regardless, that wasn't the plan. He had his special assignment this Friday afternoon, just like most other Friday afternoons. Sometimes, like now, he got lucky and caught a cute one. He explained that the fine would be around $ 175 and asked if she had that much money with her? He hoped she didn't.

"I can write you a check," she offered trying to sound as meek as possible. She was secretly annoyed with the delay. Now she'd be late meeting her girlfriend, Rhonda. They had the weekend planned starting with a party at some cute guy's house that Rhonda promised would be exciting. Cindy caught herself still drumming her fingers on the steering wheel. It was an impatient habit she had and it didn't go unnoticed by Deputy Wolfe.

"I'm sorry, Miss. We can't accept checks or credit cards. Only cash."

"I just don't have that much money with me. I'll have to call someone." Cindy put a slight whine in her voice.

"Okay. Bring your keys and purse." He motioned for her to get out of the car and follow him back to his patrol car.

Cindy suddenly realized she was in serious trouble when he put her in the back seat of the patrol car and called for a tow truck. She felt like she was in a cage. A wire screen separated the front seat from the rear, and the door handles and window cranks had been removed. There was no way she could get out.

"Where are you taking me?" she asked.

"To the sheriff's office. He'll decide how to handle your situation."

"Why can't I just follow you? You don't need a tow truck for my car."

"Can't. It's against regulations. Unattended vehicles get towed whenever they're found on the by-pass."

"Well I think your regulations suck!" She folded her arms and pouted.

Interesting choice of words, Deputy Wolfe thought to himself, being careful not to reveal a smirk. The tow job would net him a fast five, enough to pay for his dinner. And the sheriff would be pleased with this catch. It was just what he'd ordered. The deputy's shift was ending on a high note. If things went as planned, he might drop back by the office later, just to check on the prisoner. Maybe take a peek into the Honey Hole and see what was going on in there.

Sheriff Billy Hargis had been alerted and was waiting for their arrival. He acted polite and offered Cindy a seat next to his desk. The routine was well rehearsed as Deputy Wolfe turned over the ticket, pointing to the remarks section where he'd noted that the driver had not pulled over immediately. Also, the blaring sound from the radio, no doubt blanking out the sound of the siren. The county had an ordinance against excessive noise for this very reason. EMS vehicles needed to be heard before entering an intersection. Anyone playing a boomer too loud would not hear the on-coming vehicle. Deputy Wolfe enjoyed enforcing this infraction and was therefore despised by most of the teenage drivers in Harmon County.

Cindy's slouched position, folded arms and annoyed expression told Sheriff Billy he had a prize catch. This was a spoiled kid, used to having her way, and was about to experience the real world. He took her purse, opened it and dumped the contents onto his uncluttered desk, noting the plastic tampon holder was full. He was amused to also see four foil-packaged condoms.

"I see you're practicing safe sex. Are your folks aware of your sexual activity?" He continued to examine every item slowly while she watched. It was the first time anyone had ever gone through her purse and examined all her things. Even her mother hadn't searched her purse. It was an embarrassing experience.

"Just what is it you're looking for?" she asked, avoiding the question he'd just asked.

"Some kids just invite trouble, know what I mean? Pretty girl like you fits the profile. Here you are, driving too fast, not paying close attention, disturbing the peace and acting uppity about the whole thing. Sort of makes me wonder if you're doing drugs, too. What does your daddy do?" Sheriff Billy was counting the money in her wallet. There was $ 135. She also had several credit cards.

"I wouldn't know. My mother divorced him several years ago. Why, what difference does it make?"

"Well I was hoping you'd help me out here, but you seem to be hanging onto that attitude, so maybe we'll let you go through a little transition period. That will help you contemplate your situation. Then maybe later, you'll be a little more cooperative when I ask you questions. You don't seem to realize yet that you're in a little trouble here, Miss Stevens." The sheriff gave her his best smile, dumped the contents back into her purse and put it in a bottom drawer of his desk, closing it with a hard push to punctuate the situation he'd mentioned.

"Hee, hee, hee," an overweight woman snickered. She was sitting at another desk in the corner. Cindy hadn't noticed her. The woman's name was Eulla Stump. She was the dispatcher, collector of fines, phone operator and confidant to the sheriff. She was one of his loyal followers who did whatever he asked. She also kept him informed on everything she heard when he wasn't around. If she would just apply some heavy blue eye shadow, she could pass for Mimi, the plump actress and co-star on the Drew Carey Show on television. It was her favorite program and proved without a doubt that fat people could be stars.

At 35, Eulla was still single and the prospects for any change in her status didn't look promising. She didn't hide her 185 pounds very well. She did have a pretty face. She knew a lot about the sheriff's activities, his friends and sources of income. It was rumored that she gave the sheriff oral sex however nobody actually believed the rumor.

As long as she kept her mouth shut about what she knew, she had a lock on her job. Because Sheriff Billy Hargis was one of the most important men in the county, it made Eulla's position all the more significant. She took pride in being the sheriff's right arm. She also knew all about the Honey Hole and what went on there. In fact, she'd peeked more than once, enjoying the voyeuristic moments. She considered it one of the perks to her job.

One of Eulla's frequent dreams was being arrested and put in the Honey Hole and later being ravished by the sheriff. She didn't even mind that Deputy Wolfe was peeking from the office on the other side of the wall.

Anytime any *porno-graphical* material was confiscated, Sheriff Billy would leave it in the lower right hand drawer of his desk. That way, when he was out, Eulla would know exactly where to look. The other deputies also knew about the cache and borrowed the reading material from time to time on their way to the toilet, which everyone shared. To complain about anything would have been futile. Sheriff Billy and his cadre of deputies liked things just the way they were, and nothing was about to change. Eulla had accepted that fact a long time ago.

The transition was fast. One moment Cindy was sitting in a hard wooden chair beside the sheriff's gray metal desk, the next she was being escorted by the deputy through a door and down the hallway to a cell in back of the office. They passed two empty cells along the way making what seemed like a u-turn.

"Why am I being held in jail?" Cindy whined.

"Because you don't have enough money to pay the fine," the deputy said.

"But isn't a judge, or someone supposed to talk to me first?"

"Yeah, but that won't happen until Monday morning."

"You mean I'm going to be spending the whole damn weekend in this rotten place?"

"That's not my decision, Honey. Maybe the sheriff will go soft on you. Work something out. But not before you change that attitude. He's the one person around here you don't want to piss off, if you get my meaning."

"I need to call my friend and tell her where I am. She's expecting me. She'll be worried when I don't show up soon."

"Okay. Give me the number and I'll call her. As soon as I get her on the line, we'll let you talk to her."

Cindy gave him the phone number in Chattanooga, hoping she wouldn't have to spend too much time here. Her suitcase was still in the trunk of her car. She hoped they wouldn't search it and find the bottle of Jack Daniels she'd taken from home.

Her mother kept several extra bottles around, so it wasn't likely she'd miss just one. Cindy had helped herself to her mother's private stock on several occasions and nothing was ever mentioned.

Deputy Wolfe wadded up the piece of paper with the phone number, keeping it in his pocket. In an hour or so, someone would inform the prisoner there was no answer.

That was the procedure for Honey Hole occupants.

Meanwhile, Harvey Hargis would have the Mustang convertible in his protected yard beside his garage. Harvey was Billy's older brother. He owned two tow trucks. The red one had his name on the side. The black one didn't have any name on it. He used the black tow truck when he, or his son, Bobby Lee was picking up abandoned and broken down, unattended vehicles on the highway, or the by-pass. Harvey had an arrangement with a local chop shop that also posed as a junkyard, outside of town. Unattended vehicles quickly disappeared in Harmon County.

Cindy didn't know it yet, but the towing bill would be $45. Storage was $ 10 per day, or $ 20 overnight. It was a high rate, but anyone caught and ticketed, wasn't in any position to do much complaining. Harvey and Billy had a good thing going. Any deputy who called in an abandoned vehicle to Harvey got a little something extra later that same day. Harvey called it a finder's fee.

The local townspeople never paid much attention to what went on at Harvey's garage, unless they needed repairs.

Strangers didn't seem to stick around too long once they picked up their towed and impounded vehicle. About the only person they might complain to would be the attendant at the Exxon station just outside of town, if they stopped there for fuel. Otherwise they just left town in a hurry, aware they'd been victimized and nothing they could do about it, except be extra careful on their return trip.

At 6:30 P.M., Eulla walked back to Cindy's cell carrying a tray with a glass of milk and three oatmeal cookies with raisins. The rest of the cookies Eulla had eaten earlier.

"Doesn't seem to be anyone answering at that number you gave us. Is there another number we can call?" Eulla asked. She passed the tray through a small access to Cindy. "If you don't like milk, I can get you a soda. The coffee here is terrible." It was her job to appear friendly and learn anything important, so she could report back to Sheriff Billy. Officially Eulla was off-duty. She hung around knowing there would be some interesting action later, she didn't want to miss any of it. Deputy Wolfe had left for the day, but indicated that he might stop back later for a quick peek.

"I hate milk," Cindy complained, taking a sip. She ate a cookie then took another bigger sip. She was trying to remember her Aunt Carol's phone number in Cookeville. She gave Eulla the name and said information would no doubt have the number. It wasn't unlisted. Cindy hated the idea of calling her aunt. She was still hoping the sheriff might let her off with just a scolding. She had already decided to act polite the next time he talked to her. She finished the cookies and milk and shortly after started to feel sleepy. She curled up on the bunk and closed her eyes.

In her dream, Cindy saw the sheriff come into her cell and sit on the bunk close to her. What was he doing? She could feel his rough hand working its way between her legs. Now he was removing her shorts and panties. The dream seemed so real. She wanted to tell him to stop, but the words wouldn't come out. Now he was pushing her legs apart, exposing her crotch and pubis. The sheriff was breathing rapidly, whispering something she couldn't quite make out.

Cindy could smell his sour breath. It was a combination of stale smoke and coffee. He was kissing her and fondling her breasts. She tried to wiggle free, but his weight held her in place. Cindy could hear the springs beneath the thin mattress and feel the undulating motion.

When Cindy woke, she felt groggy. She had a headache and upset stomach and immediately vomited into the toilet. She noticed it was dark outside. She had no idea what time it was, and had to think about the recent events in an attempt to get oriented. She was having a difficult time trying to remember the bad dream she'd had. While sitting on the commode, she discovered her panties were on backwards!

It was 8:30 Saturday morning when Eulla brought Cindy some orange juice and a sweet roll.

"Take my advice, young lady and act polite when you speak to the sheriff. If you get nasty, he can get real mean. You get what I'm trying to say?"

"Yes. Do you think he'll let me go?"

"Sweetie, I can't answer that. Just be nice and maybe he'll go easy on you."

"Did the sheriff come to see me last night while I was sleeping?"

"No, the sheriff wasn't here last night. Why, is something wrong?"

"No, I guess I just had a bad dream."

"Well that's understandable, you being in jail all night. Just remember what I told you. Once you get out into some fresh air, you'll feel a whole lot better."

This time Cindy sat up straight in the wooden chair, hands clasped together, looking down at her knees. Her pelvis was sore. She wasn't expecting her period for at least another week. She tried to put the bad dream out of her mind, but it kept coming back and seemed so real. And there was that distinct scent of sex. She wasn't a virgin, so she recognized the smell when she woke. Sometimes when her mother arrived home late from a date, Cindy could smell that same musky odor, and knew her mother had been screwing around with someone. "Got lucky," was the way her mother would put it the next morning when Cindy would inquire. Now the only scent Cindy could smell was the sheriff's strong aftershave.

"Well now, did you sleep okay?" Sheriff Billy asked.

"Yes, Sir."

"No bad dreams?" He'd been listening to Eulla talking to the young lady in the cell a few minutes earlier.

"No, Sir." Cindy decided not to mention her bad dream.

"Good. I've decided to let you go with just a fifty-dollar fine. I see you have enough cash for that. If you want a receipt, then we'll have to send an arrest report to the state, and it will go on your record...."

"What if I don't want a receipt?" Cindy asked hopefully.

"Then we'll just forget this ever happened. You'll still have to pay to get your car out of the storage lot. They'll take a check, we can't for obvious reasons." He returned her purse and car keys. "Oh, and we had to confiscate that bottle of whiskey you had in your car. Consider yourself lucky

14

young lady. A judge wouldn't have been so easy on you." The sheriff said this with a smile leaning back and putting his boots on his desk. He was holding a cup of coffee in a mug that displayed two words, THE BOSS.

Another deputy drove her to Harvey's protected lot, next to his garage. Cindy wrote a check for $ 65 for the towing and overnight storage. She left feeling hungry, dirty and angry. It was the worst experience she'd ever had. She never wanted to see this place again. On her return trip home, she planned to take a longer, out of the way route to avoid the town, just as many others had.

* * *

"Do you think he had sex with you?" Cindy's girlfriend, Rhonda asked, after hearing about the incident in detail.

"I don't know. It feels like it, but I didn't wake up, so maybe I just dreamed it. It's all kinda fuzzy you know? Like maybe it happened, but I can't be sure."

"I'll bet they put something in the milk to knock you out. They're always talking about that date rape drug, Ecstasy that kids are using on college campuses. Maybe they slipped you something like that. Do you want to go someplace and get examined?"

"No! I just want to forget it ever happened. Don't tell anyone, okay?"

"We need to register a complaint. They can't just hold you like that," Rhonda said.

"How do you know? You're not a lawyer."

"Then maybe we should talk to one and find out."

15

"No! I'm just going to forget about it. And I'm never going back there. Just forget I ever told you about it." Cindy got up and took another shower, scrubbing every inch of her body.

Later when she checked the contents of her purse, she noticed one of the condoms was missing. It was enough to convince her that she'd been raped while sleeping, even if she couldn't prove it. She didn't mention this to her friend, or to her mother later. It was a bad experience that she hoped would soon vanish from her memory, but it wouldn't go away.

Rhonda suggested going to a party one of her friends was having, but Cindy wasn't in the mood, so they stayed home, rented a movie and made popcorn instead. That night, Cindy slept with a lamp on beside the bed.

Before falling asleep she thought about her aunt Carol in Cookeville. Cindy had always been able to confide in her aunt.

Perhaps she'd mention the incident in Paradise Valley and see what her aunt made of it. Cindy was unaware that her Aunt Carol had a close friend, Nick Alexander, who was a private investigator and former police detective.

Chapter 2

Ken Pruett was cautiously watching the gas gage rapidly drop on his cousin's '96 Chevy Silverado pickup. He knew the gage was unreliable and hoped he could make it into Paradise Valley. He couldn't afford to fill the tank, but he could buy enough gas to get him back to Soddy-Daisy, just north of Chattanooga. He had a job interview waiting there. He was concentrating on how he would explain having so many jobs in the past two years. It was difficult telling people how rotten your luck had been, but it was true.

He was 46 years old with three failed marriages and a recent bankruptcy. It was a lot of baggage to carry around. Hopefully a new start was waiting for him. His luck had to change. Just when he thought things couldn't get any worse, it usually did.

When the Chevy's engine started to sputter, Ken knew he was out of gas. He pushed in the clutch, shifted into neutral, easing over onto the shoulder of the road. Taking the keys with him, he got out and started walking. Paradise Valley was two miles ahead. While walking, Ken counted his money. He had enough to buy $ 5 worth of gas. He'd have to leave his watch as a deposit for a gas can. He hated being so broke.

Bobby Lee Hargis was Harvey's oldest son. His uncle was Sheriff Billy. When things were slow at the garage, as they were today, Bobby Lee would cruise the highway and by-pass in the black unmarked tow truck. He'd been riding around for a half hour when he spotted the dark blue Chevy pickup on the side of the road just north of town. When it came to a quick snag and drag, Bobby Lee was among the best. He could complete a hookup in less than three minutes flat and be traveling.

The Chevy's warm hood told him the driver either had recent engine trouble, or was out of gas. All the tires had air. Flat tires were a pain. For Bobby Lee, this truck was a sitting piece of cake. The doors weren't locked, saving him a few extra seconds to release the emergency brake and put the vehicle into neutral. The license plate indicated the truck was registered in another county.

To avoid any possibility of the returning driver seeing him, Bobby Lee made a quick u-turn driving in the opposite direction from town. He turned onto the first crossroad and took a parallel road back into town. He'd enter the yard from a back street entrance. It was a good strategic maneuver to avoid being seen by the truck's owner.

Later, when it was dark, Bobby Lee would deliver the pickup to Dent's chop shop across the river. It was about five miles away, hidden by a ridge and a thick stand of trees. Any stranger driving down that road would only see a junkyard. However, most strangers would be wise not to wander too far down that road. It was a dead end in more ways than one. No trespassing signs were posted on both sides of the road.

Dent didn't deal with anybody he didn't know. It was a precaution against snooping investigators. If Dent didn't know ya, then he didn't have what you were looking for, simple as that. Any strangers looking for a junkyard were never directed to Dent's place. In fact, strangers asking too many questions were usually directed to the sheriff's office.

Back at the garage, Bobby started rummaging through his collection of spare GM keys until he found one that fit the ignition. He quickly discovered the problem and put two gallons of gas in the tank, started the engine and smiled. He wouldn't even have to tow it to Dent's place. He'd drive it there and make an extra ten bucks. As a precaution against the driver discovering his pickup in the storage yard, Bobby Lee draped three large plastic tarps over the vehicle.

After leaving his watch as a security deposit, Ken walked back to where he'd left the truck. His arm ached from lugging the heavy gas can. Not seeing the truck, Ken continued to walk, puzzled that he didn't see it yet. He was pretty sure of the spot. When he finally realized the truck was gone, he swore, threw the gas can into the nearby brush and kicked the ground. Just when he thought it couldn't get any worse, it did. It damn sure did. Walking around in a circle, shaking his head, Ken looked up and saw an approaching sheriff's patrol car. He waved for it to stop.

"I need to report a missing truck," he yelled excitedly.

"Uh huh, how long has it been gone, Sir?" The deputy asked.

"Hell I don't know. I left it here about fifteen, maybe twenty minutes ago. I ran out of gas. When I came back, it was gone!"

"If it was out of gas, I doubt that anyone could have driven it away…."

"Well I don't know what to do."

"So where is the gas you were bringing back for the truck?"

"Over there in the weeds someplace."

"Uh huh, and what's it doing over there?"

"I threw the can, okay? I was pissed. I'm still pissed. You gonna help me, or not?"

"Just calm down. Go get the can and bring it back here, or I'll give you a citation for littering."

"Are you serious?"

"Want to test your luck?"

"Nope. My luck has already run out."

"Yes, it sort of looks that way." The deputy thought the man was acting a little strange. The deputy had a pretty good idea where the missing truck was, or would be soon. He regretted not having spotted it sooner so he could call it in to Harvey and earn a finder's fee.

Ken Pruett reported the truck stolen, filled out the report, signed it and called his cousin. He needed a ride, he needed a shave and he needed a break. For Ken's cousin, this was a final confirmation that Ken truly was a loser.

"Who'd want to steal a used pickup truck?" Ken asked while waiting to be picked up by his cousin.

"Probably someone who didn't have one, I guess," Eulla answered, trying not to giggle.

When he mentioned the truck was out of gas, she knew instantly where his truck was, or would be soon. Bobby Lee must have been out cruising, she thought.

"Does this happen very often around here?" Ken asked.

"Hardly ever," she lied. "Can I get you a cup of coffee while you're waiting?" Eulla had a soft spot for losers. She wondered if Ken was single? Despite needing a shave, she thought he looked rather handsome.

While Ken was drinking Eulla's coffee at the sheriff's office, Bobby Lee was checking out the Chevy pickup. Registration and insurance papers were in the glove box, along with an expensive-looking aluminum flashlight. Behind the seat he found a box socket set and jumper cables, both were handy items he could use. Then he went to work on removing the spare tire underneath the bed of the truck. He had to use a bolt cutter on the lock. Because the truck was in good shape, engine sounded strong, Bobby Lee was tempted to keep it. All it would need is a quick paint job and he could drive it for a year, get rid of it later. When he mentioned this to his dad, Harvey wouldn't have any of it.

"Don't even think about it! Being careful is important. One slip and we could all go to jail. Just because your uncle is the sheriff, doesn't mean you can act reckless. The state cops could come sniffing around, and you don't want to get caught with your pants down. Don't make me tell you that again, hear?"

Nevertheless, it was still tempting. A good four-wheel drive truck was good for deer hunting, driving up some back roads in the mountains, all kinds of things. He had a Ford Ranger, but it wasn't as new, or as nice as this one. The Chevy's seat was big enough for some serious necking with his girlfriend, Robin.

Bobby Lee and Robin had managed to go about as far as they could without actually having intercourse. They were both willing to go further, but both were also afraid of the consequences if her father, Dent ever found out. That fear was the only barrier. Consequently Bobby Lee would sometimes sneak around to the valley's low-rent development near the railroad tracks, keeping an eye out for Reba, a cute, light-skinned black girl.

Reba was just 16, could pass for 18, and was always willing to go for a ride, if she was outside walking around, or

21

looking out her window when he cruised by. When she'd see him pass, she'd walk over to the Mini-Mart at the corner and pretend she was talking to someone on the payphone outside until he pulled up. Then she'd hop in and give him a big knowing smile and say something like, "Your girlfriend didn't give you any, huh?" or "That's okay, baby you know Reba's got what you want." Sometimes she'd be unzipping his fly while he was still driving... driving him crazy.

Reba's mom worked nights at the shirt factory so Reba never had to worry about what time she got home. Her dad was serving time in Brushy Mountain Prison for incest with both his daughters. Reba's younger sister, Rita was 14 and already showing interest in older men, just like her sister. And while Reba was doing it for free, Rita had already gotten $ 5 and a free candy bar from the clerk at the Mini-Mart for giving him a hand job in the storeroom.

Rita was smarter than her older sister and had already decided that whenever a man wanted to fool around, he'd have to pay. It would never be free. She'd learned early that money was hard to come by. Her mother worked hard for minimum wages and never had any left over to give to the girls.

* * *

Ken Pruett's cousin wasn't happy when he arrived. He had already contacted his insurance agent and learned that he had a $ 500 deductible clause on the policy. The other bad news was he still owed the finance company $ 7800. The insurance agent estimated the loss value at somewhere around $ 6500 to maybe $ 7,000 tops. He also knew that Ken didn't have any money, even to pay the deductible portion of the loss.

"You're costing me some serious money here, Ken."

"I know, I'm sorry. I'll make it up to you... somehow." Ken thanked Eulla for the coffee. She winked at him as he waved goodbye, promising to stop back sometime.

"What? You got something going with that tub of lard back there?" Ken's cousin asked seeing the departure wink and wave.

"Nah, she was just being nice to me. First person in a long time, too."

"I don't know, Ken. I think there's a bad luck cloud hanging directly over your head, so don't sit too close."

About the time Ken and his cousin were leaving the sheriff's office, Bobby Lee was leaving the storage yard in the missing Chevy pickup. Dent was waiting for him. Had Bobby left a few minutes sooner, he might have been seen by the truck's owner, it was that close.

The gate was open and Dent was standing to one side when Bobby Lee drove through the fenced area. Dent closed and locked the gate as soon as the young man passed through. He drove past the yard office to a big barn in the rear of the yard. Dent's son, Robby was waiting and had the door open so they could drive directly inside the barn. The door closed behind them. Dent and Robby could dismantle the truck in less than two hours.

Bobby Lee stood and watched Robby lift the hood and quickly remove it. At the same time, Dent was removing the doors. Both were using air wrenches. An overhead winch attached to a reinforced rafter would lift the engine and transmission, once the grill, fenders and accessories were removed and the drive shaft unbolted. In less than an hour Bobby Lee was looking at a bare chassis. The engine and transmission were sitting on a wood pallet. Robby would spray some degreaser on it and make it look good as new.

"I got a buyer for the engine. He'll be here in the morning to get it," Dent said, handing Bobby Lee an envelope that contained $ 800. "Don't forget to give that to your daddy."

Dent's daughter, Robin was waiting to give Bobby Lee a lift back into town. She was 19, two years younger than her brother, Robby, and four years younger than Bobby Lee. She had ridden with Bobby Lee in the tow truck a few times when he was out cruising. They knew every secret place to park and neck in the entire county. Lately, the necking was getting pretty serious and Dent warned his daughter that if she got herself knocked up, he wasn't keeping her under his roof. He hoped it was enough to scare her. Dent had also mentioned his concern to his best friend, Harvey, Bobby Lee's father.

"Dent, when you and I were his age, we were getting it from every available skirt in the county. It's a wonder half of them never got knocked up." One of them actually had, Bobby Lee's mother.

"Look, I like Bobby Lee and I don't mind him seeing Robin, but you tell him to keep his pecker in his pants or I'll kick the shit out of him. It don't bother me none that your brother is the sheriff," Dent said.

"Tell him yourself, Dent. He's old enough to know better. Sometimes all the talking in the world won't make a speck of difference, you know that." Harvey knew it was only a matter of time and he'd be hearing that Robin was knocked up.

He couldn't blame his son. Robin was cute and she sure was sweet on Bobby Lee. If they got married, he'd let them live in one of the rent houses he owned. He hadn't discussed this plan with his son, thinking it just might encourage him, rather than wait one more year. It was obvious the kid's hormones were out of control, just as his had been at that age. Harvey understood his son better than Dent understood his daughter.

"Just want you to know how I feel about this. Those kids want to get married, that's okay, too. But I got my principals." Harvey thought that was sort of ironic.

Dent and Harvey had this same conversation several times earlier. Each time it ended with them taking a few pulls on a bottle of special moonshine made close by. Paradise Valley Syrup was some of the finest moonshine made in the state of Tennessee. Bovis Tinch was the master chemist of Paradise Valley Syrup. Much of that prized product went to clients in Chattanooga and surrounding counties.

Robin drove Dent's Ford F-350 diesel to the Dairy Queen for a chocolate sundae with nuts and lots of whipped cream. Bobby Lee had a strawberry milkshake. He hated it when she drove her dad's big truck leaving him on the passenger side. It made him feel foolish with all the other guys watching and snickering. Robin had promised to get back with the truck within the hour, which meant they had to hurry if they were going to mess around. Robin seemed to be taking an extra long time finishing her sundae. Didn't she know the clock was ticking? Maybe she was getting tired of his dry-humping and wanted something more. He certainly did, but she refused to take off her panties and it was driving Bobby Lee crazy. All his friends were envious and wondered how long it would be before they got married.

"Just drop me at the shop," he said annoyed at not being able to keep the Chevy pickup, annoyed that Robin was driving her dad's big truck, not letting him drive, and annoyed that she seemed to be teasing him, knowing that they didn't have enough time to get into some serious stuff. He was feeling particularly horny and wanted to find Reba and let her work on his problem. If Reba wasn't around, maybe her kid sister, Rita, would be willing to go for a ride. He'd seen her give him that big smile a few times. She knew what was going on, he was pretty sure. Reba might not like her younger sister cutting in, but right now, he didn't much care.

"What's your problem?" Robin asked, pulling up to Harvey's garage.

"Nothing you can do anything about," he said jumping out, not bothering to lean over and give her a kiss.

As soon as Robin disappeared, Bobby Lee got into his pickup and headed for the Valley Villas, the subsidized low-rent project. In his haste to get there, he'd forgotten to leave the envelope with the money in Harvey's top desk drawer as he usually did. He did remember to lock the office door, close and lock the gate.

On his way to the Villas, he was once again aware of how much more room there was in the Chevy pickup he'd just delivered than in his Ford Ranger. A bigger truck with a wider seat would allow for some serious sexual activity. The Chevy Silverado was sure worth a lot more than the $800 Dent paid Harvey. In pieces, Dent would probably get $5,000 at least.

Somewhere along the line Sheriff Billy would get a small cut. Bobby Lee wasn't exactly sure how much that cut would be because a lot of that transacted when he wasn't around. He suspected it happened at the Saturday night cockfights that took place at Bovis Tinch's big barn. Bobby Lee and Robin usually went out somewhere on Saturday nights so he rarely went to the cockfights. They didn't appeal to him all that much and the place reeked of moonshine, cigarette and cigar smoke. All the ingredients were there for a good fire, he thought. It was an ominous flash of insight that he never mentioned.

Chapter 3

Bobby Lee made two passes around the low-rent complex without seeing Reba. He didn't like to dwell on the fact that she might be with someone else, but it was possible. He hadn't seen her in at least two weeks. Just as he was about to go back to the garage, he spotted Rita coming out of the Mini-Mart. She had her hair in pigtails, making her look closer to 12 than her actual age, which was 14.

"Hey Rita, want to go for a ride?" Bobby Lee asked.

"Why would I want to do that?" She walked over to his truck smiling, holding a half-empty soda bottle. She was wearing a short dress and pink flip-flops on her bare feet.

"Well, since I don't see Reba around anywhere, maybe you'd like to go park somewhere with me. Maybe mess around a little."

"You got any money?"

"Why are you asking me that? Something you want?"

"Uh huh. You want to mess 'round with me, you gotta pay me some money. I don't do it for free like my sister." She leaned into open driver's side window giving him a big innocent-looking smile. Her white teeth a sharp contrast to her walnut skin. She and her sister were both light-colored black girls with well-defined features. Reba also had a well-developed chest while Rita was only showing a hint of development.

"So you want to go, or not?" Bobby Lee asked. He was a little nervous sitting there where anyone could see and recognize his truck.

"Uh huh, you got any whiskey?"

"I've got a little shine, you want a sip?"

"Uh huh, and I want five dollas. You don't pay, you don't play. Ha, ha, hah." She sounded like a regular street hooker, surprising Bobby Lee.

"So what do I get for five dollars?"

"Mostly I does hand-jobbin'. What you lookin' for?" Rita gave him a wide knowing smile. "But you gotta promise to bring me back here when we're done, okay?"

"Get in," he had the passenger door open, waiting for her. He looked around to see if anyone noticed. The thought of getting it on with such a young girl excited him. First, he had to find a place where they wouldn't be seen. Everyone in town recognized his pickup truck and it would be embarrassing to be seen with a young black girl. His uncle would take a dim view and so would his father.

* * *

Bovis Tinch had a good thing going in Harmon County. He was a big man in several ways. He was six-feet tall and weighed 300 pounds. He was always seen wearing a plaid flannel shirt with bib overalls, regardless of the season. He controlled most of the betting on the cockfights held at his farm every Saturday night. Admission was $ 5 and he had to know you, or you weren't allowed in. The only exception was when one of the regulars brought a friend along and vouched for them. The new guest was always frisked as a precaution then given a free sample of Tinch's finest so there were never any hard feelings. Once sampled, most serious sippers ordered a few jars to take home with them after the festivities.

All the orders were ready for distribution by the time the last fight was over. As a precaution, the cockfights were always protected by Sheriff Billy's presence. For his services, he enjoyed a minor percentage of all the proceeds. His presence was enough to keep things orderly and controlled. It also allayed any fears that the place might be raided.

Whenever Sheriff Billy bet on a given bird, he did it through his brother, Harvey. That way no one was the wiser on how he felt the outcome would be. He also made sure two of his deputies were on duty patrolling nearby. Saturday night was always a prime time to pickup drunk drivers. An exception was made for those coming from the Tinch farm. Win or lose, all the betters, visitors and partakers held the sheriff in high regard and usually waved as they left.

Bovis Tinch's barn was the largest barn in the county. It held the old bleacher seating from the high school gym that was replaced in 1994. On a good night, the barn could hold 250 people. That would net Bovis $ 1250 on admissions and Sheriff Billy's 10 percent cut amounted to $ 125. Plus he got a small cut of the betting, and as much syrup as he wanted. Bovis knew the sheriff wasn't greedy, never took undue advantage of his position and never questioned the actual amount of money bet. He trusted Bovis. He had to. Bovis was also a county commissioner. Anyone questioning the sheriff's activities had to go through the commissioners to whom the sheriff reported. Anyone questioning Bovis's activities out on his farm, had to go through the sheriff. Consequently there was rarely a question that couldn't be quickly satisfied by one or both parties.

This Saturday night the barn was packed. A fighting rooster from Dalton, Georgia was being touted for a succession of recent wins. Those patrons from Chattanooga knew of its reputation and were betting heavily on this favorite. Bovis made sure it was slated as the last fight of the night to keep everyone there as long as possible. The Dalton bird was kept in his cage with its owner standing close by, talking to the bird. The steel spurs wouldn't be put on until just before the fight. Sheriff Billy walked over to examine the colorful bird up close.

"Looks like he's got that killer instinct," the sheriff said to the owner.

"He sure does. He's got a few scars, but he knows how to fight. I wouldn't bet against him if I were you."

"Oh I don't bet. How would that look, me betting on a bird at a cockfight?" They both laughed at the remark. Billy tested the bird by dangling his fingers close to the cage. Immediately the rooster flew at his fingers, which he withdrew quickly.

"Aggressive bugger ain't he?" Sheriff Billy felt pretty sure this one was indeed a winner.

"You just wait and see what he does in the ring. I got him trained good. Had a guy down in Atlanta offered me two thousand bucks for him."

"That right? Why didn't you sell him?"

"Hell, he's already made me twice that much. I ain't ever going to sell this bird. He's a champion, you'll see."

Billy believed him. The bird did have a killer instinct. It all depended on which bird he was matched with. Billy walked around the outer edge of the barn surveying the crowd, nodding to those who looked his way. He was looking for his brother, Harvey. He wanted him to bet $ 100 on the Dalton bird.

He found Harvey and Dent sitting together on the third tier of seats on the left hand side, where they usually sat. Since there was seating on three sides of the small ring, there were no bad seats. He didn't have to pass any money over to his brother, just nod and whisper into his ear. Then he had to spread a few comments around that "the Dalton bird looked a little sick," to get some action going.

Parking at the farm was sometimes a problem. Having so many vehicles parked near the barn could cause suspicion. For that reason, Bovis had a sign by the entrance, which was a gravel drive, indicating:

PRIVATE AUCTION -- BY INVITATION ONLY

It was there as a precaution, should a passing motorist become curious. It had only happened once, but that was sufficient to warrant having the sign in place on Saturday nights. It was Billy's duty to make sure it was out there.

The cockfights were always over by 11:00 PM. Any later and some of the men wouldn't make it to church the following morning, which in turn would reduce the attendance the following Saturday. The plan was to keep everyone happy. After the crowd left, the sheriff took his percentage, compared notes with Bovis on how things had gone, picked up his jar and left for the office, where he'd catch a few hours sleep in the Honey Hole. It was another reason it had a better mattress.

* * *

Bobby Lee drove north, crossed the railroad tracks and pulled behind an abandoned barn that was about to collapse. He reached under the seat and found a pint whiskey bottle almost half-full with Tinch's PV Syrup. He unscrewed the cap and took a swig before passing it to Rita. She hesitated,

31

smelled the open end of the bottle, then took a small sip, closing her eyes and making a grimacing face.

"It doesn't take much to get you really mellow," Bobby Lee said taking the bottle from her and twisting on the cap.

"You gonna give me five dollas now?"

"How about later? After you make me feel good." That way she'd be inclined to put out so she'd get paid. He was still having a hard time believing she wanted money. After all, she was still just a kid and not really old enough to know much about sex. For just a fleeting second it occurred to him that if he was ever caught in a compromising situation with someone under the age of 18, he could go to jail and do some serious time. But since his uncle was the sheriff, it wasn't likely.

Still, if Robin ever found out, it would be the end of their relationship. Dent probably wouldn't want much to do with him, and he'd have to listen to his dad tell him again how dumb he was.

"No way! You gotta pay me first. If you don't pay me, I'll tell the man at the market you tried to rape me, and they'll send you to jail."

"Got it all figured out, don't you? Okay, here's your money, now get over here." Bobby Lee pulled out a $ 5 dollar bill from his pant's pocket and gave it to her realizing she had a problem. She didn't have a pocket, or anyplace to put it. She took the money and squeezed it in her hand, moving closer to him.

"Don't you think you should take off them pants? They gonna get all messed up and your momma's gonna be mad atchou." She said knowingly.

Smiling at her logic, Bobby Lee lifted up and slid his jeans and shorts down around his ankles. As he did this, he was unaware of the envelope with the $ 800 falling out of his back pocket onto the floor of the truck.

"So who you like better, me or my sister?" she asked. She was sitting beside him, jabbering away, acting like nothing unusual was happening.

"Don't talk." He was nervous and wishing this was Robin, not some street kid hitting him up for money. He hoped she wouldn't brag to her sister and spoil the good thing he had going with Reba who was smart enough to keep her mouth shut. Her younger sister might start running hers. If Harvey or Dent got word, he couldn't dig a hole deep enough to hide in from the embarrassment. He was thinking about this while the kid continued to jabber.

"That's enough. Move over," he mumbled, reaching down for his pants. It was dark inside the truck and he didn't see the envelope lying on the floor.

Rita had to pee, but she was afraid of getting out of the truck, he might drive off and leave her there, so she held it. She'd dropped the money on the floor. When she reached down, her hand felt the envelope. She wasn't sure what it was, but picked it up with her money. While Bobby Lee was driving she tucked the envelope inside her panties. She'd look later. Maybe it was a love letter from his girlfriend. And maybe she'd show it to Reba to make her jealous.

"Just drop me off at the market, okay?" Rita sat next to the door so she could jump out the minute he stopped. Going over all those bumps, she was sure she was going to pee in her panties, something she really didn't want to have happen, because then he'd never take her for another ride.

When they arrived at the market, Rita jumped out of the truck and ran into the store. Just as quick, Bobby Lee drove off, hoping nobody witnessed his hasty departure. Unfortunately an unsavory dude in an old Ford LTD four-door was sitting across the street hoping to score some dope. He saw the young black girl jump out of the truck and run into the market, and the truck take off.

He had a good idea what that was all about. He'd seen the truck around town, but he didn't know the driver, except he was a white dude messing with a young black girl. That small bit of information was worth a few bills. Sitting there, waiting had paid off, even though he hadn't scored anything yet. Watch long enough and you can learn what's going on, was his motto.

Inside the toilet, Rita pulled down her panties, sat on the commode and studied the envelope and its contents. She counted the money twice. Bobby Lee would surely discover it missing soon and come looking for her. She had to hide someplace. She debated whether to tell her sister. She decided she couldn't tell anyone. She'd hurry home, hoping Reba wasn't there to see her hiding the money. She had an old stuffed teddy bear that might work. The $ 5 bill was in a tight ball when she approached the counter. The clerk, who was also white, gave her a big knowing grin.

He wanted to ask her to go back in the storage room with him, but there were several customers in the store. "Why don't you stop back later... and maybe we can do some more business." He whispered in a low nervous voice, arching his eyebrows. She nodded. Hurrying out the door with a candy bar he'd given her. She was unaware of the black man in the old Ford across the street, still watching.

Bobby Lee drove back to the garage, planning on leaving the money in Harvey's desk. As soon as he got out of the truck, he knew something was wrong. He felt in all his pockets for the envelope. Then he got the new aluminum flashlight he'd taken from the Chevy pickup, and checked the interior of his truck carefully. Could Rita have stolen it? She wasn't that slick to be a pickpocket. That was something a pro might do, but then he wasn't about to pay some whore $ 800 for a quick 15 minutes of fake love. Not when he could get it free from Reba, and pretty damned soon from Robin.

He was still standing beside his truck when an old Ford LTD passed by slowly, the driver checking him out. Bobby Lee became alert instantly and made sure the front door of the garage was locked. He'd stop by later just to check on things. Harvey kept a loaded shotgun in the office. Bobby Lee considered unlocking the door, and taking it with him. He was hungry. The milkshake wasn't enough, and his mother would remind him that if he wanted to eat at home, he had to show up when she was preparing dinner, not three hours later. Harvey would be at the cockfights with Dent.

Jerome was aware that he'd made the young man nervous as he slowly cruised down the street, scoping out the garage, like maybe he'd hit the place later. Jerome enjoyed acting cool and making people nervous. He wore dark shades just like the cool dude in that movie, Shaft. He also shaved his head so he'd be bald, and had to do it every three days to keep from looking like an ex-con. When he drove, he kept the seat way back and leaned toward the center. It took a little practice.

Jerome was 34, still single and presently renting a room from a black lady. She was a widow and old enough to be his mother. She said she had a son his age, working somewhere in Nashville. The first two times he tried to hit on her, she pushed him away, reminding him, 'she could be his mother'.

The third time she didn't resist too much, so he kissed her and pulled her close, so she could feel his excitement growing. She didn't resist and Jerome made sure she liked it, taking his time. When they were finished, she reminded him that he would still have to pay her the $ 50 a week rent for the room, 'regardless of any social arrangements'. That was cool. He felt pretty sure he could get her to do his laundry and maybe fix a few of his favorite meals. He knew older ladies liked having someone to look after, particularly when they were lonely.

He also knew he could be late with the rent for a few weeks now, before she'd start to nag him. She had never asked for references when he moved in with just two suitcases and a cardboard box full of books and magazines. Now she was asking him all kinds of things, like was he ever married? Did he have any kids, shit like that. He'd paid the first week's rent in advance, telling her he was looking for work, which was true. He was also hiding from a dude he'd ripped off in Knoxville a week earlier.

Prior to taking a sudden unannounced leave of absence, Jerome was working as a detail man for a new car dealership in Knoxville. The manager of the place was a real prick. He made all his people work from 8:00 in the morning until 8:00 in the evening. On Saturdays they stayed open until 5:00. Jerome was constantly busy. Whenever things got slow, he was suppose to wash the boss's car, which was several times a week at least.

All Jerome ever got out of it was $ 7 an hour and some leftover pizza whenever the salesmen were too busy to eat on Saturdays. Cleaning and detailing cars and trucks had a few advantages in that he sometimes found money, cigarette lighters and even a gun left under a seat. He still had the gun, a small 25-caliber automatic. Nobody had ever come around looking for it, and he never mentioned finding it.

Jerome also had access to all the keys for all the new and used vehicles on the lot since he was constantly moving them into the wash bay inside the service area. Every Saturday afternoon he'd select a late model used car he wanted to drive on Sunday and he'd keep that key hidden, along with a spare dealer tag.

As long as the vehicle was back on the lot by late Sunday night, nobody would know that he had it out overnight. Nobody ever checked the mileage on the used vehicles. He always picked one that had at least a half tank of gas. He figured they owed him that for all the grunt work he did around the place.

Then last Saturday, the manager left early with some of his drinking buddies. He left instructions for one of the salesmen to lock up and left his keys on his desk. The salesman, who was supposed to lock up, got busy with several customers in a row and didn't notice Jerome walking around in the offices and showroom.

There was a small metal cashbox in the bottom desk drawer of the manager's office. He kept a stack of hundred dollar bills in it that he used for daily bonuses to the salesmen, when he felt they needed an added incentive to sell a particular vehicle that had been on the lot too long. With the keys, Jerome was able to count the $ 2300, all in hundreds. It was just too tempting to pass up, so he took it, leaving the keys on the desk where he'd found them.

Jerome spent Saturday evening getting his stuff together, moving out of his two-room efficiency, without paying the rent that was overdue. He waited until after midnight to depart so the landlord wouldn't see him leave. He was heading for Atlanta when he stopped to get gas in a small town that turned out to be Paradise Valley. He liked the looks of the place... and the name.

Since he wasn't expected anywhere, he decided to stay for a while. Because it was a small town, it was easy to spot strangers. Anyone looking for him would stand out. Meanwhile, he was learning some things about his new neighborhood.

It appeared that the white dude who worked nights at the Mini-Mart was hitting on one of the little black girls. She was the same girl he saw getting out of that pickup with the other white dude behind the wheel. She looked way too young to be a hooker, but there was something going on with her.

Jerome made a mental note to check her out later. Maybe he'd flash the gun and scare her a little, make her believe he was a truant officer or something like that. Scare her enough to give him some free sugar and fill him in on what was going on with the white bread in the mini-market. One thing could always lead to another. Right now Jerome, soon to be *the man*, was looking for new opportunities.

Atlanta could wait. He wasn't in any particular hurry. Now that he was on intimate terms with his landlady, Jerome expanded his small bedroom to include the use of most of the house. And, he was enjoying a few free meals. Just for showing the old lady a little affection. It was a great trade. He also liked the slower pace of this small town compared to the big city.

Chapter 4

Cindy Stevens continued to have bad dreams. Before leaving to return home, she called her favorite aunt, Carol Mayberry in Cookeville. Cindy could talk to her aunt openly, something she couldn't do with her mother without some constant distraction. Her mother was too preoccupied with things that only mattered to her, not Cindy.

"I was wondering if I could stop by and visit you? Maybe stay overnight before I drive home," Cindy said on the phone. She explained that she was visiting a friend in Chattanooga.

"That would be wonderful. What time would you be arriving?" Carol knew there was an hour's difference because of the time zone that split the two areas even though it was only an hour and a half drive. Carol also sensed there must be a problem because it was quite unlike her niece to call so unexpectedly. It wasn't a holiday or a birthday. Carol was also a little critical of the way her younger sister allowed Cindy so much freedom.

"I was thinking about leaving in about an hour, so I guess I could get there around noon. Would that be okay?"

"Noon is perfect. We'll find someplace nice to have lunch. We have a Cracker Barrel here, is that okay with you?" Carol asked.

"Sure. I don't really care. I just thought we might catch up. You know, we don't see that much of one another and

Mom isn't going to be back until Tuesday so there's no sense staying home alone."

"I agree. See you when you get here."

They had to wait for an available table since it was such a popular place to eat. Carol was patient and didn't ask any questions. She knew it would take time for her niece to tell her whatever it was that was bothering her. She hoped it wasn't an announcement that the young girl was pregnant. Anything else she could easily handle, or so she thought.

Carol barely had time to bake a pie after her niece's call. She had a piecrust in the freezer and quickly assembled all the ingredients to produce her niece's favorite desert, apple pie. She would stop by the grocery store for some vanilla ice cream after lunch. She also cut a bunch of cornflowers from her garden and put them in the guest bedroom. Cindy Stevens was her only niece; and therefore, was sufficient reason to spoil her a little.

"I keep having this same dream and I'm not sure if it really happened, but I'm pretty sure it did," Cindy told Carol what she suspected while sitting in the living room after a pleasant lunch followed by a later helping of Carol's apple pie with ice cream. The desert alone made the trip worthwhile for Cindy.

"You must understand this is a serious charge, Honey. I don't for a minute disbelieve anything you've told me, but it may be difficult to prove," Carol said. She found it hard to believe that any law enforcement officer would dare do such a thing. Was the young girl having some sort of fantasy? Maybe she was pregnant and scared. That might explain why she was making up such a preposterous story.

"I don't care about proving it. I just want the bad dreams to stop. And I knew I could talk to you and you'd understand. Mom would just think I was making it all up. I can see her now driving back down there to check out the sheriff. Maybe if she spent a night in that jail cell, she might be convinced." Or maybe she'd enjoy getting laid by the sheriff, she thought. He wouldn't even have to waste a pill or whatever it was he used to drug Cindy on her mother. And Paradise Valley was a lot closer than Las Vegas.

Later that evening, after Cindy went to bed, Carol called her close friend, Nick Alexander. Nick was a retired police detective who now did private investigations. The company Carol worked for, McDermitt Manufacturing, had hired Nick to do some background checks on department managers and key staff members. Later the company used him to recommend and supervise the installation of a new security system. That's how Carol and Nick had met.

Over time, the relationship went from friendly to intimate. Carol was a widow and Nick was divorced. They enjoyed each other's company. Nick visited Carol in Cookeville whenever he had business in Atlanta, stopping on his way down and again on his way back. It was the main reason he drove instead of taking a commercial flight.

Carol made several trips a year up to St. Clair Shores, Michigan, where Nick still lived in a leased apartment on the lake. Lately he was spending more and more time in Cookeville and it was Carol's secret hope that one day he'd move south. Nick had hinted several times that a move was likely and Carol was being patient. They sent each other email messages and spoke on the phone several times a week. The romance was continuing to blossom just like a long engagement with each discovering something new about the other every time they got together. It was a comfortable relationship.

"I don't know what to believe," Carol said to Nick after relating the scenario her niece had told.

"Without seeming to pry, try to get as much detailed information from her as you can. I'd like to know the name of the sheriff and the arresting deputy if she can recall it. Be sure to get the exact time and date this was suppose to have happened. I'll be down your way next week and I can check it out on my way to Atlanta," Nick said.

"Oh Nick, I hate for you to get involved in something that may not have actually happened."

"If you're concerned, then I am, too. Nobody should be subjected to that type treatment, particularly a seventeen-year old girl. Spending a night in jail had to be a horrible experience for her. I'll be discreet. I don't plan on having a confrontation with a small town law officer where I don't have any influence."

"Thank you, Nick. Do you really have a scheduled appointment Atlanta, or are you just using this bizarre incident as an excuse to visit?"

"Yes and yes. That's what is so nice about being my own boss. I can reschedule my time when it suits me." Nick was aware that teenagers were prone to telling tales to divert attention or get it. Either way, the story needed to be corroborated. Carol had given Nick some background on her niece. She was spoiled and used to having her own way. Her mother was preoccupied most of the time leaving Cindy pretty much alone to do whatever she wanted to do, go wherever she wanted to go. Nick agreed with Carol that the young lady needed more parental supervision, but it seemed a little late for that. Too much freedom and free time made it easy for kids to get into trouble, regardless of the family's economic status or ethnic background.

* * *

42

Frank Gibson was a special investigator for Puritan Insurance. He started as a claims agent. Five years later, he was promoted into his present position, which he'd held for the last 12 years. His office was in Atlanta, but most of his time was spent in the field. Stolen vehicles were his specialty, even though he investigated other types of claims involving fraud. One of the company's claims agents reported the theft of a pickup truck in Harmon County, Tennessee.

Ordinarily one theft wouldn't get his attention, but it was the third theft claim for the company in the past year in that area. None of the stolen vehicles had ever been recovered, which was a bit unusual. It suggested that a chop shop operation was involved. It was time for Frank to become better acquainted with Harmon County and do some personal checking.

Frank's company car was accumulating a lot of miles. It was due for a tune-up, oil change, tire rotation, and some other minor repairs. He decided to schedule it into a repair shop and rent a car for a week while driving up to Paradise Valley. The rental agency didn't have any new models available, so he consented to driving a year-old Pontiac Grand Am 4-door. The insurance company received a special discounted rate.

His first stop was the sheriff's office to inspect the stolen vehicle report on the Chevy pickup. Frank had a copy, but wanted to be sure it matched the report that was filed locally. Sometimes there were discrepancies. He also wanted to talk to the deputy who wrote the report. He decided not to reveal that he was working for the insurance company. He had a cover story to use instead. He knew he'd get less cooperation, but he'd also see how they treated the average inquiring citizen, and keep any warning flags from going up prematurely. The sheriff would undoubtedly see through the cover story fast enough and start worrying.

Frank wanted him to worry. He also wanted to see what had been done by the sheriff's office in attempting to locate the missing truck.

"This guy was kind of odd. I saw him waving at me standing beside the road." The deputy explained.

"What was so odd about that?" Frank asked the deputy.

"Well he'd just thrown a full can of gas into the weeds and I ordered him to retrieve it."

"Uh huh. What else?"

"He wasn't real sure about where he left the truck. I thought maybe he'd been drinking at first."

"Where do you think the truck went?" Frank looked directly at the man, giving him his best knowing smile.

"Kids probably took it for a ride and ditched it someplace."

"But it hasn't been found yet. You figure the kids were riding around and just happened to have some extra gas in a can with them?"

"That doesn't seem likely," the deputy responded.

"I guess that's my point. If it was stolen, which I'm inclined to think it was, where would it wind up?" Joy rides were usually found nearby the next day. Frank knew the statistics. "Any chop shops operating around here?"

"Uh, my guess is it would be heading south to Atlanta somewhere. Hard to spot with all that traffic they have. And I don't know about any chop shops. This is a small community. Anything like that wouldn't last long here. We'd know about it."

"Uh huh. Any junkyards around here?"

"Yeah, there's a couple. Waste of time looking though. Most of the stuff they have is real junk, ready for the scrap heap."

"What about body shops? I'll bet you have a few of those." A fast paint job would be enough to disguise the truck."

The deputy gave him the names and addresses. He'd alert the sheriff as soon as he found him that a stranger was sniffing around, asking a lot of questions about the missing Chevy truck. Presumably the man was from the finance company. Their claim to the insurance company had been denied, so this guy was trying to locate the truck so the finance company could recoup some of their loss. That was the story Frank had given. He even produced a fake business card he sometimes used.

Frank had a lot of experience with small town politicians, law enforcement officers and local businesspeople. The prevailing attitude was not to give a stranger too much information. The deputy appeared cooperative, but there was a slight hesitation when asked about chop shops and junkyards. It was enough to tell Frank to look beyond the list he'd been given.

The place he was looking for would not be on the list. His next stop after making the perfunctory visit at the sheriff's office was the local barbershop for a trim, then the café he'd spotted earlier. Both were on the square. Barbershops and diners were good places to overhear local gossip. All he had to do was plunk down, pick up a newspaper and keep his ears open. Something Frank was good at.

Lou's Barbershop was straight out of the '40s with three old-fashioned barber chairs, mirrors and cabinets that had stood the test of time. A line of chrome and vinyl chairs lined the opposite wall. An assortment of hunting and fishing magazines were piled on the one side table. Frank removed his tie, picked up a magazine and waited his turn. He listened to the local gossip, much of which didn't matter to him.

From time to time the barber lowered his voice and would look in Frank's direction. It was obvious to everyone present that he was a stranger just passing through town.

Covertly, each occupant, including Lou, was checking him out with furtive glances. No attempt was made to engage him in conversation.

By the time it was Frank's turn, he'd learned that someone named Mary Lou Haslette was circulating a petition to have the parking meters removed around the square. He also learned that nobody paid them any attention, parked free and ignored the signs indicating a fine. This was because there was no one available to check the aging and often broken meters. Lou, the barber thought maybe there was a hidden agenda to Mary Lou's cause. She was 44, never married, a librarian and therefore well read, and looking for small annoying things to draw the sheriff's attention to her. The conclusion was that she was sweet on the sheriff who never seemed to take any notice of her, except when she delivered one of her silly petitions.

"Why doesn't she just bake him a blueberry pie or something and take it over to his office as a peace offering," one of the customers suggested.

"Probably because Eulla would eat the pie before the sheriff ever knew it was there," another responded, getting a few laughs.

"Eulla's not going to let any competition get too close to the sheriff without a good fight. I doubt Mary Lou is any match for Eulla," Lou said glancing over at Frank. Lou doubted the stranger knew anything about what they were discussing.

Finally it was Frank's turn and he had to answer the normal questions a barber always asks a new customer. "Yes, he was new in town, yes he was just here for a short visit, no he didn't have any relatives living in Paradise Valley, and no he wasn't a Republican." Once the questions were over, Frank managed to mention that he was looking for a missing truck. Once he stated his mission, the shop became very quiet. Not another word was spoken until he asked how much he owed. It wouldn't take long for the word to travel throughout the town that someone was asking about a missing pickup. It was good gossip stuff.

Millie's Mug & Skillet Café had all the looks and smells it suggested. There was a long counter behind which was the grill, a stove and a sink. The other side of the room was a collection of tables, chairs and booths. Nothing appeared to match, including the silverware. Frank's experience led him to the counter, the best place to carry on a casual conversation with the cook. Melissa Jane Haggerty inherited the café from her mother, Millie 12 years earlier. The café remained the same as the day she passed away. The only improvement was a new toaster. Frank noticed the café was only open for breakfast and lunch. Anyone wanting something to eat after 2:30 PM was out of luck. Frank had just made it, since it was now 2:15.

"Whatcha havin' Sweetie?" Melissa asked, hands on hips, giving him the once over. She could smell the lilac water Lou always used despite the aroma of grease in the air. She gave him her best afternoon smile, which took a little effort.

"Cup of coffee and a piece of cherry pie, if you have any left," Frank said giving Melissa a similar once over.

"Saved it just for you." She turned and walked over to the coffee pot, still half full. He was a stranger who was comfortable in strange places. He was either a salesman or a state inspector, she guessed. Either way, she subconsciously patted her hair and gave him another smile while she poured his coffee. He looked up and for a full 30 seconds they maintained eye contact. Frank felt an old tingle of anticipation. Something was going on here.

"Just passing through, visiting kin, or are you planning to stay a while?" she asked. Melissa still looked good for her 50 years. When she took the time, she could still flirt with her customers, feigning interest that always assured her of a few good tips. She rarely flirted with anyone after 1:30 because by then she was too tired to make the extra effort. Most of her customers were the same every day, and only a few left a decent tip, much to her chagrin.

"A little of both. I'm lookin' to buy a good used pickup truck. I heard there might be some good deals around here. Any idea where I should look?" Frank asked.

"Sweetie, I don't know nothin' about trucks, but I know a little about pick ups, ha, ha, hah." Melissa shot him a wink, laughing at her own joke. Then she turned to see if Maria was taking any notice. Maria washed dishes, cleared tables and mopped the floor. She rarely said anything to anyone, even Millie who had known her for more than 20 years. Maria truly minded her own business, something rare in Paradise Valley.

"Mind if I smoke?" Frank held up a pack of Marlboros.

"Only if you light one for me, too. Not supposed to smoke in here, but it's almost closing time and there's no one else here to complain, so be my guest."

"Good for you. I like a woman with spunk, and who's willing to break the rules once in a while for a good cause."

"Oh I got plenty of spunk left in me, Sweetie. I don't know about the cause part."

"I'll bet you do have a lot of spunk. How about having dinner with me?"

"As long as I don't have to cook it, I'm willing. When?"

"How about tonight? I can't think of a better time. Where's a good place to go?" He didn't think the question would offend her since the café wasn't open for dinner.

"Now that's a problem. Only good place that serves dinner is about fifteen miles from here. Think you can handle that?"

"That's fine with me. So where will I find you?" Frank avoided using the term, 'pick you up'. He had to be careful not to assume too much with this lady, regardless of the flirting. Frank's girlfriend in Atlanta was hinting that she was tired of waiting for him to take the next step and pop the question. She'd been waiting three years and wasn't getting any younger.

Frank didn't see any reason to hurry. It also gave him a guilt-free conscience when he was traveling, like now. He wasn't exactly cheating he was still prospecting, making a few comparisons and enjoying his last bit of freedom. He'd been married once and wasn't in any hurry to make the same mistake again. He was convinced that once married, the romance wasn't as intense or as often.

Melissa gave him her address and instructions on how to find her place. It was only two blocks away. Melissa usually walked to work everyday leaving her car at home. When Frank finished his coffee and the pie, he stood up and left $ 3 on the counter against her objection. Since he had some time to kill, he headed for the used car lot she had mentioned. Then he'd find a local motel and check in. His original plan wasn't to stay over, but now he was feeling lucky. A good dinner and some companionship would put a nice finish on the otherwise boring day. He could take his time tomorrow checking out the area before heading back to Atlanta, which was a good three and a half-hour drive.

Melissa was pretty sure he was a salesman. He flirted like a salesman, and he'd left a really nice tip, so he wasn't a cheapskate. She noticed that he drove a late model car. Maybe this wouldn't end up as an exciting one-nighter. So far, they only knew each other's first name. Over dinner they could become better acquainted. She also thought he looked a little like Clint Eastwood with that receding hair line and the same crooked smile. When she had turned her back to get his coffee, she could almost feel his gaze on her backside, which was still one of her better features.

"Flaunt it while you still got it, Honey" she said into the mirror. She took a long soaking bath hoping to eliminate the kitchen stink that seemed to hang in the air at the café. Mostly it was the smell of grease and onions. When you work in a smelly atmosphere long enough you no longer recognize it until the outside fresh air hits you. Sometimes Melissa walked home without noticing the difference because she was so tired. Standing on her feet most of the day sapped a lot of energy. The thought of having a date with a good-looking guy revitalized her. She hoped he wouldn't get cold feet and be a no show.

Harmon County was a dry county. It would remain so for as long as Bovis Tinch was a commissioner. Every once in a while, Bovis would stop by her café and leave a small jar of PV Syrup for her under the counter. Even though Bovis was much older, he had a soft spot for Melissa. She still had the better part of a jar sitting in the refrigerator at home. She wondered if Frank would be offended by her bringing it along for later. It was crystal clear, smooth, 140 proof and guaranteed to give you a good buzz in no time at all. If Frank had the foresight to get a motel room, then they could have a good old time getting loose and getting it on. While she soaked in the tub, she wondered what she'd wear?

While Melissa was still contemplating her wardrobe, Frank was wandering around in Happy Harry's used car lot. He concentrated on the used trucks, ignoring the automobiles.

"What kind of truck you lookin' for?" Harry asked walking over to the stranger, not holding out his hand for an introduction.

Harry had been watching the man for the past few minutes trying to determine his interest. He never rushed right out to greet people. He allowed them to look around for a while, then he'd mosey over to them, hands in his pockets and maintain a laid back attitude. That's what it took to sell some of the farmers. Get too pushy and they'd just walk away. Harry was robust, wore suspenders and a big smile all the time. If Harry ever had a worry, it never showed. Consequently everyone knew him as Happy Harry and never even thought about his last name, which was Ferguson... now.

Originally it had been Finkle, when he still lived in New Jersey. Living in this little hideaway town, Happy Harry was good enough for everyone... except maybe the sheriff, who didn't know Harry all that well, but still regarded him cautiously since Harry hadn't grown up in Paradise Valley.

The only people the sheriff trusted were those few who he'd gone to school with and knew their family. One thing was for sure in Paradise Valley. Everyone who lived there was either: a relative, a school friend, or afraid of him. It was amazing how many of the Hargis clan remained in Harmon County. The sheriff could run for re-election and not worry, because half the votes would come from kinfolks. The other half wouldn't get counted.

"I guess I'm looking for a good, used Chevy pickup. Something like a ninety-six Silverado," Frank said.

"Well now, I just might have what you're lookin' for in the back." Harry introduced himself and took Frank into the small repair shop behind the mobile home office. There were three work bays, each with a separate overhead door.

Inside the shop, Frank saw the exact model truck he was looking for, except it was silver. The hood had been removed and the engine was missing. Looking around, Frank spotted the engine in the rear of the shop dangling from an engine stand, leaking oil on the concrete floor.

"I've got another engine coming to replace this one. It's got a bad crankshaft. Hardly worth rebuilding a blown engine anymore. I could have this one ready and running first of next week," Harry offered.

"Right model, wrong color. You get a blue one in like that, give me a holler." Frank wrote down his home phone number and gave it to Harry. He didn't want to use a business card.

"You're a long way from home ain't ya?"

"I get up this way now and then. Prices are usually better once you get outside the city and the high rent districts."

"Uh huh. And you're up here lookin' for a blue, ninety-six, Chevy Silverado pickup. What make tires does it have to have on it?" Harry chuckled. "What happened, somebody steal your truck?"

"Well you pegged that pretty darned fast. Yeah, a friend of mine had it stolen around here about a week ago. I thought maybe I could find it for him."

"Son, you're a little late to be lookin' now. It's probably somewhere down in Chattanooga, or maybe even in Atlanta. It wouldn't stay around here, and I wouldn't touch something like that. It's got to have a clean, clear title before I'd take it. This is a small community. Everybody knows everybody else, or they're related, so there aren't many secrets. Know what I'm saying?"

"You're probably right. I'm just curious how it could run out of gas, then disappear so fast."

"Kids. They go joy ridin', try to impress their friends, they'll do just about anything. I've had 'em in here tryin' to steal the wheels off a car... in daylight!"

"What did you do?"

"Turned 'em over to the sheriff, that's all I could do. Can't hit 'em, even though you'd like to."

"So what does the sheriff do with them?"

"Oh he's got a way to get their attention. First he locks 'em up for a few hours then he calls their parents to come get 'em. Before they leave his office, they sign a paper admitting to what they did, promising never to do it again, and they also promise to put in ten hours of free labor after school. He makes them clean up the park, pick up trash and paint the public toilets in the courthouse. They can't complain about it either. They get smart with him, he wails the tar out of them. And the parents don't say a word about it. For a little fella, the sheriff has a lot a juice in this town. He knows everyone and what's going on. Not someone you want to get crosswise with."

"It sounds like he pretty much rules the community here."

"You got that right."

"So is he pretty competent as a sheriff?"

"Small community like ours, you accept whatever and whoever gets elected. He's no better, or worse than any others. Job doesn't pay much, but he gets a lot of respect. I'd be careful askin' too many questions around here about the sheriff. He'd get wind of it real quick. Like I said, he knows everything that's going on."

"Any place where I can buy you a drink?" Frank asked.

"Yeah, follow me." Harry took Frank into his office, opened a drawer and took out a jar of Paradise Valley Syrup. "Best there is around here. Some folks even drive up from Georgia to buy it." He passed the jar to Frank.

"Ooooh that's goood." Frank whispered savoring the unique taste. He'd had shine before, but nothing this good.

"Ain't it though?" Harry took a swig and sat back in his chair. The man sitting across from him made him curious. Harry was pretty sure there was more to the story than he was letting on. His curiosity about the sheriff was his first clue. Harry suspected the man was probably from the state's TBI. That stood for Tennessee Bureau of Investigation. Harry was aware of the numerous thefts and had a pretty good idea where some of them went. Dent had an engine for him, and he'd come up with it pretty fast. No telling where it came from. Harry didn't want to know either as long as the price was right. While Happy Harry wasn't exactly a local boy, Dent always treated him fairly.

"Well I'd better get going. I got a hot date waiting."

"Good for you. I reckon she's not from around here."

"I just hope she's no kin to the sheriff. I forgot to ask."

"Don't forget what I told you about the sheriff. Be real careful who you talk to about him. He's like a copperhead snake and twice as mean when he wants to be. If I was you, I'd forget about that truck and let the insurance company pay for it."

How many times had Frank heard that?

* * *

"My, my, my! You're looking mighty pretty in that dress," Frank said standing in the doorway, watching Melissa as she grabbed her purse and a brown paper bag.

"Well thank you!" I had to get that kitchen stink off me. It's a wonder you even asked me out, I smelled so bad."

"I guess I asked you because I love the smell of onions." They both laughed at that remark. Frank was feeling mellow already after taking a few pulls on Harry's jar. He thought the name, Happy Harry's was particularly fitting.

"Before I get in your car, I want to ask you something. It's personal."

"Okay, ask away. I promise to be truthful." He was expecting her to ask if he was married.

"After dinner. You got something else planned?"

"Wow, that's straight forward enough. Yeah, as a matter of fact I do. I was thinking that maybe after dinner we'd stop back at the motel where I'm staying and maybe we'd get a chance to get to know one another better. Talk a little. You know, take it slow and easy like." Frank was trying to be careful in choosing his words. The syrup was working.

"Just talk? I thought maybe you had something else in mind." Melissa was feeling randy. It had been a while since she'd had any male companionship.

"Yeah I do, but can we talk about it later, after we eat? I hardly ever get horny on an empty stomach."

"Fine, I'll save the rest of my questions for later, when you're full and feel like talking. Do you like these shoes?"

Frank looked down at her bright green satin shoes. They matched the green pattern in her dress. They were a little loud. If his girlfriend had asked that question, he'd have rolled his eyes. "They're very nice. And so are you." He opened the door and she got in, showing some bare leg in the process, which did not go unnoticed. It had been some time since anyone held the door open for Melissa and she was enjoying the extra attention. So far things were moving along nicely. Frank was easy to be with, and he was definitely thinking the same thoughts as she was, without being crude about it.

"What's in the bag?" he asked. They were driving south on the main highway, passing Happy Harry's place. Frank tooted his horn and waved as they drove by. Anyone watching would have thought he was a local.

"It's a surprise for later. I brought along dessert. I hope you like it." She took the jar out of the bag and held it up for him to see.

"Oh my, this is going to be quite a night. That stuff will melt your socks," Frank said smiling.

"Well just take it easy then. I don't want anything below your belt to melt," she giggled. Frank thought that was funny and laughed loudly. Then he reached over and patted her leg and leaned close enough to kiss her on the cheek.

After a surprisingly pleasant dinner of meatloaf and mashed potatoes, Frank drove directly to the motel. Without any pretense, they undressed and crawled into bed and snuggled like an old married couple, pulling up the blanket. Then they watched TV and sipped from the jar. For Frank, it felt good just having a nice warm, naked body lying next to his. The syrup hit him pretty hard and he had a difficult time getting out of bed to go to the bathroom. He stumbled like a drunken sailor on rough water, weaving his way into the other room.

When he returned, he turned out the lights, turned off the TV, crawled back into bed, snuggled against Melissa's backside and listened to her snoring. With all the syrup he'd consumed, there was no way he could be Mr. Wonderful tonight. Never the less, he fell asleep content with one arm draped over Melissa's hip. The fragrance from her bubble bath still lingered. Just before falling asleep, Frank decided this investigation might take a few days to complete. There was no hurry to get back to Atlanta now.

The next morning was the first time in five years that Melissa was late opening the café for breakfast. Frank drove her home then met her at the café. He needed a caffeine fix. He had a hangover that wasn't too bad, considering how much syrup he'd polished off, first at Happy Harry's then at the motel. Sooner or later, he'd find out where he could buy some to take back with him. It was the best moonshine he'd ever tasted, and by far the most potent.

When Melissa poured his coffee, she pretended to be avoiding his stare. He whispered, "Did we have fun last night?" He had a hard time hiding his smirk.

"Hush, remember you're a stranger to these folks. Don't embarrass me, or I won't go out with you tonight." She smiled as she walked away, knowing his eyes were following her. Tonight they would start earlier, and she'd make sure he didn't drink as much as he had last night. She was pretty sure they hadn't had sex, so she planned to remedy that oversight tonight. And, she'd remember to set the alarm clock. Considering all she'd had to drink last night, she felt pretty perky.

She hadn't been out on a date in over a year. She liked Frank's confident attitude without being too pushy. He didn't seem to be in any hurry. She liked that. When they had climbed into bed she remembered he wanted to snuggle and didn't want to immediately jump her bones. She decided that Frank was someone she could like a lot.

Sheriff Billy walked into the café and ordered a big breakfast. After testing his coffee, he turned and looked directly at Frank, sitting two stools away.

"You the fellow that's been asking about the famous missing truck?"

"Don't suppose you know anything about it? Nobody else seems to," Frank said.

"Just what you saw on the report my deputy showed you. If it was me, I wouldn't have a wasted the trip up here, a phone call could have gotten what you wanted."

"I never pass up a chance to get out of the office. I enjoyed the trip. Very scenic."

"Yep, and it'll be just as scenic on your way back. Now that you've discovered your missing truck isn't anywhere around here, I guess there's no real reason for hanging around is there?" The sheriff gave Frank a cold, insincere smile.

"That just depends. It's a nice town you have here. I thought I just might stick around for a few days and take in the sights." He was thinking about Melissa's comment about seeing him again tonight. He was glad he hadn't bothered to check out yet. He could justify staying another day or two. There were a few junkyards to check out. The sheriff seemed a bit testy.

"You can do all that in less than an hour. What's the real reason for your visit?"

"Don't know as I have to have another reason. What's your big interest in me, Sheriff? You worried I might find the truck, or the person who stole it?"

"Oh I seriously doubt you'll find the truck. I'm not even convinced there ever was one here. My deputy tells me the driver may have been hitchhiking and made up the whole story. He probably sold the truck up in Harriman, or lost it in a card game. We should have checked to see if he'd been drinking, but we felt sorry for the guy. Didn't want to give him a hard time. Now I'm thinking maybe we should have taken a closer look at him. Is he a friend of yours?"

"Not really."

"So what is your interest?" The sheriff's breakfast was sitting in front of him untouched.

"I know the man who owned the truck. The insurance company is giving him a hard time about it. I told him I had to be up this way on business and that I'd ask around for him. See if anyone saw anything."

"Uh huh. And just what is it you do, Mr. ahh...."

"Gibson. Frank Gibson. I do some contract work for a finance company. Whenever there's a problem with the insurance on an open loan, I try to help them out. Make sure all the paperwork is correct, that sort of thing. Sometimes my curiosity gets the better of me and I poke my nose into files, ask a lot of questions, see who gets nervous. Not unlike what you do I suppose." Frank gave the sheriff a big smile, but mentally giving him the bird. He remembered the warning Happy Harry had given last night, to be careful.

"But you don't really have any business here, right?"

"Not yet, but you never know."

"I'm telling you, there's nothing here for you. No reason for you to stick around. You think maybe there's a hint in that message?"

"If there was, it flew right over my head. The Chamber of Commerce wouldn't be too happy to hear the way you talk to visitors. You know, people like me who might be thinking of buying a place here, or starting a business here maybe? People like that are used to having the red carpet treatment, not the bum's rush."

"Well until I'm convinced otherwise, you're just snooping around. If that missing truck were here, my deputies would have found it by now. They know every inch of this county. That's an advantage you don't have. So like I said, I'm not buying any of your hooey and I'm not shy about telling you. So if I was you, I'd cut my visit here real short and take in the scenery on my way home, wherever that is."

"Hey Mellie, these eggs are cold! Bring me something hot." The sheriff turned and talked to several other patrons,

60

ignoring Frank and the conversation that abruptly ended with a warning.

Melissa brought Frank a refill. She gave him a frown. She'd heard everything and was trying to send Frank a warning to be careful. She put another plate in front of the sheriff. She wished Sheriff Billy hadn't used her nickname, Mellie in front of Frank. It suggested they might know each other on a friendlier basis, which at one time, they had.

They hadn't been romantically inclined toward one another for the last three years. She did wonder from time to time where Billy was getting it, since he never seemed to have a date. The local rumor she'd heard about Eulla servicing the sheriff was just something silly to laugh about. She didn't believe the rumor could be true. She also knew that the librarian had an interest in the sheriff. She was a much prettier candidate. However Billy never seemed to show much interest in any of the available women locally.

Just then the door opened and a very large man filled the doorway. His big shiny bald head actually brushed against the top of the door frame. He was wearing an old faded denim jacket without sleeves, showing well-muscled tattooed arms. He wasn't wearing a shirt, revealing a hairy chest and flat, muscled abdomen.

His jeans and boots were dirty. Frank thought he looked like a biker, even though he hadn't heard any motorcycle noise outside. Or the man could be a professional wrestler. He looked a lot like Jesse Ventura, former wrestler and former governor.

"Hey Billy, what's going on?" The big man said sitting several stools away from the sheriff. It was rare for anyone to call him Billy, except his brother.

"What are you doing around here, Darius?" The sheriff didn't look happy to see the big man. Frank was happy for the intrusion. It took the focus off him. Frank was able to discern a noticeable change in the sheriff's demeanor.

"Lookin' for a bad dude, what else would I be doing in a burg like this?"

"I didn't notice you drive in."

"That's 'cause I didn't. I hopped a freight train coming this way. Dude I'm lookin' for is a drifter. Beats me how he ever managed to make bail. Now I gotta find him and bring him back, so he can stand trial for aggravated assault with a weapon."

"What makes you think he's around here?"

"I'm not for sure he is. I just got tired of riding the rails and I was hungry for some of Melissa's good grub. You going to eat those eggs? If not, slide em over here. Man, I'm powerful hungry!" Without waiting for the sheriff to answer, the man stood up and reached over and grabbed the plate in front of the sheriff.

"Help yourself, I was just leaving. Stop by my office later, I want to talk to you."

"I'll have to check my calendar and see if I have a spare fifteen minutes. Ha, ha, hah." The man laughed loudly. His presence dominated the café. "What are you looking at?" He said to a couple in one of the booths. The man enjoyed making others feel uncomfortable. Frank doubted anyone would be foolish enough to stand up to him. Even the sheriff was reluctant to stick around.

"Hey Melissa, bring me a piece of pie and put all this on Sheriff Billy's tab." When he finished, he got up and left, failing to leave a tip. Frank was nursing a third cup of coffee, waiting for things to get quiet.

"How'd you manage to get the sheriff so pissed at you?" she asked Frank.

"I don't know, but he sure is nervous about me looking around. Makes me think he's got something to hide."

"We better forget about tonight. You just skeedaddle, and stop back real soon. Here's my phone number in case you want to call me." She handed him a piece of paper folded.

"Thanks, but I'm not letting that little power-hungry sheriff run me out of town. I haven't done anything wrong, so he has no reason what so ever to arrest me, or even question me. I know a little about what my rights are. He likes to push people around...."

"Don't do anything foolish. He makes his own law around here and gets away with it. You stand up to him, he'll put you behind bars with a few bruises and nobody can do a thing about it. Take my word on it, he's not someone to play games with."

"You know him fairly well, don't you?"

"Oh yeah, we go back a ways together, not that I want to think about it. There was a time when I used to think he was cute. Now I know him a lot better and all I can say is he's a cheap sumbitch. Always tells me to put his meal on his tab. Hell, he ain't got no tab, never did have one. Doesn't leave a tip, either."

"So he just eats here free?"

63

"Has been for a long time. He doesn't pay for anything anywhere here in town. Just tells everybody the same thing. 'Put it on my tab'."

"It sounds like he has everyone right where he wants them."

"You never heard that from me. And I already warned you about him. So please be careful and don't make no trouble, or I'll have to visit you in jail and bring you a piece of pie 'cause that's the only piece you'll be getting' in there."

"I'm going to remember that. What about that bounty hunter that was just in here?"

"He's one mean machine. You saw the way he was with the sheriff? He ain't afraid of nobody. He pops in here once or twice a month. Likes to beat up on those drifters that ride in the boxcars. Railroad is just a couple blocks away. We get a dozen trains a day pass by here, hauling freight."

Frank promised to call Melissa later in the day. He wanted to see if there were any more junkyards or body shops around that weren't on the list he had. He showed the list to Melissa after she took another order. When she came back, she hesitated then told him he might find another junk-yard outside of town, across the river. She gave him directions and he left, leaving another large tip. The woman was working too hard for little money, he thought.

He also planned on staying over another night and spending it with her, regardless of the sheriff's warning. He waved to the dishwasher, Maria as he left and she waved back wondering what was going on. Nobody ever paid her any attention.

"Now don't you be flirting with the customers," Melissa joked. Maria was married, unshapely and had a visible mustache. When her hair was pulled back she could pass for a homely man.

"That one has eyes for only you. I saw the way he looked at you. I think he's sweet on you," Maria said.

"Really? He probably has a steady girlfriend back home," Melissa said. Once again she smoothed her apron and wished she could have a cigarette. She was glad she had thought to jot down her phone number for Frank.

Chapter 5

It took Frank a few minutes to find the gravel road leading past Dent's junkyard. The fact that the deputy had deliberately not mentioned it was reason enough to suspect the place. Frank drove by slowly. He noticed an old rusting school bus loaded with parts. He continued on until the gravel became dirt then the hint of a turnaround. He couldn't find a suitable place to park without being seen. There was a tall stand of trees on the side of a hill that looked like a good place. Getting there posed a problem.

Frank returned down the road, past the junkyard again and made a left turn onto the intersecting road at the bottom of the hill, overlooking the river. A few minutes later, he found another similar road going back up into a wooded area. He saw a singlewide mobile home sitting on concrete blocks and a small barn with a cleared area that might pass for a garden.

Continuing on, he found an old abandoned farmhouse on the left with a gravel drive overgrown with weeds. Frank pulled in as far as he could. He hadn't seen anyone, or heard anything. He hoped his arrival went unnoticed. Frank took a pair of binoculars from the trunk, pulled on a baseball cap and circled around the old house to the rear. He detected a foul stench as he passed by the house. There was a hint of a path leading up to a hill and more trees. He walked quickly by the old outhouse and continued in the direction of the same hill he'd seen from the other side. It took him 10 minutes to reach a good observation spot. He sat down, with his back to a big Poplar tree, focused his binoculars and waited.

Frank wasn't a natural outdoors person. He didn't hunt animals and he had a natural fear of snakes so he was careful to check the surrounding area before getting into a more relaxed sitting position that was well shaded. The junkyard was easily seen from this higher elevation. It was less than a half-mile away. With the help of high-powered binoculars he was able to read the license number on a truck parked next to the barn. There was some activity going on in the barn, Frank saw a young man go in and out several times. Then he saw the barn door slide open and the truck backed into the barn, leaving just the cab portion outside.

Adjusting the focus, Frank could just make out that two people were hoisting an engine and transmission into the bed of the truck. Frank was tempted to go back to his car and wait at the bottom of the hill and follow the truck. He wondered if the destination was Happy Harry's. If so, the engine came out of a similar Chevy truck and the rest of it was no doubt in pieces inside that barn. Frank wondered if perhaps Happy Harry knew more than he had let on earlier.

Enjoying the surrounding scenery, Frank spotted a red-tail hawk circling around overhead periodically screeching his unique sound. Through the binoculars Frank observed the bird. Only its head seemed to move as it searched the terrain below. Its wings remained spread riding a gentle thermal.

A slight breeze picked up from the valley below, and for the first time in years, Frank considered the real benefits of camping. Being outside in the woods on a nice day was a refreshing break from the hectic busy streets in Atlanta. Frank was concentrating on the activity inside the barn again and never heard the silent footsteps behind him. Whoever it was, knew how to stalk prey in the woods.

"Get up slow and easy and put your hands where I can see 'em," the voice ordered. "Do something foolish and this shotgun will blow you down to that holler in pieces." It was a husky, serious-sounding voice.

"You don't know who you're dealing with," Frank said. He was startled and surprised that he was so easily found since he was fairly well hidden. The man must have seen him arrive and followed him.

"Guess I don't care, either," the man said.

With a shotgun pushed into the middle of his back, Frank was forced to walk through the tall grass back to his car, with his hands raised like the captured Taliban prisoners he'd seen on TV. Somewhere along the hike, Frank remembered that he'd left his binoculars beside the big Poplar tree. He hoped he'd have a chance to retrieve them later. For now, it was a trespass situation, which he hoped he could talk his way out of. When they arrived by Frank's car, he was told to stop. He opened the driver's side door and was beginning to hope the man just might let him go, when he was hit in the head by the shotgun's stock.

Frank fell forward onto the seat unconscious. The man removed Frank's wallet, car keys and money. Then he pushed Frank's bent body to the other side, got in the car and started the engine. He noticed the gas tank was almost full. He backed the car carefully out onto the gravel road. In two day's time there wouldn't be much trace of a car ever having parked there, particularly if it rained. It was an unfitting end to Frank's curiosity.

* * *

"Sheriff's office," Eulla announced, answering the phone.

"Looks like a car on fire out near the quarry on Yancy Lane. Pretty good blaze going, so I can't tell if anyone is in it, or not," the caller said. "Oh shit, it just exploded!"

"I'll send a fire truck and a patrol car right away. You stay there they'll want to talk to you. What's your name?"

"Don't have time to stand here and chat with ya. Gotta go." Click. Whoever had called, hung up. Eulla had an idea who the caller was. She thought she recognized the voice. She got Deputy Wolfe and directed him to check out the fire. Yancy Lane was the gravel road that led to the community dump, which was an old stone quarry the Yancy family owned for years. It was a remote area, across the river. And because of the constant smell coming from the dump, it wasn't a favored place for kids who wanted to park and neck. But it was a good place for target practice on rats.

When Frank didn't call, Melissa knew something was wrong. He didn't seem like the type to split without saying goodbye. It was 6:00 in the evening when she drove to the motel to see if he'd checked out. His Pontiac wasn't there. The blinds in his room were open just enough for her to peek in and see the bed made and Frank's suitcase was still open on the low cabinet. So he was still in town. Her next stop was the sheriff's office. There was a good possibility that Frank had another run-in with Sheriff Billy and was spending a few hours behind bars, courtesy of Harmon County and her ex-boyfriend. She wondered if perhaps the sheriff was showing just a little bit of jealousy.

Eulla told Melissa that all the holding cells were empty. Sheriff Billy was over at the railroad-switching yard with Darius, they were looking for a bail jumper who'd been spotted in that area by some of the hobos that rode the Iron Highway. Darius maintained a friendly relationship with the 'bos. They were a good source of needed information in his line of work. They never gave him any trouble.

Then Eulla told Melissa about the call on a car on fire out on Yancy Lane in the stone quarry. It was only about two miles from Dent's junkyard and Melissa knew, without being told, that the car would be a white Pontiac Grand Am 4-door. She hoped Frank wasn't inside, and if he wasn't, then he'd no doubt be in some shallow grave somewhere out there, or possibly in the quarry. He was probably snooping and got caught, she thought. It didn't matter who caught him, dead was dead. She felt an instant chill and her body shook for a brief moment.

Once more Melissa had looked for love and lost it before anything worthwhile could get started. She felt bad about Frank. She took a deep breath and tried to put the whole episode out of her mind. To ask any more questions would be too dangerous, even for her. She felt a tinge of guilt, because she had pointed Frank in that direction. Dent's name wasn't on the list Frank had shown her, and she'd been quick to point that out... and it probably got him killed. She didn't explain any of this to Eulla knowing it would go right back to Sheriff Billy.

"Was this guy you're looking for a new boyfriend?" Eulla asked. Eulla was aware that Billy and Melissa had been an item a few years ago. She guessed the problem was Melissa was about five feet eight inches tall. In any kind of heels, she'd be taller than Billy. Eulla didn't have to worry about that. She was four inches shorter than Billy... and always would be.

"No, nothing like that. He just... oh forget it, it isn't that important now." Melissa didn't have a good story to tell and she wasn't that good at making up things quickly. Anything she said would be taken the wrong way, so she just left, hoping that Eulla didn't read too much into her stopping by. No doubt she'd report the visit to Sheriff Billy when he returned, and he'd wonder what was going on and no doubt ask her in the morning, while eating breakfast. That's the way he would do things, just show up and start asking questions, not concerned about who overheard. He liked having an audience. It added to the embarrassment of the moment and gave him a decided advantage, not that he needed one.

* * *

"So, did your new boyfriend leave town?" Sheriff Billy asked, just as she had expected. He was sitting at the counter in his usual spot. Hat on, big smirk on his face, turning to make sure that everyone in the place could hear his question.

"He wasn't my boyfriend, just someone passing through. He asked me to have dinner with him last night, but he didn't show up. Since you gave him such a hard time in here yesterday, I figured he was visiting you at the Hard Rock Motel."

"Uh huh. Well I guess he took my advice and cut short his visit. Sorry if I cost you a free dinner and a little fun."

"It's no big deal." Billy hadn't mentioned the car fire, so she didn't bring it up, or ask about it. Maybe Eulla hadn't said anything about that part of their conversation.

"You're right, it isn't. When a stranger like that comes into town and starts asking a lot of questions, just refer them to my office and we'll handle it, okay? I didn't like the guy first time I saw him. Something about him wasn't right, know what I mean?"

"No, he seemed okay to me. Didn't ask me any questions." Melissa knew what bothered the sheriff. Frank hadn't displayed any concern or fear, that's what it was.

"Oh yes he did. He asked you out, didn't he? Ha, ha, hah. Gotcha!"

"Did you and Darius find the man he was looking for?"

"Not yet. If I was a fugitive, I sure wouldn't want Darius out there tracking after me. He's just like a Bloodhound. He ever ask you out, Mellie?"

"No, and I wouldn't be interested, if he did either."

"Really? Now that's interesting. You'd go out with that nosey stranger you didn't know, but you wouldn't go out with Darius. And he's been coming 'round here for some time. Why is that? You got something against bald-headed men?"

"Darius scares the hell out of me, that's why. Now can we drop this dumb subject?"

"A little touchy this morning aint' we? Okay, subject's closed. Put this is on my tab." The sheriff tipped his wide-brimmed hat forward, grabbed a toothpick and sauntered out. Melissa knew she'd hear all about the car on fire by the time her lunch crowd started to arrive around 11:00. She didn't want to appear too interested, but she was never the less.

The lunch crowd arrived early. Melissa heard several versions of the car found on fire that subsequently exploded and continued to burn. Eventually someone mentioned that they found a charred body inside, burned beyond recognition. The sheriff would have to send the remains to Chattanooga to be identified. Melissa had a difficult time getting through fixing and serving lunch.

She closed promptly at 2:30 and drove back to the motel. Maybe Frank left something that would help her notify a relative, or his employer. It was the least she could do. Her conscience still bothered her. There was also a remote possibility that the car that exploded wasn't Frank's. Even if he just skipped their date and left town, it was better than him being dead.

"Sorry, Melissa, we don't have anyone registered here under that name," the owner told her.

"He stayed here. He was in room one oh five last night."

"I'm afraid you're mistaken. Room one oh five wasn't occupied last night. If you have any information about this missing person, I suggest you talk to the sheriff," he said.

Melissa wished now that she hadn't come back to the motel. Frank was murdered, and somebody was covering it up. Now she had to be careful because she knew the truth and it scared her. There was no one she could turn to for help. She spent a restless, sleepless night thinking about everything that had happened. Frank said he was looking for a missing truck that belonged to a friend. That was the reason he'd given her for coming to Paradise Valley. Billy didn't seem to believe him. So maybe there was more to the story. He was looking for junkyards.

If she hadn't agreed to have dinner with him, he would have left… and would still be alive. That bothered her. And Sheriff Billy had obviously checked the motel and had given instructions not to say anything to anyone. It was as if Frank had never visited Paradise Valley. Eventually someone would come around to check on Frank's disappearance. Melissa wasn't sure what she'd say if asked. She had a difficult time driving her old Honda Civic back to her house. Her hands were shaking so bad. Once inside her house, she locked the front door immediately and checked the lock on the back door as well. She rarely worried about security, or the sheriff… until now. For the first time in years she didn't feel safe.

* * *

"Good morning Mellie. Just coffee today, Sweetheart." Sheriff Billy sat at the counter and took off his hat, something he never did. And, he never called her 'sweetheart'. Those two simple acts made her tense. "I hear you've been playing detective, asking questions about that nosey guy who was sweet on you. What's the matter, didn't he leave you his phone number?"

"As a matter of fact he didn't."

"And you're thinkin' maybe he's the one that burned up in the car, at the quarry huh?"

"I guess it's possible, I don't know."

"That's right, you don't know. And anything you do know, you should be telling to me, since I'm in charge of the investigation, unless you think there's someone out there better qualified. Am I getting through to you, Mellie?"

"Yes. Anything else?"

"Not for now. I hear that you're asking any more questions about this guy, I'm not going to be happy with you. It never pays to be on the wrong side of the sheriff now does it?"

"No, it doesn't."

"Good. Try to remember that." He picked up his hat, squared it on his head and walked to the door. "Oh, and put the coffee on my tab." He chuckled lightly as he left. Melissa was glad no one else was in the café, except Maria to hear that conversation. The sheriff timed it just right.

* * *

"Harvey, we got us a little problem. That guy who was snooping around, looking for a blue Chevy pickup? Well guess what? He was an insurance investigator." Sheriff Billy was not happy. Giving his older brother this news wasn't something he looked forward to. The sheriff had gone through the contents of Frank's suitcase and briefcase and found documents, reports and forms. The sheriff hated being lied to and didn't regret that the nosey guy, trying to pass himself off as somebody else, had run into some trouble. Sheriff Billy didn't regret it for a second.

"That right? No skin off my butt what he was. I don't have the damned truck. Why are you getting crosswise with me?"

"Because you gotta tell Bobby Lee to stop cruising in the tow truck for a while. I'm going over to talk with Dent, too. I got a hunch they'll be sending someone in here real soon to check us out, and we gotta look clean as the Monday wash hangin' on the backyard line."

"I think you're over-reacting, Billy. So what if he was an insurance dick. He had a little accident while poking around up there in those hills. Probably ran across a moonshine still and found out, that arriving unannounced, can get you killed. Least that's the way I see it," Harvey said.

"Uh huh, and what do you suppose he was doing up there? He sure wasn't looking for any moonshine."

"You tell me little brother, you're the sheriff. What'd you put down in your report?"

"I'm still workin' on it. Say he drove up some strange road, thought it was peaceful and decided to take a nap. Some dumb yahoo sees a deer and takes a shot, but misses. You know some of that high-powered ammo travels a long way. Might have hit the car somewhere near the gas tank and it exploded. Just dumb bad luck to be sitting out there at the wrong time, and no witnesses. By the time anyone finds the wreckage it's too late."

"So did you find a bullet hole in the car?" Harvey hadn't bothered to look closely. What he had hauled back to the yard was an almost unrecognizable hunk of twisted, burned metal that stunk worse than any outhouse. He'd towed bad wrecks before, but nothing as bad as this one had been.

"Not at first, but there's one in it now, just for safety's sake." Billy Hargis thought his version of what might have happened sounded plausible enough.

"Uh huh, well I guess that's as good as any other story. When I hauled it down here I didn't notice a bullet hole, course I wasn't looking for any, either. Not much left to examine. You figure someone will come get it?"

"Bet on it. As soon as you talk to anyone who's looking around, call me, and talk to Bobby Lee, hear?"

"Yeah, yeah. I think you got your shorts in a knot over nothin', but it's none of my business."

"It sure as hell is your business! Don't start with that. Bobby Lee grabbed that pickup. Later, he drove it over to Dent's place and they tore it to pieces, so don't act like this isn't anything to do with you. We all got something to protect here. Trust me, we haven't seen the last of this incident." It had been a long time since Billy had ever spoken harshly to his older brother. When he drove off in his Bronco, he laid some rubber on the pavement. It was his way of adding an exclamation point to his parting statement.

Harvey picked up the phone. He thought he'd better warn Dent that Billy was on his way over with a bee up his ass. What annoyed Harvey the most about that pickup was

Bobby Lee claiming he lost the $ 800 that Dent had given him. He wanted to believe his son, but he still had doubts about the money. Now, that same truck was causing a lot of serious trouble with an insurance investigator getting killed. He must have found something for Dent to kill him the way he did.

Billy was doing his best to cover it up. Harvey walked out to his storage yard for another look at the burned out hunk of twisted metal. It was difficult to even identify what type vehicle it was. He wanted to confirm for himself there was a bullet hole somewhere close to the gas tank that was now split into pieces. He could still smell the stink of burning flesh as he approached the charred carcass of what was once a 4-door automobile.

* * *

"Dent, you got anything left of that Chevy pickup Bobby Lee brought over here?" The sheriff asked.

"Sure, but nothing that can be traced. The engine went over to Happy Harry's. Sold the front clip to a dealer up in Rockwood. They came and got it, so there isn't much left."

"Well get rid of everything that is left. I don't want anything laying around that someone might suspect came from that truck."

"Whoa, just a damned minute. You mind telling me just when you became my new partner? That car burning up must have really got you spooked."

"Dent, I'm everybody's partner in this town, and now isn't the time for you, or anyone else, to start second guessing me, or telling me how to be sheriff. There's going to be trouble coming our way. I know it just as sure as I'm standing here."

"Well then move someplace else, cause I'm not foolish enough to throw out anything worth some money and you know it. Just take a look around and what do you see? Junk, parts and scrap. It would take an expert to recognize some of the stuff I got laying around here."

"And that's just my point. My guess is there'll be several experts breathing down our backside pretty soon. They find one small piece they think is part of that stolen truck, they'll haul your sorry ass off to prison and there won't be a thing I can do to stop them."

"Yeah? Well you better make damned sure that doesn't happen then... partner!"

"Will you listen to me!" Sheriff Billy screamed. "What do you think I'm trying to do right now? I'm out here trying to protect you, and you're worried about losing a few dollars over some junk parts. Get rid of 'em, and do it today. This whole damned mess has given me one big headache."

"You find out who torched the car?" Dent asked.

"I got a pretty good idea. I'm also pretty sure there was someone up on that hill over there watching what was going on over here. I found a pair of binoculars under a tree across the hollow."

"Oh yeah? Maybe he was watching that red-tailed hawk that keeps circling overhead." Dent didn't seem to be very worried that someone had been watching him and his operation. "So how long before these dickheads show up?"

"Don't know. They may not check in with me, but I'll know just as soon as they hit town. I got spies everywhere."

"Does this mean there won't be a cockfight Saturday night?"

"Oh shit! I'd completely forgotten about that. I'll speak to Bovis and see what he thinks. He'll be really pissed, but he's nobody's fool." The sheriff could imagine the domino effect that could take place if anybody said or did the wrong thing. He needed to put someone behind bars fast. That might just take the focus off everything else.

* * *

Ely Slocum lived alone in an old, patched singlewide mobile home about a half-mile from where the car exploded. Ely spent a lot of time walking in the woods searching for Ginseng. When he was younger he was known for being a peeping Tom. He was always a little different. Sheriff Billy was pretty certain that Ely was responsible for the car burning. If not, he surely knew who was.

The problem was catching Ely at home. Sheriff Billy had stopped several times only to find the place empty and filthy. Ely was still living there, that was evident by all the dirty dishes in the sink and on the counter. Garbage was on the floor and the trash was piled out back.

Putting Ely behind bars for a few days was probably a good idea and would enhance his image as a sheriff who was doing his job. He didn't care what Harvey or Dent thought. They needed him. He was more concerned about what Bovis might think. They had been friends for a long time and Sheriff Billy hated to think this one incident could tarnish his reputation. Too bad the nosey investigator hadn't taken his advice, he thought. Then none of this would have happened. Paradise Valley didn't need any outside publicity or investigation that might focus on his procedures.

Sheriff Billy was kicking at the trash with his boot behind Ely's place when he heard a dog bark in the distance. He remembered that Ely had a dog. Maybe it was his dog barking. If so, then Ely must be somewhere close by. Sheriff Billy went back to the Bronco and waited, listening to the breeze in the tall trees and the birds chirping. He even heard the hawk screeching somewhere beyond the stand of Poplars. He was getting tired of waiting. He had better things to do than sit out here waiting for a dumb ass trash picker like Ely. He'd let one of his deputies pick him up.

As the sheriff backed out of the gravel drive he turned and drove on up to where the abandoned farmhouse stood. Once again he saw evidence that a car had been in the drive recently and could see where some of the tall grass was tracked down. The path led to the hill a few hundred yards behind the house where he'd found the expensive binoculars and saw a fresh candy wrapper. It was enough evidence for him to conclude that Frank Gibson had been covertly watching Dent's place. Someone caught him there by surprise. It was the only logical reason for the man to leave the high-powered binoculars behind.

Ely could have done it, but he was never known to be dangerous or violent, just a loner and a little strange. Or, it could have been Dent.

Walking past the old deserted farmhouse, the sheriff heard a dog bark again. This time it seemed to come from within the farmhouse. Sheriff Billy walked around the house. High weeds and briars made his progress annoyingly slow. When he stepped onto the broken down porch, the dog barked continuously, telling him the animal was somehow trapped inside. The sheriff kicked at the side door and it opened allowing a terrible stench to escape, along with the mongrel dog that appeared happy to see him.

A putrid smell emanated from inside. On the kitchen floor, Ely was curled up on his side in a fetal position. The man had been dead for several days judging by the number of flies buzzing around the corpse. Sheriff Billy wished he'd never found Ely. Now he had a real problem on his hands. In the living room there was evidence that someone had spent time there. A half-burned candle was inside a soup can on the floor along with a piece of worn carpet. Surely Ely wouldn't spend the night here when he lived just down the road. So maybe he saw or heard something that caused him to come take a looksee. And whoever was hiding here caught him by surprise.

That same person must have taken Frank Gibson by surprise, too. Only one other suspect came to mind. For a fleeting second, Sheriff Billy considered burying Ely's body somewhere where it wouldn't be found. That way, he could blame this whole mess on Ely. Case closed.

The sheriff called his office and told both deputies on duty to meet him. He wanted his camera for some pictures. The Medical Examiner would have to come from another county, so that would take a few hours. While Sheriff Billy was waiting, it suddenly dawned on him that Ely had an older vehicle and it wasn't in his drive, and it wasn't here. So where the hell was Ely's car? And what make was it? Sheriff Billy couldn't recall, so he called and asked Eulla to find out for him.

All this time, he'd felt sure that Dent was responsible for killing Frank Gibson. Now he had to search for someone else. The farmhouse was a good five miles from town and the railroad tracks. The fugitive Darius was looking for could have made it up here easily enough without ever being seen. The lit candle must have gotten Ely's attention. Nobody else lived close enough to ever see it.

"Darius, how dangerous was your fugitive?" The sheriff asked back at his office. He was glad Darius was still hanging around.

"Any man who's on the run from the law is dangerous. If this guy killed someone up there in the hills, then that makes this hunt all the more interesting. My warrant is for missing a court hearing on an assault charge. Hard to believe he'd kill someone to avoid that, but who knows? Guess I'll stick around a little longer. You just might need my help."

As in any small community, the word spread quickly about Ely's murder. The man had been strangled and the only witness was his dog. Suddenly another missing vehicle was insignificant. Sheriff Billy had two murders on his hands, and they appeared to be connected. He had to notify the state police. Meanwhile, Eulla was able to learn that Ely's vehicle was listed as a '92 Plymouth Acclaim 4-door. Sheriff Billy was surprised because he always thought Ely drove a small, foreign-brand pickup truck.

Billy regretted Ely's death because he would have made an excellent suspect for the burned car and charred corpse. Now the focus was on a fugitive from another area. At least he could tell Bovis there was a solid suspect they were looking for. And he didn't have to worry about covering for Harvey or Dent. Either one of them was capable of running off the insurance investigator, or worse shooting him.

Chapter 6

Special Agents Greg Mathews and Noah Cody arrived in Paradise Valley from Chattanooga in a black Ford Taurus 4-door. Agent Carl Daniels arrived in a year old Honda Accord EX 4-door equipped with a sunroof, alloy wheels, V6 engine and a CD player with 6 speakers. It was metallic champagne color with South Carolina license plates. Insurance statistics indicated this model was among those most frequently stolen.

Usually the TBI didn't get involved in any local criminal activity unless a police chief, sheriff or district attorney requested their help. No one from Harmon County had ever sought their help until now. An anonymous letter to the Chattanooga office of the Tennessee Bureau of Investigation created some interest. The note indicated that an insurance investigator had recently disappeared. Apparently he was checking on a missing, presumably stolen, pickup truck and had been asking questions about chop shops in the area. TBI agents quickly established that a Frank Gibson had indeed been assigned to investigate several recent stolen vehicles in Harmon County. It was sufficient cause to take a first hand look.

Agent Daniels left the Honda sitting on the shoulder of the by-pass with the flashers blinking, and the doors locked. Under the right rear wheel well he placed a magnetic transponder that would allow the TBI team to track the vehicle.

Agent Mathews was the lead investigator. He parked his Ford Taurus in an obscure area of a small shopping center where they waited drinking coffee.

* * *

Nick Alexander spent the weekend with his friend Carol Mayberry, who told him what she was able to learn from her niece Cindy, when she was there the previous weekend. Now he was on his way to Atlanta, with a slight detour. Paradise Valley wasn't that much out of the way as it turned out. Nick was still driving a Ford Crown Victoria. He was fond of the car from his days on the St. Clair Shores police force where he drove a similar vehicle. The few changes were all nice improvements.

To get a feel for the area, Nick drove through the town, around the square, and back out to the highway then the by-pass where Cindy was reportedly stopped. He noticed the obscured speed limit sign, but only because he was looking for it. Otherwise it would have gone unnoticed. It was definitely a trap situation, he could see that quickly enough. He also noticed a county patrol car giving him a careful look as it passed him going the other way. Instinctively Nick slowed down and watched in his rearview mirror as the patrol car did a quick u-turn and proceeded to follow him at a distance.

Nick drove back into the square using a different street than before and noticed the sheriff's office. It wasn't in the county courthouse where he expected it to be. Instead, it was at the end of a row of stores on a side street a block away from the square. There was a large parking lot adjacent to the sheriff's office with plenty of available parking. However, the sheriff's white Ford Bronco was parked at the curb in front of the office. Nick decided it was like a doctor's sign informing patients that he was open. The sheriff would be in his office.

* * *

After waiting an hour, the three agents drove into town in the unmarked Ford Taurus. Their first stop after circling the town square was Millie's café for a sandwich. They sat in a booth and spoke softly. Melissa made several trips to their booth to refill their coffee cups. It was better service than most of the regular customers saw. She overheard one of the men mention something about the burned car.

She didn't know a lot about automobiles, but she did know that Frank Gibson had been driving a late model Pontiac Grand Am 4-door. These men had to be investigating Frank's murder, she felt certain of that. She thought about calling the sheriff's office to warn Billy then decided he didn't need a warning from her. Let somebody else do it.

While the agents were eating lunch, Eulla was busy receiving phone calls from Sheriff Billy's spy network. Three strangers, all well dressed, were seen driving around the town, checking it out. Sheriff Billy gave Eulla a nervous smile. He knew this moment would come sooner, or later. His black cowboy boots had a high shine, his khaki pants were neatly pressed. All the pornographic magazines and junk had been cleared out of the desk, ready for any inspection. He had Eulla alert the deputies to stay out on patrol and not to call in, unless it was really important.

Harvey was at the NAPA parts store when the black Ford Taurus cruised by. Because he had his back to the window, leaning on the counter, he failed to see it.

Bobby Lee was on his way to work at the garage when he spotted the Honda beside the road. It was a beauty. No flat tires. He hurried on to the garage and jumped into the unmarked tow truck. He was back to the Honda in less than 10 minutes, hooking to it. He had to jimmy the lock to get inside to release the hand brake. Without a key, he couldn't shift it into neutral, so he hooked to the front of the car instead of the rear. He was pulling the Honda into the storage yard when Harvey arrived and saw him.

"Just what the hell do you think you're doing? Don't you remember what I told you? Your uncle Billy put out the word to cool it, and here you are dragging in another one."

"But Paw, just look at it, it's like new. Even has a premium sound system and CD player."

"Billy, you need a good lesson in listening. Now back that car up to the fence and leave it there. Don't think about driving it, and don't think about taking it to Dent's place. You do, and he'll kick your ass and I'll do even worse."

"I don't see what the big deal is. We been doing this shit for a long time. So why is it that we have to stop now?"

"Boy you don't have the brains you were born with. That's a fact!" Harvey wasn't the fool his son was. He sensed something about the car. It was an expensive model with all the options. He couldn't fault his son for liking it. Any other time Dent would be delighted to have it. But this one smelled like bait. Harvey called the gas station to see if anyone had run out of gas recently? Then he called his brother, Billy to tell him what happened.

"Doesn't that kid of yours listen? This smells like a set up to me. Three strangers just arrived. My guess is they're state cops, so be very careful what you say to them if they come around asking questions. Better yet, don't say anything, send them over here to me and let me handle it. And tell Bobby Lee to keep his damned mouth shut. That kid has caused more trouble for us lately. I've just about had it with him. You tell him that."

Harvey had just hung up the phone when a well dressed stranger walked into the messy office. It was a rare moment to ever see Harvey worried, but this was one of those times and it showed.

"Help you with something?" Harvey asked.

"Yeah, I'm here to get my car. It's the beige Honda you have parked in your yard."

"What happened, you run out of gas?" Harvey was trying to be casual.

"I don't know what's wrong. The engine just died on me. It's got plenty of gas. I walked down the road to make a phone call and when I got back, you guys had already towed my car."

"Well... we try to help people who break down out there on the by-pass...."

"I didn't call you, so there was no reason for you to take my car."

"The sheriff authorizes us to make any tow that's required. We don't need your permission."

"And when did the sheriff call you to pick up my car?"

"Ah, he didn't. That's just a standing agreement, I mean order that we have."

"So you're telling me that the sheriff authorizes you to tow any vehicle that's in trouble on that by-pass?"

"Yes Sir, if it's unattended, we can tow it."

"Show me something in writing that says you have that authority."

"Now listen, I'm trying to do the right thing here. I don't want any trouble and just so you know there's no hard feelings, I won't charge you for the tow. If you have the keys with you, and you can get it started, you're welcome to drive it on out of here."

"How much to leave it here overnight?"

"That will cost you ten dollars."

"Fine. Then leave it set right where it is. I'll stop back for it tomorrow."

"Do you need a lift somewhere?"

"No I'm just walking over to meet the sheriff and see if what you just told me is really true. I'm sure you have insurance coverage in case there's any damage."

"Of course we have insurance. And I don't see any damage."

"We'll discuss that later. I left the car locked and somehow you managed to get inside, so if anything is broken, or stolen I'll hold you responsible."

The man walked out before Harvey could get his name. The man seemed to know the law and he was definitely trouble. The only person he could blame for this was Bobby Lee. And the kid still hadn't found the missing money. Dent said he'd given him a white envelope with the money inside. It wasn't sealed, not that it mattered. Somewhere between Dent's place and the garage, the money disappeared, unless Bobby Lee stopped off someplace along the way. Harvey was beginning to think there might be a little more to the story than he was told so far.

Agent Greg Mathews knew he had the man at the garage worried. His next stop was to visit the sheriff who was probably waiting for him to arrive. Noah and Carl drove up to the sight where the burned car was found. Greg's plan was for the sheriff to learn there were three men in town, but he would only be meeting Greg. This would make him wonder where the other two were, and what was going on. The car snatch would be a distraction and an annoyance, setting the stage for Greg's visit. He also had the feeling that they were expected, so this wasn't an entirely surprise visit.

Sheriff Billy was sitting at his desk, hat on, pretending to be reading something when Greg arrived. Eulla greeted him at the counter. The sheriff didn't bother to look up, supposedly concentrating on something more important.

"I'm looking for Sheriff Billy Bob Hargis, is that you?"

"Name's not Billy Bob. Folks around here call me Sheriff Billy, or Billy Hargis if they've known me a long time and we went to school together. What can I do for you?" The sheriff put down the piece of paper and tuned to the man, not offering him a seat.

"The man at the garage told me that he was instructed by you to tow my unattended vehicle from the by-pass. Since I only left it unattended for thirty minutes or so, I was wondering why you felt it was necessary to do that?"

"He's authorized to assist motorists who need help out there. When he finds a vehicle unattended he usually waits a few minutes for the driver to return. And sometimes he'll check with the gas station to see if anyone there owns the vehicle. If they're at the station, he'll give them a lift back and make sure it starts. More or less a courtesy you might say." It was a lot of fancy smoke, and Eulla had a difficult time keeping her giggle subdued.

"Well he was pretty quick to snatch my car, and he didn't do any of those nice things you just mentioned."

"I guess I'll have to get on old Harvey. He must be slipping."

"The fellow I spoke with at the garage, his name was Harvey Hargis. He any relation to you, Bubba?"

"You're talking awful disrespectful for someone who might want my cooperation. How about showing me some ID before we go any further. I like to know who I'm talking to." The Bubba bit really got him unnerved and Eulla became alert that something just might happen here.

"Sure thing." The agent opened his case displaying his badge and photo ID, all the while standing and looking directly at the sheriff who remained seated.

"I had a hunch you might be dropping in. Why did you feel the need to plant the car out on the highway?"

"We wanted to see how long it would sit there before someone snagged it. That seems to be happening a lot lately in Harmon County. Of course you'd know all about that, Harvey being your brother and all."

"If you know so much, why bother asking me anything? You come into town to play games? Or to give me some help?"

"Just what kind of help is it you're asking for, Billy Bob?"

"If you're going to continue to be antagonistic, we might as well put a halt to this conversation right now."

"I'll be the judge of when this conversation ends, not you. Where do the vehicles go after old Harvey impounds them?"

"They don't go anywhere. They remain there until the owner pays the bill and claims the vehicle."

"I see. And how much of cut do you get from that?"

"I resent your question. While Harvey is my brother, he doesn't give me a thing, and I wouldn't expect it."

"So you don't get a piece of the action? I'm having a hard time swallowing that one, Sheriff. But at least we know the first part of the system. Let's suppose the owner doesn't show up to collect the vehicle, for whatever reason, what happens next?"

"If after a week or so, its still there, we try to locate the owner, run the VIN number, check the registration. See if it's stolen." As soon as he said this, Billy realized his error.

"Uh huh. Does that happen very often?"

"No, not too often."

"So you don't locate the owner. What do you do, put it up for auction?"

"Not right away. It would have to remain in the impound area for ninety days before we'd do anything like that."

"Show me some records where you've done that. Just pick one out of your file, so I can see the dates and the procedures you took."

That caught Sheriff Billy by surprise. So far he was scooting along nicely, then this agent lowered a hammer on him. There weren't any such records to show and he had to stall this line of questioning.

"I guess I'd have to see a court order before I'd be able to dig up those files, and it would take a while to find them."

"I can get all the court orders I need, that's not a problem. So, I suggest you start looking after I leave. I'll check back with you tomorrow. By the way, where are you storing the vehicle that recently burned? I want to take a good look at it, maybe take a few pictures."

"Not much to see. Gas tank exploded and popped it into the air, landed upside down and flattened out pretty good. Poor fellow inside didn't have much of a chance. Burned him to a crisp. We sent the remains to Chattanooga. My guess is you already know all this."

"You said, 'poor fellow', are you certain it was a male occupant?"

"Well, call it an educated guess. We had this guy here last week asking a lot of questions about a truck that his friend said was stolen around here, only we don't have any stolen vehicle report on file...."

"Why is that?"

"The driver was kind of zippy, didn't know what planet he was on, or where he left the truck. Told my deputy that he ran out of gas. He picked him up walking down the road. For all we know, there wasn't a truck, or he smacked it up somewhere and thought he'd try to get away reporting that it was stolen, hoping the insurance company would pay. People will try anything, you know that."

"Uh huh, so you didn't bother to write a report?"

"We had very little information to go on. I think we took down the details he gave us, and of course we drove around looking for the alleged missing truck...."

"But you didn't look too hard, because ... like you said, it was probably in a ditch somewhere, out of your jurisdiction. Did you check with any of the surrounding counties? You know, just on the off chance the guy was telling you the truth?"

"Yeah we asked around, nothing."

"So who is this guy that came around asking all the questions?"

"He said he was a friend of the guy who owned the truck, but the owner wasn't the one driving it. Supposedly he loaned it to his cousin, the guy we picked up out on the highway."

"The cousin is the zippy guy?"

"Yeah. So now you got the picture?"

"No, not really. But we'll get there eventually. Any chance your brother, Hot Wheels Harvey could have snatched it and maybe forgot to tell you about it?"

"If he picked it up, I'd know about it, okay? He didn't pick it up, you can trust me on that."

"Sheriff, anyone tells me that, I immediately reach in my back pocket to make sure my wallet is still there."

"Well then, believe what you want. You asked me a question, and I gave you my best answer. What more do you want?"

"To see some reports showing the procedures you take on missing or abandoned vehicles for openers. You can work on that later. Right now, let's take a ride. You can show me exactly where you found the burned vehicle, and bring along any pictures you may have taken. You did take some pictures didn't you?"

"Of course we did. You think I don't know how to handle an investigation?"

"I'll have to get back to you on that, after I've had a look around."

"Fine. You trust me to drive? Or do you want to go in your car?"

"You drive, it's your turf."

"About time you began to realize that!" The sheriff finally stood up. The agent was a good four to five inches taller. Eulla knew what they meant. Billy hated looking up to anyone.

One of the deputies had used a can of spray paint to outline where the burned vehicle was found. It was just an oval outline painted blue, since it was the only color he had in his garage at the time. There wasn't much contrast. White or yellow would have been better.

"Looks like a pretty deserted area for a stranger to drive to," the agent commented, getting out of the sheriff's Bronco.

"Yeah, that's what I thought. Must have gotten lost."

"Okay, orient me here. Which way was the vehicle facing when you found it?"

Sheriff Billy was getting exasperated with this investigator who seemed to be trying very hard to prove his importance. The sheriff had a hunch the man already knew more than he was letting on, maybe trying to catch Billy in a lie, or trap him in some way. He'd have to be careful how he answered the man's annoying questions. Billy had already concluded that the man was deliberately trying to aggravate him, calling him Billy Bob, then later, Bubba. The sheriff was aware of those tricks, he'd used them himself, when he wanted to get someone aggravated enough that they became sidetracked, or unglued.

Now he had to remind himself to be careful. The agent was playing the same game with him. And Billy had already made a slip he wasn't sure went by unnoticed by the agent. It was about checking to see if a vehicle was on the stolen list. The vehicle shouldn't sit impounded for a week before checking.

"When we arrived, the fire was almost out. The vehicle was upside down, lying on its roof, which was flattened like a pancake. Front of the car was pointed that way," the sheriff pointed in the direction of the quarry entrance.

"Any idea on what might have caused the explosion?"

"It could have been this guy, whoever he was, didn't know the area very well and came up here by accident. Being a strange vehicle, he might have been in the wrong place at the wrong time. I found a bullet hole in the rear of the car. That could have hit the gas tank causing the explosion, which must have blown him up into the air."

"You're suggesting he may have happened onto something. What would that be, a still?"

"Maybe. Or it could have been a stray bullet from a hunter shooting at something else."

"This isn't hunting season."

"Well, for some folks up in the hills, there's no such thing as hunting season. They see a deer someplace, they shoot it and nobody's ever the wiser. Pretty hard to control that sort of thing."

"Okay, let's go look at the burn-out. Your brother Harvey keeping it secure?"

"Well, it's in his storage lot, and he keeps it locked. No reason for anyone to fool with what you're about to see. Stinks to high heaven."

"Did you know the man asking questions about the missing truck was an insurance investigator?"

"No, sure didn't. He never identified himself other than to tell me his name."

"And you didn't bother to check him out, right?"

"No reason to. He wasn't breaking any laws, just asking a few simple questions, then went on his way." They were back in town now approaching Harvey's garage. Sheriff Billy was glad the white tow truck wasn't there. He was also glad to see a tarp had been put over the burned vehicle. He hoped Bobby Lee wasn't anywhere close by.

The agent removed the tarp and walked around the bent and mangled metal remains examining it from every angle. He took several pictures, then kneeled down to examine the bullet hole. The metal was indented toward the inside around the hole. The agent wrote in his notebook, closed it and nodded that he was finished.

"So what do you want to do with this hunk of twisted scrap metal?" Harvey asked.

"Oh, we'll send a truck to get it. Our lab people will want to go over it in more detail." He wasn't about to comment on the bullet hole. However it got there, it didn't cause the explosion. He felt certain the lab would confirm his suspicion on that.

Someone added that touch after the explosion to cover up something. Not only did the wreckage smell bad, so did the way the investigation was going so far. There would be little cooperation from the sheriff, his deputies, or the brother. Small communities were like that toward anyone who was an outsider. That included uninvited TBI agents.

Agents Greg Mathews, Noah Cody and Carl Daniels re-convened at Millie's Mug & Skillet Café for a late lunch. They compared notes on the burn site. Greg gave his two associates a report on the burned vehicle in the storage lot.

"I think someone is yanking our chain here. That burned up piece of metal and melted plastic is the remains of an older model Plymouth or Dodge, early to mid-nineties. No VIN number by the windshield and no evidence that it had been removed, but that's difficult to determine right now."

"Why would an insurance investigator be driving an older model car?" Noah asked. Melissa was approaching with fresh coffee and overheard the question.

"If you fellas are investigating Frank Gibson's recent disappearance, for your information he was driving a Pontiac Grand Am. It looked like a new model."

"And how is it you'd know that?" Two agents asked the same question at the same time.

"Because he took me to dinner in it." She went on to tell them where they had dinner then mentioned that he was staying at a motel just south of town. She also mentioned that when she went back to check on Frank, because they had another date, the motel owner was emphatic that Frank had not stayed there.

"Maybe you had the wrong motel," Agent Noah offered, writing down all the points she was making.

"No Sir, it was room one oh five. I ought to know, I spent the night there with him!"

"Hmmm, now that's interesting. Why would the motel owner want to get involved in this cover up?" He spoke the question in front of Melissa, but it was directed to his associates. "Miss, is there anything else about this Frank Gibson you can tell us?"

"No, but if you say the burned car was an older model Plymouth, then it may not be Frank who was in that fire. And if it is Frank, then he was in a different automobile and someone had to put him there."

"I agree with your observation. Can you think of any reason he'd be up in that area?"

Melissa wiped her eyes and sat down at the table. The café was empty except for the three agents. She was glad for the opportunity to get some of the guilty feelings out in the open. She told the agents she was responsible for pointing Frank in that direction. She mentioned seeing the list of junkyards and happened to mention that Dent's place wasn't on the list.

Now it was starting to make more sense. Agent Greg Mathews had a point of departure to work with. Noah and Carl would work on the motel guy while Greg paid a visit to Dent's place. Melissa gave him directions and then asked to be kept out of it.

She feared a reprisal, from most of the town, many of whom were her customers, if it got out that she'd been talking about this, particularly after the sheriff had warned her not to. When they left, she worried about whether she did the right thing, talking to the special agents. In a sense she'd broken the unspoken code about giving strangers too much information.

* * *

Soon after Agent Mathews and Sheriff Billy left for the quarry, another stranger walked into the sheriff's office. Eulla decided he was another TBI agent until the man gave her his business card. It indicated he was a private investigator.

"We sure are getting our share of investigators today," Eulla said.

"What's going on to cause that to happen?" Nick asked.

"Well first we had this missing truck, then some guy came around asking a whole lot of questions. Turns out he was an investigator for the insurance company. Then he turns up missing. And there was a car caught on fire up in the quarry and there was a body in it, so everyone seems to think it was the missing insurance fella. Then the TBI shows up. Now you. So what part of all that are you interested in?" Eulla asked. Once she'd started the litany of what happened, she didn't know where to stop.

"None of it, but it sure sounds like you've got your hands full right now. Will the sheriff be back soon?"

"Honey, your guess is as good as mine. He left with one of the TBI agents a few minutes ago so I wouldn't expect him back anytime soon. Something I can do for you?"

"I realize all your records are confidential, but I'm interested in a recent arrest of a young lady that was charged with speeding."

"You'll have to be more specific than that. We catch a lot of young people speeding."

"This one spent the night here in jail. Her name was Cindy Stevens. She was driving an older model Mustang convertible. Does that ring any bells?"

"The name sounds vaguely familiar. When did all this happen?" Eulla asked. She was trying to be careful. Sheriff Billy didn't need any more problems right now and this had all the makings of a big problem, if the girl's family had hired a private investigator.

"Just a little over a week ago. I just figured you might remember something about it."

"Nooo, not really. I can look through the arrest records, but the sheriff is the only one authorized to release any of that information. I suggest you stop back a little later and speak with him."

"Thank you. I'll be sure to do that. Please see that he gets my card. Tell him I'd like to have a copy of the arrest report and how it was finalized." Nick sensed the woman was worried. Her pupils got larger when he mentioned Cindy's name and she looked to her left, meaning a lie was being formulated.

Had she looked to her right, or up, she would have been trying to remember. It was an old technique Nick used when he was still a police detective. Face to face always gave you signals that were invisible over the phone. Nick had once taught a course on interviewing techniques at the police academy.

Nick drove past the garage and storage area where Cindy said her Mustang had been kept overnight. The name on the garage jumped out at Nick. The sheriff's last name was also Hargis. No doubt in a small town like this they had to be related. Rather than wait around, Nick decided to head for Atlanta. He'd stop back on his return trip.

A picture was beginning to form in his mind. These small communities set up speed traps and collected big fines. And from what he'd just learned, it seemed that trouble was definitely brewing in Paradise Valley.

The sheriff was up to his eyeballs with investigators right now. Nick wondered how he could learn if anyone else had spent time in the jail, and had been molested or raped? That was always difficult information to come by. It wasn't something people volunteered. Arrest records might provide a few clues, if he could get access to them.

Chapter 7

Dent saw the black Ford Taurus pull into his yard. The gate was open and he knew who the occupant was. Billy had called earlier, and so had Harvey. The local alert system was working fine.

"Help you?" Dent asked, trying to act casual.

"Here to look around." Agent Mathews flashed his badge and walked right past Harvey, not asking any questions.

"Wait just a damned minute there. I didn't see any search warrant. You want to go pokin' around my place, you better have all your paperwork in order."

"Okay, if that's the way you want to play it, I'll get the search warrant and tear this place to pieces."

"Oh yeah, on what grounds? I got nothing to hide here, it's just what you see, a plain old junkyard with lots of stuff just setting around collecting rust and dust."

"Is that right? If that's the case, why are you so sensitive about me having a search warrant when there's obviously nothing here that would interest me, or cause you any concern?"

"'Cause I'm a law-abiding citizen, and I expect everyone else to be as well. Just what is it you're lookin' for?"

"First of all, are you the one who hauled that burned-out hunk of scrap to Harvey's storage lot?"

"Nope. Harvey picked it up. I saw it though. Not much left to look at. Sure did stink!"

"How do you suppose the bullet hole got there? You been doing any out of season hunting lately?"

"Don't know anything about a bullet hole. All I got here is a shotgun, and I ain't had no time to go hunting this past year."

"Business that good, huh?"

"No, but I manage to keep busy hauling scrap."

Both men started walking toward the shop where Dent's son Robby was working on an old tractor. The young boy didn't show any interest in the visitor who was looking around.

"What's in the barn over there?"

"Parts mostly. Anything worth keepin'. I got a few engines and some axles," Dent was trying not to show too much concern. "Go on, take a look if you don't believe me."

What Dent didn't realize was, he'd just given the agent permission to search the place without a warrant, which was exactly what Agent Greg Mathews hoped would happen. He could get a warrant with probable cause, but so far, he didn't have much to go on. He might have trouble getting back in a second time without the warrant, so he had to spend the extra time now checking out the place.

As soon as he slid open the barn door, he knew it was a chop shop. The door opened easily and had an oversized hasp and lock hanging through the loop. It wouldn't be necessary for an old barn like this, particularly since the entire area was fenced in. The next thing he spotted was the wench and pulley suspended from an overhead rafter. It was perfectly arranged to pull an engine. The oil and grease on the dirt floor below confirmed that.

All the doors, hoods and fender sections were neatly stacked against one wall. It was too neat. Along the other wall was a workbench with a few tools. Under a tarp, he found a large air compressor. He continued to look in boxes until he found the air impact wrenches he knew were hidden somewhere close by. Dent was standing in the doorway watching him, not making any comment.

"It looks like you have two separate workshops here. Why two?"

"Well, sometimes we got more than one project going at once. I can't afford to let an old tractor tie me up when I need a part off one of my units out there. If it's raining, I just drag it in here. Easier that a way." Dent knew the agent was suspicious by the way he was taking his time looking at everything carefully. He was glad now that Billy had insisted they get rid of the Chevy truck chassis. He hadn't exactly thrown it away, just dragged it down to an old creek holler and left it there along with some other stuff that he'd retrieve later when this blew over. Dent never threw anything of value away...ever!

* * *

While Special Agent Greg Mathews was checking out Dent's place, Jerome was checking out the Mini-Mart from across the street. The market attracted a lot of younger kids and a few teenagers hung outside by the phone. He hadn't seen the one young girl who got out of the truck in several days. He found that interesting. Maybe she was hurt. He'd asked around and learned her name was Rita, and her older sister was Reba. Reba was the one he'd seen getting out of a car last night. He was having a hard time accepting these two young girls were hookers; but if they were, then maybe he'd buy a little action and maybe learn more about the dude that worked at the garage in town.

Jerome was concentrating on the market across the street and didn't notice the sheriff's deputy pull in behind him. He was startled when the deputy appeared by his window.

"Mind telling me what you're doing parked here?" The deputy asked.

"Ah, I'm just sitting here enjoying the day, Officer. Is there a problem?"

"Yeah, we've had several complaints about this car parked here with you sitting in it. We got a park down the road where you can enjoy your day and nobody will bother you."

"Okay, good idea. Thanks." Jerome was about to start the car.

"Hold on, Sport. Before you go anywhere, let's see your license and the registration for this car. You the owner?"

"I know it's old lookin', but it does the job. Gets me where I need to be." Jerome was acting cool, using his hands for emphasis. Then he pulled out his wallet and carefully extracted his license, handing it out the window. While the deputy was looking at the license, Jerome leaned over and opened the glove box carefully remembering that the automatic pistol was also in there. He didn't want the deputy to see it, or have it fall out. He was being overly careful, looking for the registration.

"Sir, I'll have to ask you to step out of the car."

"What for? I didn't do nothing wrong. Just give me a minute, I'll find the damned registration. It's in here some-place." He was wishing he'd put the pistol under the seat. Suddenly the gun fell out onto the floor in plain view. Jerome tried to put it back when he the deputy ordered him to "freeze!"

"Hey Man, just let me explain something okay?"

"Save your story for later. I'm sure the sheriff will hang onto every word you have to say. Right now I have a suspicious character with out of county plates, watching a Mini-Mart for the past two days, and there's a gun in your possession. What do you suppose that looks like?"

"If I was white, you wouldn't be doing this."

"If you were white, you'd know better than to hang around in this part of town. Get in the patrol car."

"This here automobile is mine, and the gun is just something I found a few weeks ago. I wasn't planning on robbing no market. I was just checking out the chicks that hang around there. That's the truth." And for the most part it was, but the deputy's version sounded more convincing.

The deputy called Harvey's garage and told him to pick up the old Ford LTD parked across the street from the Mini-Mart.

At the sheriff's office, Jerome shifted from his Shaft persona, which didn't seem to be working too well lately, to that of a quiet, innocent man who was unfortunate enough to be visiting a cell. With any luck they wouldn't be in touch with his former employer, so he decided to be patient, not that he had many options.

What Jerome didn't know was the arresting officer was currently at Harvey's storage lot examining the contents of the Ford's glove box where he found several paycheck stubs from a car dealer in Knoxville. He borrowed a crowbar from Harvey and left it in the trunk and listed it as one of the items found. It never hurt to have more than one item listed when you had a suspicious character like Jerome in custody. The sheriff had taught him that trick. They might be able to hang a few B and Es on him as well.

Going over the interior of the car one more time the deputy hit pay dirt. He lifted the rear rubber floor mat and found an envelope with twenty, $ 100 dollar bills. The envelope had the same car dealership name and address on it as the paycheck stubs.

"Sir, this is the Harmon County Sheriff's Department calling. We're holding a man here in custody that might have worked for you recently...."

"You caught Jerome? Well I'll be! That sum bitch have any of my money left?"

"We found two thousand dollars, all in one hundred dollar bills in his car, would that be the money you're talking about?"

"Well there was a whole lot more than that. I already reported the money stolen to my insurance company, and to the police, of course."

"Uh huh. How much did he take?"

"A little over five thousand I believe. When can I get my money back?"

"Difficult to say. For now we have it here. You'll need to fax us a statement of what you've just told me so that we can use it when we take him before a magistrate. Are you missing a gun by any chance?"

"Maybe. What kind of gun was it?"

"Small caliber handgun, twenty-five millimeter."

"Seems to me we might have had one like that in one of the desks here. I'll have to ask around." The manager decided to make a list of missing items, real or imagined, and send it along. He'd make a copy for an insurance claim as well. And, he'd have to make a police report, which until now he hadn't bothered to do because he'd have to explain where the money came from. It was kickback money from the wholesalers who bought the less desirable trade-ins. He never kept any old beaters on his lot.

"It seems you're in deep shit up in Knoxville, Jerome," the deputy said. Jerome was now behind bars in the holding cell.

"Why would you call the people I used to work for? They ain't gonna tell you the truth about me. That's why I quit. The man's a crook, that's a fact!"

"Uh huh. He said you stole five thousand dollars from him. Maybe the gun, too."

"He said that? He's lying! It was only twenty-three hundred dollars. And I found the gun under the seat of a used car I was cleaning. He didn't know jack shit about the gun because I never told him about it. See, I told you the man was a liar. Got no use for liars!"

"Me either, Jerome. I got no use for thieves, either. So you took twenty-three hundred and skipped town, is that it?"

"Yeah, that's it. I still got most of the money, but I'd hate for you to send it back to him. He don't deserve it."

"Well, that will be up to someone else to decide. Right now, the sheriff is kinda busy. We got a couple of murders on our hands. You didn't happen to be up around the dump any time recently, did you?"

"Man, only dump I know is where I'm paying rent."

"I'm talking about the other side of the river, up in the hills. You ever been up that way?"

"Yeah, I been up there. Gave a man a lift, dropped him off over there by the river."

"Where did you pick him up?"

"Let me think, he was hitchhiking south of town by the railroad tracks. He said some big white dude was chasin' after him."

"So this was a black man, right?"

"No, I think he was a Latino, or maybe Puerto Rican. He had an accent, but spoke English pretty good."

"So you weren't afraid of him, nothing like that?"

"Shit, what's to be afraid of? We all runnin' from somethin' ain't we? At first I thought he was a brother, but he wasn't."

When Sheriff Billy returned, the deputy relayed what he'd learned from Jerome. It put the fugitive bail jumper in the vicinity of the car burning. Now they would have to hold Jerome as a material witness. And then there was the matter of the stolen money found in Jerome's Ford LTD.

"Did you enter the gun and the money found into the log yet?" The sheriff asked the deputy.

"No, Sir. I know you usually like to do that after examining everything first. I don't think Jerome is in any position to claim any of it, and I think his former employer exaggerated the amount he took. He's got insurance to cover that loss. So how do you want to handle this guy?"

"First we check the gun's registration. See if it's been reported stolen. If it's clean, we'll just hang onto it as possible evidence against this guy. We know he was checking out that market on the other side of the tracks, so we probably prevented a robbery there. And the money... well, we've been needing a new copier here for a long time. That would just about buy one now wouldn't it?"

"Yes, Sir, just what I was thinking."

"Good. We're on the same wavelength then. Let's get a written and signed statement from this Jerome. Tell him to keep his mouth shut about the gun and stolen money and we might go easy on him."

Special Agent Greg Mathews walked in and sat down without being invited. He no longer cared if the sheriff liked it or not.

"We put out a BOL on that white Pontiac Grand Am four-door. The rental agency gave us the license number. With any luck the guy is still driving it. I doubt he'd stick around here. If he was headed south originally, he's no doubt still going in that direction. Somebody might snag him."

"Yeah, well I was just about ready to do that. Guess I owe you one."

"You owe me an explanation on that bullet hole in the burn-out. You put it there?"

"What! Why would I do such a foolish thing?"

"I don't know. I was hoping you'd tell me. See, if that bullet caused the explosion, there would be scorch marks around the hole. And since the hole is clean, that means the bullet entered the metal after the fire."

"I guess somebody could have taken a shot at it while it was still burning and before we got there. You find any other bullet holes?"

"No, how many times did you shoot?"

"Ya know, I'm starting to get tired of your attitude. I appreciate that you have a job to do, just like me. And I don't have all the resources you have to investigate with, but I damned sure resent your insinuation that I'd have anything to do with a piece of burned out scrap in Harvey's yard. I don't know what the guy was doing up there near the dump. Don't even have a good guess...."

"Well let me help you out there, Billy Bob...."

"Excuse me, I'm going to tell you this one last time. My name isn't Billy Bob. If you insist on calling me that, we're not going to get very far in our cooperative efforts here."

"Fine, now answer my fucking question, did you shoot that burnout hoping to make it look like something different from what it actually was?"

"Why would I do that? You tell me."

"Because you're an elected official in a small town. You know everybody and what they're up to. Sometimes it's in your best interest to protect some of your friends. And one of those good friends may be the moonshiner that took issue with that car being there. Is any of this sinking in yet? The lab report will no doubt confirm everything I've just told you."

"Well you fellas are sure a lot smarter than me. I would never have figured that out, no Sir." Sheriff Billy was trying to buy some time. "I got a black man back there in a cell who might be able to give you some additional details on who might have done this. He gave the guy a ride and dropped him off about a half mile from where it all happened. We think the hitchhiker is a fugitive and he may have spent the night in an abandoned farmhouse up on the ridge not far from the dump. I guess that doesn't track with your moonshiner theory, but it makes more sense to me." Billy would have to revise his earlier report.

"And just when were you planning to tell me all this?"

"I just did. I wanted to hear your theory first because I know you TBI guys think we're just a bunch of hicks up here who don't know how to keep the peace, or do our job."

"I can't imagine why we'd ever think such a thing. So why are you holding this man in a cell?"

"Because he's a suspect in another case we're working."

"Is this more bullshit?"

"You tell me. Talk to the man and decide for yourself."

Eulla opened the door to the hallway and walked back with the Special Agent, acting as polite as she could. She'd never seen the sheriff act or talk the way he was doing just now. It was a sure sign that he was worried. Maybe he'd confide in her later. Maybe after everyone was gone she'd rub his shoulders and neck to help relieve some of that tension. And he was very tense right now, she could tell.

Special Agent Greg Mathews entered the cell and sat down on the bunk forcing Jerome to sit up. He waited until Eulla left before asking questions.

Jerome had trouble determining any difference between FBI and TBI. He thought Greg was a federal agent. After trying to explain the difference without any success, Greg just left him thinking he was the FBI.

"Man, I must be in some deep shit for you to come down here to see me. I'm goin' to lay it out for you straight, boss. I didn't rob no banks, and I didn't kill anybody."

"You do drugs, Jerome?"

"Sometimes, why?"

"You high on anything now?"

"No, but I sure wish I was. It would make staying in this place a whole lot better, know what I mean?"

"So tell me why do you think you're here?"

"I'm here because the man put me here. A few hours ago, I'm being cool, just sitting in my wheels digging the chicks. There's this one that's real cute. I'm thinking maybe she'd like to ride around with me, know what I'm saying? Only I haven't seen her in a while, so I keep watching and waiting for her to show." Jerome was doing his Eddie Murphy routine and really getting into it. "That's when this police officer sneaks up on me. Scares the shit out of me. Starts asking a bunch of fool questions. I guess he thought I was plannin' on robbin' that Mini-Mart, but I sure wasn't. Next thing I'm here watching the roach races."

"Was the car you were in stolen?"

"No, Sir, it's mine. I paid cash money for it last year."

"So what type work do you do, Jerome that you have so much free time to check out the ladies? You a pimp?"

"No, I'm looking for a job. I used to wash cars, but that's a drag, man. Can't get anywhere being 'the boy', know what I'm saying?"

"Was that in Knoxville?"

"Yeah. I thought I'd check out Chattanooga, but I haven't got that far yet. Stopped off here just to look around, you know, maybe find something interesting." Jerome was starting to relax.

"So you're currently unemployed. How much money do you have?"

"Ask the deputy. He took all my money. I had about twenty dollars in my pocket and another two large stashed under the floor mat in my vehicle, but he took all my money."

"Did they give you a receipt for the money?"

"They ain't give me shit, man. They didn't read me my rights or nothing. When I get out of here, I'm gonna sue those mothers."

"Okay, okay, calm down. Right now, we need for you to give us a detailed description of the man you picked up."

"Why is this dude so important to you guys, he kill somebody?"

"Something like that. Consider yourself lucky he didn't do you and take your car. He picked somebody else instead."

"Oh man, and here I thought this was a nice little town with a nice sounding name."

"Yeah, well names can fool you, Jerome... just like people and first appearances. Life is a slow learning process."

"Ain't that the truth. So you gonna help me get out of here?"

"All in good time. Right now we need you sign a statement just telling what you just said in your own words so we have a record of it. One of the deputies will come back here with some paper and have you sign it."

"Then I'm free to go?"

"Not yet. There may be some charges against you for the money you took from your former employer."

"Do you think I should get me a lawyer?"

"Probably wouldn't hurt." Agent Mathews jotted a note to check the evidence log later to see if the money that was confiscated was recorded. Right about now, he'd bet money there wasn't any record. Then again, he only had Jerome's word that there was any money confiscated.

Chapter 8

Bovis Tinch wasn't happy after listening to the report from the sheriff that TBI agents were in town sniffing around. There was no way to spread the word that the cockfights were cancelled. People driving up from Georgia and Chattanooga would be pissed making the trip for nothing and probably wouldn't return for several weeks. That translated into a lot of money being lost. Once you had the momentum going, you had to keep it going.

"These special agents you're telling me about probably won't stick around for the weekend. They'll go home. Help them find whatever it is they're looking for, so they'll be on their way."

"I'm trying, Bovis. These guys have their own agenda and make their own rules. And they sure don't miss much."

"Billy, I know how you can be sometimes when you get your shorts tied in a knot. Now listen to me. Give 'em whatever they want, be as helpful as you and your boys can be. Pretend you got nothing to hide. And if they catch you in some small screw up, just let it pass and say you're sorry for the oversight. Just don't piss 'em off." Bovis put his hand on Billy's shoulder. "We want them out of here, 'cause I'm not gonna cancel the cockfights. Now if that poses a problem for you, then you got one big problem."

"Okay, I'll do what I can, Bovis."

"I know you will, Son. Be sure your brother does the same."

The next morning Sheriff Billy was sitting at the counter in Millie's café when the agents came in for breakfast. They sat together in the same booth they always sat in. Melissa hurried over with coffee, even before they ordered.

"Hey Mellie, be sure and put their breakfast on my bill," Sheriff Billy said this loud enough so the agents could hear. When they looked up, he turned and waved over to them. "Good morning, gentlemen. Gonna be a great day, and this is the best place to get it started."

Melissa had just about had it with the sheriff's free-loading, now he was being benevolent at her expense. She was fuming and disguised her anger with a plastic smile as she approached him. "I'm sorry Sheriff, but your tab has passed its limit. I've been meaning to talk to you about that for some time now. Why don't I stop by your office later today with the bill."

The sheriff's face turned red with embarrassment. He stood up and threw a twenty-dollar bill on the counter, adjusted his hat and walked out the door. Agent Greg came over and asked for their check immediately, saying they always paid for their own meals. Melissa decided the rest of the twenty could be applied to what the sheriff owed her, which was a lot more. This was a start, however.

In the short time they'd been there, the agents were getting a good picture of the way the sheriff operated. In time, they'd make a good case against him. It was obvious to them that he was corrupt from his boots to his hat and everything in between. The sheriff enforced the rules as he saw fit, helped himself to whatever he felt was his due and probably took a cut of any other action going on. Gathering sufficient evidence and making a case took time. Meanwhile, they'd give the sheriff as much rope as he wanted.

A rollback truck arrived at Harvey's yard and picked up the burned car to take it to the TBI's lab in Nashville. One of the agents was with the driver. He took the stored Honda.

"Sheriff said to tell you there'd be no charge for leaving it here." The words almost stuck in Harvey's throat, but he was doing what he'd been told, knowing he didn't have a choice. Being grounded, Bobby Lee was working inside the garage. He wasn't allowed to drive either tow truck for several weeks, which meant Harvey had to handle any pick up requests. There would be no cruising for vehicles left on the highway unless a patrol car called it in.

Between the breakfast and lunch crowd, Melissa sat down and started to estimate just how much sheriff Billy's tab might actually be. She was amazed at how much money he owed, knowing that he'd never pay her. She figured at least 200 breakfasts in the last year alone times $ 2.45 came to a total of $ 495. From now on, she'd write out a bill. If he decided not to pay, she'd have him sign it. Sooner or later, he'd get the message, and maybe find someplace else less convenient to eat. She no longer cared if he stopped showing up, because he was costing her some serious money.

Dent wasn't happy with the way the agent's visit ended. The agent discovered the air compressor and welding torches in the barn. Air tools had more torque and were a sure give-away being in the barn instead of the shop. While the agent couldn't prove anything, Dent was sure they suspected him, which meant they'd keep him under close watch. For the next few months, he'd have to be very careful and not accept anything stolen or suspicious. The insurance investigator's disappearance didn't help. Everyone, including the sheriff seemed to think he had something to do with that. All of these recent events put him in a foul mood.

Sheriff Billy decided to release Jerome, if he promised to relocate to another place, like Chattanooga, where he had a better chance of finding work. Billy explained that since he had not received a copy of a police report yet from Knoxville, Jerome should not linger, but get out of Dodge as quickly as possible. He returned Jerome's personal effects, but not the gun or the confiscated money. He explained those would be returned to Jerome's former employer, once a complaint was received. Sheriff Billy called Harvey's garage and asked to have Bobby Lee bring over Jerome's Ford LTD. There would be no towing or storage charge, provided Jerome packed up and left town before noon.

"Well if it ain't the whitebread who was foolin' around with that cute little black girl," Jerome exclaimed as soon as Bobby Lee arrived in front of the sheriff's office.

"I don't know what you're talking about," Bobby Lee said. His face said differently and his uncle saw and heard the exchange.

"Sure you do. You been humping that little Rita and her sister, Reba. I think those girls are a little too young for you to be foolin' with. Sure hope you don't knock one of them up, you be in big trouble. Thanks for bringing my vehicle around for me... boy. You forgot to wash it. And here I just gave you a big tip, know what I'm saying?"

Jerome got into his car and drove off waving out the window, a big smile on his face. Now he had to figure out a way to say farewell to his landlady and be gone. For some strange reason the sheriff wanted him out of town fast. He didn't believe for a hot second that the sheriff was doing him any favor. It had to be something else. Maybe that FBI man put in a good word, he thought. Whatever the reason, he was glad to be out of jail.

"Come on in the office, we need to talk about this." The sheriff was annoyed with what he'd just heard, and felt certain Jerome wasn't making it up. Harvey had mentioned the missing $ 800 earlier, now this new revelation.

"Uncle Billy, I swear, I never saw that guy before in my life."

"Yeah, well he's been hanging around the Mini-Mart over in that neighborhood for the past few days. Apparently you didn't see him, but he saw you. If you've been messing around with any of those black girls over there, you could get yourself cut or shot. What the hell's the matter with you Bobby Lee? Are you doing drugs?"

"No, Sir."

"Then where'd the money go that Dent gave you to give to your daddy?"

"Jeez, everybody knows about that! I don't know what happened to that envelope. I've looked everywhere. It must have fell out of my back pocket, because I sure don't have it, and I didn't spend it, honest."

"You think somebody might have taken it out of your pocket, maybe when your pants were down and you weren't thinking straight?"

Bobby Lee's face was turning red. "Yeah, maybe. It's the only place I haven't checked."

"Pretty stupid thing to do. You're lucky I just ran that black guy out of town. He saw you all right. And he could've made trouble for you. If your daddy knew about this, he'd put a whoopin' on you. So, we're keeping this conversation just between you and me."

"Thank you, Uncle Billy."

"One more thing. Maybe you ought to think about getting married to Robin sometime soon, before you knock her up, or she catches you catting around. Your daddy and Dent are best friends, so don't do anything foolish that might spoil that relationship."

"No, Sir, I won't. Robin and me, we've been trying to be careful."

"Right now, I'm thinking she's a whole lot smarter than you. Stop fooling with those black girls. If I hear you've been messing around over there in the Villas again, so help me, I'll personally kick your ass so hard you'll have to shit out some other hole, kin or not. "

"Yes, Sir, Uncle Billy I understand. I won't cause you any more trouble, I promise. And thanks for your advice."

Eulla sat at her desk being quiet. She agreed with the advice Billy had just given his nephew. Hopefully he'd take it. She waited until the young man left before asking, "Sheriff, what are you going to do with that gun you confiscated?"

"Why?"

"I was thinking I'd like to have it, you know, for protection."

"I can't give it to you, it has to be sold at auction."

"Oh, oh well. Let me know when you hold the auction."

"We can hold it right now. Don't see many people here. I guess they didn't read the notice in the newspaper. You did send out a notice, didn't you Eulla?"

"Uh, well sure. That is, I think I did." She smiled when she finally caught on.

"Bidding starts at ten dollars for this hardly used, twenty-five caliber lady's handgun. Do I hear ten dollars?"

"Ten dollars!"

"Sold. We'll need to take it up to the dump and let you fire a few rounds, so you'll be more comfortable with it. Remember now, you bought this at the auction, so make out a receipt."

"Thank you, Billy." Eulla walked over and handed him ten dollars and gave him a kiss on the cheek. She'd give him another kiss later, maybe when they were up at the dump.

Just as Bovis had predicted, the TBI agents left town before the weekend arrived, driving away in both vehicles and without any comment. While Sheriff Billy was happy to see them leave, he had a feeling they'd be back, and by the time he knew about it, it might be too late to warn anyone.

It was pretty much agreed that the fugitive passing through had no doubt holed up in the abandoned farmhouse where Ely discovered him. The fugitive must have surprised him, maybe heard him outside.

How Frank Gibson happened to be in the same area was still speculation. Sheriff Billy hadn't mentioned finding the binoculars because that would point suspicion directly at Dent. However he was pretty sure that Frank was spying on Dent's operation from that high ridge. The fact that he chose the same deserted area as the fugitive was coincidental. Getting caught by surprise cost the man his life. Now the fugitive was no doubt driving around in Frank's rental car and maybe using his ID. Darius had the description of Frank's car and was on his way to Chattanooga, hoping to spot it there.

Sheriff Billy was glad to see Darius leave town. The big man had good instincts and tracking ability, but very little respect for others, or the law. He was too imposing for a small town like Paradise Valley. Then there was Jerome who was on his way out of town, if he had any brains at all.

The upside for the week was Sheriff Billy had netted a nice $ 2,000 surprise bonus from the search of Jerome's old Ford. The deputy who turned it in deserved a reward. Billy considered giving him $ 50 for doing the right thing.

Then there was Melissa at the café, acting entirely out of character, embarrassing him the way she did. They'd have to have a long talk about that later. He couldn't afford to have citizens treating him with disrespect. Now that the special agents were gone, things could get back to normal. He also had a little extra money to bet with Saturday night. Bovis would be happy and that was important.

Before too much time slipped by, Billy had another visit to make. Bobby Lee had lost Harvey's $ 800. The suggestion was never denied that he'd been fooling around with a couple of young black girls in the vicinity of the Mini-Mart. Jerome had been a witness to that, and for some reason, the sheriff believed him.

Chapter 9

Sheriff Billy parked his Bronco in front of the Mini-Mart. As he, got out, he noticed several young black girls hanging around the payphone outside. One was talking while two of her giggling friends were trying to listen. Sheriff Billy waved at the girls and walked into the market, walked past the pudgy clerk to the rear, where the soft drink cooler was. He selected a Dr. Pepper and brought it to the counter. He was deliberately taking his time checking out the store and the clerk.

It had been at least a year since he'd been inside. The last time was to break up a fight outside between two drunks who refused to leave the parking area. The clerk had called the sheriff's office for some assistance. This was a different store clerk. Billy didn't recognize him.

"You doin' all right today?" The sheriff asked casually. The clerk seemed nervous and had watched the sheriff with obvious curiosity. This was the first time the sheriff had ever stopped by since he started working at the Mini-Mart.

"Yeah, doin' fine. You?" The law hardly ever came around, except to arrest the black dude who'd been checking out the place from across the street. "There's no charge for the drink, Sheriff. On the house."

"Thanks, I appreciate that. I wonder if you could help me out with something. The black guy we picked up, parked over there," Billy pointed out the window. "said there was a little action going on around here...."

"Ah, I don't know nothing about that, I just work here. I don't get involved with these people. You start doin' that, they take advantage."

"Yeah, I know what you mean. I'm not suggesting you'd fool with any of them, but there's a rumor goin' around that a couple of the young girls are puttin' out. I was thinkin' I might want some of that sometime, if you know what I mean?" Sheriff Billy winked at the young man.

"Sure wish I could help you out, Sheriff. I could use some myself, but like I said, it'd be stupid, and if anyone was to get caught, well that could sure cause some trouble. I could get fired."

"Uh huh. Well you strike me as a pretty bright young man. You probably see everything that's going on around here. Ever see anyone get into Bobby Lee's truck? I hear he's been cruising around here lately, and I know for sure he got some recently, but I didn't get her name."

"I'm not sure I know who Bobby Lee is, but I did see one of the girls hop into a truck a few days ago with a white guy. I think he was driving a Ford Ranger. Maybe that was him? I try to mind my own business, ya know?"

"So which girl was it, hopped into the truck?"

"Is she in some sort of trouble?"

"Nah, I just want to talk to her, make sure she knows to use protection. We don't need any more teenage mothers around here trying to get on welfare. I don't care if they charge for it, just so long as they're careful and don't cause any trouble."

"Well... there is this one girl, I think her name is Rita, she charges five bucks I hear. She'd probably give it to you for nothing, since you're the law."

"Think so? You sell rubbers here?"

"Sure do, what's your pleasure? They're on the rack over there. I'll have to charge you for those because of inventory."

"Oh, I'm not needin' any. Just glad to see that you have them available for those who do." The sheriff leaned closer,

"Think you could point her out for me?" He had no idea how old the girl might be, or if she was among those by the phone. He thought about his last encounter, she brought along her own supply of condoms. He liked that. Made the whole encounter seem more personal.

"I don't see her. As a matter of fact, I haven't seen her around here in several days, which is strange now that I think about it."

"Do you know where she lives?"

"Not exactly, but I think she lives somewhere on the next block. You can ask around. I'm sure everyone around here knows who she is. Cute kid about fourteen, looks a little younger. Usually wears pigtails. I haven't seen her older sister, Reba either."

It was enough for the sheriff to conclude that the clerk knew all these girls fairly well. He probably gave them free candy and messed around with them in the back room. He looked the type. Another time, the sheriff might have worked on him a little, put the fear of God in him, for even having such perverted thoughts. It was disgusting.

"You're telling me it's the younger of the two sisters who's putting out? What about the older sister, you think she's screwing around, too?"

"It's a good possibility, but I don't actually know that for sure." You find out, let me know, he wanted to add, but didn't. He kept thinking that Paradise Valley needed more available young women. In fact, he wished there was a local whorehouse. Yeah, that's what the town really needed. He'd probably have to stand in line at the door and wait his turn. No doubt the sheriff would have one of his deputies working at the door, he thought.

Outside, the sheriff asked the girls by the payphone if they knew where Rita and Reba lived. One of the girls gave him directions while the other two giggled.

Sheriff Billy cruised slowly by the two-family side-by-side unit, turned around and came back, parking across the street from the house. He saw someone peeking out of the window and saw the curtains move. Slowly, he crawled out of his Bronco and walked up to the front door and knocked.

"Whatchoo want?" a young girl asked, allowing only a small crack in the partially opened door.

"I'm the sheriff, and I'm here to talk to Miss Rita, is that you?"

"Go away, I didn't do anything wrong. I don't want to talk to you."

"Is that right? Well how about I just haul your little ass off to jail then and you can talk to me there. You want me to do that?"

"I don't want nothin', and I ain't coming outside, no, Sir."

"If you haven't done anything wrong, what are you so worried about?"

"I got my reasons. Now you just go on. Go talk to somebody else about whatever it is you're needin'."

"Is your mother home?" Billy asked trying to be patient.

"No. Nobody's home, 'cept me. And you can't come in here."

"So why aren't you outside playing with your friends. It's nice outside. Come on out here and sit on the porch so we can have us a little talk." Billy sat on the steps and waited.

"What you want to talk about?"

"All that money you found the other day in that white boy's truck when you went for a ride."

"He tell you I took his money? He's lying! I didn't take that money. He lost that eight hundred dollars someplace else."

"How'd you happen to know it was eight hundred dollars? He told me it was nine."

"Well then he's lying! Besides, I didn't take it. I found it. Finders keepers, so there. You tell that white boy to stop coming around here. I ain't goin' for no more rides wid him."

"That's right, you're not. I already told him to leave you girls alone or I'll put him in jail. Now you got to do the right thing and return that money. It doesn't belong to you, and it doesn't belong to Bobby Lee either."

"Who does it belong to then?"

"The Missionary of God Church in Chattanooga. That's who the money belongs to." It was the first thing he could think of for a quick response. "They need it so they can feed a whole bunch of starving children over in Africa. Do you know where Africa is?"

"Un uh. Are they hungry?"

"Yes they are. They're waiting for their dinner, and they ain't going to get anything to eat, because someone took the money and won't give it back. Now I may have to take that person to jail, and I sure don't want to do that if I don't have to."

"Just tell them chidrens the money got lost somewhere."

"So when is your momma coming home?" Sheriff Billy was getting tired of being polite and tired of sitting on the steps, talking over his shoulder while the girl continued to talk through the partially opened door that was wider now.

"She's working. But she don't know nothin' 'bout that lost money. I ain't tole nobody...'cept you. Do I have to give it all back?"

"Yes you do, Sweetheart. I'll tell you what, you go get the money and I'll tell all those hungry children you did the right thing. We can ride down to the Mini-Mart and I'll buy you a candy bar, or a soda."

"Unh uh. I don't ride in nobody's truck unless they give me five dollars."

"Okay, just go get the money and we'll forget about the ride in the truck." He was getting exasperated with the girl. She was either dumber than a box of rocks, or she was playing with him. He couldn't decide which it was.

He remained sitting on the hard concrete steps. Several people passing by were sending questioning looks his way, so he stood up and faced the door. The girl was gone, but the door remained partially open so he stepped inside and waited. The living room appeared to be neat.

Rita came into the room holding a worn, brown teddy bear. One eye was missing and his split back was held together with a dozen safety pins, which she was now opening slowly, one by one. He stood there watching. It seemed to take her ten minutes to remove the money. He counted it. There was $ 800 exactly.

"I guess that white boy lied about the correct amount," he said smiling.

"Told ya so. He's a liar, liar, pants on fire."

The little girl didn't know just how true that was, Billy thought as he left. Bobby Lee's hormones could cause a lot of trouble for everyone if he didn't watch himself.

* * *

Sheriff Billy stopped by his brother's garage. Bobby Lee was working on a brake job and not within hearing. Harvey was in his messy office on the phone. He motioned for his brother to find a place to sit.

"Here's your missing money from Dent."

"Where'd you find it?"

"Don't ask. Some things you don't need to know."

"Well thanks anyway. It's been kinda slow around here with those special agents running all over the place."

"And I got a feeling they'll be back."

"Surely not. They already know who killed Ely and burned up the other fella. Only person who benefited from them hanging around was Melissa over at the café."

"That reminds me, Mellie and me, we got to have us a little heart to heart talk about that mouth of hers." The woman was suddenly being too talkative, not watching what she said. She must have had a thing for that missing insurance investigator. Did she really think some stranger would waltz into town and sweep her off her feet and become a steady boyfriend? It wasn't likely unless pigs had learned to fly recently.

Billy had to admit that Melissa still looked good for her age, but in the last few years, Billy's taste had gone toward younger women and quickies. He wasn't interested in a long term relationship where he'd be obligated to buy flowers on the woman's birthday, put up with her in-laws, be home at a certain time and listen to a lot of nagging about a leaking faucet or a commode that didn't always flush properly. Women like that needed to marry a plumber.

Chapter 10

"Hey Deputy Dog, d'ya know what day it is?"

"Yeah, it's Friday, Sheriff Billy. I was just about to set up out there on the by-pass."

"Well don't forget to be polite. And bring back a nice one, hear?"

"I didn't hear any complaints about the last one I brought in. She was a real looker."

"No, you did good that time, Son. Try doing it again. I need to feel lucky for tomorrow night. Big crowd coming up to Bovis's place." He flashed back to the night Cindy was brought in. Just like the others, she had been happy to be turned loose and never registered a complaint. His supply of Ecstasy was getting low. It was about time for him to make a trip into Chattanooga to replenish his supply and get a few new magazines for Eulla and the guys. He had to keep his team happy.

As if on cue, Marsha Lane was becoming annoyed with the slow moving truck in front of her on the by-pass. It seemed to be poking along at 50 mph. She decided to pass the truck and pushed down on the accelerator of her almost new red Chevy Monte Carlo, which responded instantly. She shot past the truck momentarily doing 75. She didn't see the patrol car parked off the shoulder partially hidden and obscured by the truck she was passing.

"Shit," she muttered as soon as she saw the flashing lights behind her. Now she knew why the truck was poking along.

"Okay Miss, let's see 'em," the deputy was giving her a good going over, all the while smiling. The sheriff was going to be pleased with this one, he thought.

Her license indicated that Marsha V. Lane was 24 years old and lived in Red Bank, a suburb of Chattanooga. She explained that she was passing a truck when she momentarily exceeded the speed limit, hoping the deputy would understand. He was leaning into the open window and could smell her perfume. He seemed to be taking his time trying to decide how to proceed. She wondered for a moment if he was waiting for her to offer a bribe.

"I'm gonna' hafta write you a ticket for speeding, Miss. Sure do hate to do that to a pretty woman like you... out here all by yourself, miles away from home and all, but...."

"Can't you just give me a warning and let me go?"

"I'm afraid I can't, and this here ticket is going to be an expensive reminder to take it easy on this highway. We're trying to prevent accidents. If you had lost control of this vehicle while passing that truck, it could have been a really bad one."

"So how much is the ticket?"

"Two hundred dollars."

"What? Why that's ridiculous!"

"I don't make the rules, I just enforce them."

"I hope you accept credit cards, because I just don't have that much on me right now." Marsha knew she had about $ 75 in her wallet, which wasn't enough. Maybe if there was an ATM machine around, she could withdraw the rest from her account.

When she was forced to sit in the back of the patrol car while a tow truck was summoned, she began to get worried. She'd heard stories of small communities that thrived on events just like what was happening to her now. Her first opportunity to make a phone call, she would call her fiancée, Ralph Goodwin and have him take care of everything. Ralph's father was a prominent doctor in Chattanooga. The family had numerous important contacts. One phone call and this would be settled, she felt certain.

The sheriff wasn't in the office when Marsha and the deputy arrived. Having to wait in a holding cell was another unnerving experience. She gave Eulla Ralph's phone number, somewhat surprised that she wasn't allowed to dial the number herself. She became increasingly worried when she was told there was no answer. Surely they would leave a message.

"Did you leave a message on his answering machine?"

"No. We don't know who might pick up that message and we don't want you to suffer any additional embarrassment," Eulla explained through the cell bars. Marsha was quite attractive and smartly dressed, wearing a knee length shirtdress, leather belt and matching high heels. Eulla was a bit apprehensive about detaining this young lady. Sometimes it was better to pass on the really smart ones, regardless of how attractive they were. This one could be trouble.

When the sheriff returned, he went through Marsha's purse without her being present. He'd already inspected her car and found it to be clean. While it was an illegal search, the owner wasn't aware of it and therefore couldn't complain. Nothing was taken and nothing was damaged.

Billy was in a randy mood while talking to Marsha. In heels she was as taller than he. He kept admiring the outline of her ample breasts. She was fully aware of his ogling. She asked to call her fiancée again and was told that he'd try the call later. When she started to insist that he do it instantly, he became irritated and told Eulla to escort her back to the Honey Hole and give her something to drink. It was still late afternoon. He might allow her to leave later that night, rather than wait until morning.

Marsha's daily workouts kept her body in excellent shape. She had a high tolerance against colds, viruses and infections. Consequently the effects of the drug she was given wore off sooner than expected. When she woke up, the sheriff was still actively engaged, bouncing on top of her. She was helpless at this point, not quite sure if she was dreaming, and decided to keep her eyes closed and hoped the moment would pass quickly. She could hear and feel his heavy breathing and soon realized what was actually happening. She was being raped after being drugged.

Two hours later, when she looked at her watch she realized that she must have fallen back to sleep. It was now 8:00 PM in the evening. When she called out, Eulla arrived and offered her coffee, which Marsha refused. She was thirsty and sipped some tap water instead.

Eulla gave her a receipt for $ 75 after making her sign the speeding ticket and told her that the sheriff was releasing her with a reduced fine. Her car was parked at the curb, because Harvey's garage was already closed. There was a bill for towing, and Marsha wrote a check, accepted her keys and left without saying goodbye. She wanted to say something more like, ' you haven't heard the last of this', then decided not to say anything, just get out of town quickly.

The sheriff was parked across the street in his white Ford Bronco. He watched her leave as she passed by him.

Marsha made sure she didn't exceed the speed limit all the way home to Red Bank.

Unlike Cindy, Marsha didn't take a shower as soon as she arrived home. She called her fiancée, Ralph, who was already worried about her and had been making calls. When she told him what happened, he became furious. When he calmed down he began thinking about evidence and talked Marsha into going to the hospital for an immediate exam. They would also test her for drugs and take DNA samples.

* * *

Bovis had a record crowd show up for the cockfights on Saturday. There was a slight problem with parking. Normally Bovis had his nephew outside helping direct people where to park, but this weekend he didn't show up, so vehicles were parked in a more helter-skelter fashion, thus taking up more space. Bovis was exceptionally busy collecting fees and taking orders for his syrup.

Sheriff Billy was busy inspecting the birds, trying to decide which ones he liked. He planned to bet heavily, having come into some extra money during the week. Harvey was in a similar good mood now that he had the lost money. He and Dent were sitting in their usual spot on the third tier, swapping lies with their neighbors and telling bad jokes.

Right after the first bout, one of the visitors became agitated, claiming someone had switched birds just before the fight. Bovis stepped in and tried to assure the man that nothing like what he was claiming took place. The man appeared to be drunk and wasn't satisfied. He took a swing at Bovis, who managed to step back in time so the man missed. Sheriff Billy arrived, grabbed the man from behind and ushered him out of the barn with approval from the crowd.

"Time for you to get. Give me any more trouble, and I'll lock you up for the night," the sheriff announced. He stayed outside and watched the man stagger over to his truck and drive away. It was rare that anyone caused a scene out here, even when they had been drinking. Walking back to the barn he heard a loud cheer from the crowd and wondered if his bird had won. If so, he'd be $ 200 richer than he was an hour earlier.

Later that night, after everyone had left, a man walked across the field to the barn carrying a gas can. He splashed gas against the barn on the three sides not facing Bovis's house. He opened the big door and splashed more gas on some dry hay, threw the can into the center where the fights were held, ran outside and lit several matches, making sure the barn started to burn before running off in the same direction he came. He stumbled and fell on his way back to his truck parked a half-mile down the road.

Before driving off, he looked back and saw the barn was totally engulfed in flames. He was gone before the first patrol car arrived, followed by several pieces of fire equipment.

The roof of the burning structure collapsed within its frame while the walls remained glowing with heat and flames. The metal bleachers were scorched, but remained intact as the surrounding area disintegrated quickly. By the time flumes of water were being sprayed, the building was a stark skeleton of charred timbers. Bovis stood beside Sheriff Billy shaking his head over his loss.

"You know who did this, don't you?" He growled at the sheriff. "It was that drunk you threw out tonight. The one who took a swing at me."

"I think you're right about that, Bovis. I'll have to check around and find out who he is. I've seen him before, but I don't know his name." The sheriff knew the man wasn't from Paradise Valley, or Harmon County, or he'd know him. "You got insurance, don't you?"

"Of course I got insurance, but that doesn't cover my future losses. All it will do is pay for a new barn, which will take months to build. Meanwhile all those people will go somewhere else, and some of them will never come back. When you find that guy, kill him, or bring him to me and I'll do it. Either way, he ain't standing no trial."

"Let me handle it. Right now, you got other problems to face." The sheriff was trying to recall the truck the man was driving. He was pretty sure it had Georgia plates, and it was a Dodge, not one of the new ones, maybe an early '90s model. Then he remembered it was gray. Not a lot to go on, but it was a start.

His first stop would be the Exxon station that was open all night. It occurred to Billy that a lot of unusual activity had taken place recently. He wondered if it was a sign of things changing? If so, they weren't changing for the better. He was glad the TBI boys had left town before the fire or they'd be snooping around, asking more questions, getting Bovis upset.

"Maybe we can borrow a few inmates from the prison to do a little chain gang work around here. Get a half dozen strong men for a few days and we can get this place cleaned up," Bovis said.

"Okay. You want me to make the call?"

"No, I better do it. I got a few favors owed me, and a few markers to call in. You just keep looking for that yahoo who got match happy. Maybe we'll have us an old fashioned lynchin' party." That would send a strong message to anyone who thought they could fuss with Bovis Tinch and get away with it. Bovis was the most important man in Harmon County and all the locals were well aware of his power. While an outsider might not have that awareness, the lesson to be learned would be costly.

Billy was hoping that Bovis wouldn't pursue the lynching idea. A reward for information and a conviction was a better idea. Once caught, a short trial and a prison sentence would put things right. Billy was willing to bend the rules for Bovis, but hanging someone, without a trial, bothered him. The last thing he wanted was be at odds with Bovis.

Chapter 11

"I guess the price of pee vee syrup will be going up," a customer in Lou's barbershop was heard saying the following Monday.

"Good thing Bovis didn't have any livestock in that barn," another responded.

"I'm surprised it hasn't happened sooner," another customer added. "All those people out there getting all liquored up, watching a bunch of chickens scratch at each other. Why they act plumb crazy sometimes."

Similar comments were being made in the café over breakfast. It was the biggest tragic event to ever hit Paradise Valley since the flood of '79. The sheriff hadn't been around the café since Melissa reminded him that he didn't have a tab. Several patrons commented about his absence, since he could usually be found there any weekday morning between 7:30 and 8:00 AM.

The Harmon County Bugler came out once a week on Thursdays so readers could take advantage of any discount coupons in the newspaper. Fifteen years ago, it was called *The Weekly Shopper*. When Edgar Ames took over as editor and publisher, he changed the name, hoping to make the newspaper into something more than grocery ads and flea market announcements. Edgar was still working on the front page featuring Bovis's barn burning to the ground. Edgar had an earlier photo showing the barn intact, then two enlarged photos of the barn ablaze, one of which showed the bleachers in sharp contrast to the flaming walls. Two additional photos showed the charred ruins with Bovis standing to one side examining the rubble. The headline would be: *Auction Barn, Going, Going, Gone!* It was sure to get a lot of readership and precipitate a lot of comments.

The editor was well aware of what went on at Bovis's barn every Saturday night, along with many of the local residents. Literary sophistication would be lost on most of the readers, but Edgar still had dreams of producing a better publication to higher standards.

In the brief editorial, it was mentioned that during the auction, one of the patrons was drunk, became unruly and was removed by the sheriff. There was some speculation that the removed man was the arsonist, who came back later Saturday night, or early Sunday morning and torched the barn. Bovis Tinch was offering a reward of $ 500 to anyone who knew the man and his present whereabouts. The sheriff gave a brief description of the man and the gray Dodge truck he was driving. The reward would get more attention than the photographic essay.

Edgar was an amateur photographer and took pride in the photos he took. His digital camera was his pride and joy. It took exceptional photos, which could be imported directly into the computer and later arranged to fit the page. He no longer needed to use a darkroom. The digital photos enhanced the final product, but only a few readers, like Mary Lou Haslette, the librarian, appreciated his efforts. He hoped she'd make some favorable comment on this special issue.

Edgar wore wire-framed glasses and always wore a plaid sports coat whenever he was outside. Many residents thought he looked like a college professor. Lou at the barbershop thought he looked a lot like the actor, Robin Williams if he'd just smile more. Lately, he'd been spending time at the library pretending to do some research, hoping Mary Lou would notice his polka dot bow tie and make a comment.

He was two years older than Mary Lou and they had known each other in high school. During that period, Mary Lou wore braces on her teeth and Edgar had a face full of pimples. Neither was particularly attractive or attracted to each other. Like Sheriff Billy, Edgar was also single. Unlike Sheriff Billy, Edgar had a personal interest in Mary Lou. He was also aware that she had an unexplained interest in the sheriff, whom Edgar didn't hold in high regard. Never had.

Both Hargis boys were troublemakers when they were younger. Both were wild when they started to drive, racing on all the back roads, raising a lot of dust. Harvey always drove modified cars with loud mufflers. He was the one who also had the most girlfriends. Between the two, Edgar couldn't determine which of the brothers was the meaner. Both had won their fair share of fights growing up.

To be in trouble with one of the Hargis boys meant you were in trouble with both. While the Hargis boys were driving around in hotrod cars, Edgar was still riding a bicycle and silently wishing his father would allow him to drive. For boys in Harmon County, it was a right of passage in the transition to becoming a man to drive a car. It was all the more meaningful if the car was your own, not your father's. Thus the Hargis boys always had their pick of girls.

Edgar had to be careful in his editorials not to condemn the sheriff openly for negligence, or incompetence. He was fully aware of what really went on out at Bovis Tinch's barn on Saturday nights. One couldn't live in Paradise Valley all their life and not know about the cockfights and the infamous PV syrup. Both had made Bovis a very rich man by local standards.

Edgar sent the anonymous letter to the TBI. Their subsequent arrival in Paradise Valley had given Edgar a good reason to feature their visit, along with mentioning the car burning and the disappearance of an insurance investigator. He also worked in a quick mention of a fugitive being sought by police as well as Darius Ott, a bounty hunter from Knox-ville who thought the fugitive might still be somewhere in Chattanooga. Readership would certainly increase for this special edition, Edgar thought. He had mistakenly taken a photo of a man leaving the sheriff's office he thought was one of the TBI agents. It was Nick Alexander, but Edgar didn't know the man's name.

Bovis Tinch ordered 500 additional copies of next Thursday's edition to be sent to surrounding communities. *The Bugler* was also printing 200 posters offering a reward.

* * *

Ralph Goodwin worked for a hardware wholesaler in Chattanooga. He was in charge of warehoused inventory. He and Marsha Lane were planning on an October wedding with a honeymoon in Williamsburg, Virginia. His father was a prominent doctor and was disappointed that his son hadn't finished medical school. The entire family was upset over the rape incident in Harmon County. Their lawyer cautioned everyone to stay away from the sheriff, not to discuss the incident outside the family and to remain as calm as possible. Ralph wasn't about to follow that advice. He and some of his friends felt the justice system took far too long to correct the evil that currently existed. Ralph felt it was his personal obligation to punish the man who had soiled his property. It was a matter of honor in the southern tradition he'd decided.

While Ralph hadn't finished medical school, he had done considerable reading, mostly about underground mili-tary activity. He was considering joining an extremist group that was forming. Ralph had attended a few casual meetings held at the firing range where Ralph demonstrated his ability to obliterate a bull's eye from 300 yards using a special scope.

He wasn't yet a member of the group but he was accepted into their gathering and was regarded as a prime candidate. Ralph's views on the increasing encroachment of Hispanics and African-Americans in the United States, and in Chattanooga were consistent with the group's views. At home, Ralph didn't voice these opinions. Nor did he talk about them in front of Marsha.

At the warehouse, Ralph eventually weeded out the three 'undesirables' working there. He had to be careful not to be labeled a racist. He had to have a solid reason for firing each African-American working with him in the warehouse. Merchandise started to disappear only to be found later in one of the cars. Some items were never found because they were hidden in a storage locker Ralph had rented a few blocks away under a different name. Now he had an all white crew and they all got along well. Ralph would frequently joke that he was an Anglo-American and everyone in the warehouse would laugh.

Ralph's hatred for what happened to Marsha was intense. He took a week's leave of absence, left Marsha a note and left for Harmon County. His rage bordered on insanity, which he kept disguised behind a forced grin and gritted teeth. The mental anguish was almost more than he could bear. Marsha worried that he might do something foolish after reading his note. She knew he was angry and felt guilty about the incident, even though it wasn't her fault. She wished it had never happened. And, she wasn't sure it was the smartest thing she'd ever done telling Ralph about it.

Ralph's camo-painted Jeep Wrangler had 4-wheel drive. He was an avid hunter and camper, so the outdoors, and strange surroundings didn't bother him in the least. He had his camouflaged tent and sleeping bag, hiking boots, survival kit, high-powered binoculars, high-powered rifle with scope, large Bowie knife plus a 20-gauge shotgun that kept the shot pattern tight. If he were stopped, he would appear to be a normal camper. Before leaving, he made sure he had a detailed map of Harmon County, a good compass, a sharp axe and shovel. He also had enough ammunition to stage a decent small war.

His plan was to spend a day or two learning the topography of the area surrounding Paradise Valley, camping out in remote areas. After he had a good feel for the place, his next step was to watch the sheriff's movements and determine if he had a predictable routine as most people did, regardless of their occupation. The sheriff would never know he was being stalked.

Once he could predict where the sheriff would be, Ralph could select the best spot to take him out. There would be no confrontation, no discussion and no warning. And there would be no witnesses, so if he staged it properly, it might appear to be an accidental shooting rather than an execution.

While driving down secondary roads, surveying the area, Ralph came upon an abandoned farmhouse and saw yellow tape across the back door, indicating it was a crime scene. Being a stranger to the area, Ralph had no knowledge of recent events. However, it was a remote place that the sheriff had no doubt visited recently. Maybe he'd make a return visit. Ralph drove his Jeep into a wooded area a quarter mile past the farmhouse then looked around for a good observation spot.

The Jeep was well hidden in its present spot behind a large rocky hill, so he left it there and started hiking. He crossed a high ridge, worked his way through a dense stand of trees and came upon an old stone quarry and dump. He watched from a hidden pile of boulders as several residents parked and threw their trash onto a growing pile. A big green dumpster was partially filled with metal cans, and another had cardboard boxes. Ralph couldn't hear their conversations, but did notice they were looking at a painted oval on melted black top. Something no doubt happened there, or it was planned for something.

An hour later, a white Bronco appeared with the sheriff driving. His passenger was a shorter, heavyset woman. The sheriff appeared to be showing her something then Ralph realized they were taking target practice. The quarry echoed the shots. It was the perfect time to shoot the sheriff, except for the woman with him, and he'd left his rifle in the Jeep. Ralph hadn't anticipated this chance opportunity, but the observation gave him some good intelligence. He now knew the type vehicle the sheriff drove and would be on the look-out for it.

* * *

Chattanooga was one of Nick's favorite stopping spots between Atlanta and Cookeville. There was an abundance of good eating establishments in the downtown area along Market and Broad Streets near the aquarium. Parking was easy, and he liked the atmosphere. On an earlier visit, Nick had taken some extra time and toured the aquarium on the river. He also spent an hour marveling over the antique vehicles in the museum featuring tow trucks.

The heritage of the Civil War was everywhere with Lookout and Signal Mountains nearby. He thought about bringing Carol here for a weekend, so they could do the tourist thing at Rock City and Ruby Falls. Later they could take a ride around the downtown area in a horse-drawn carriage. Chattanooga was only an hour and a half's drive from Cookeville, going over the mountains, providing some magnificent valley views along the way.

On this return trip to Cookeville, Nick deviated from his normal route and once again drove through Paradise Valley. He liked the quaint old buildings that made up the town square. There was an abundance of antique shops. It was a

146

larger version of what he considered the famous village of Mayberry to be, but there was no bumbling Barney Fife and likeable sheriff. Instead they had a despicable little man who had too much power and not enough common sense. Nick couldn't judge him as corrupt because he didn't know enough about the man... yet.

Nick found a parking spot on the square, got out and walked around. When he spotted Millie's Mug & Skillet Café he was compelled to check it out. It was just a few minutes before closing time.

"I got the grill shut off, Hon, but I still have some pie left," Melissa said. She wondered if he was another TBI agent. He also reminded her of Frank Gibson, but looked more like the actor, Peter Strauss. She'd recently seen him on television advertising a garden fertilizer.

"A piece of your cherry pie and a cup of coffee would be great. This is a very nice town you've got here," Nick said. He picked up a copy of *The Bugler* scanning the front page.

"Yeah it can be. I guess you don't appreciate it as much when you live here all your life," Melissa said.

"Consider yourself lucky."

"Some days I do. Where are you from, Hon?"

Just as Nick was about to answer, Sheriff Billy walked in, interrupting their conversation. He sat several stools away from Nick, gave him a quick once over and ordered coffee.

"Well, if it isn't our glorious sheriff. Haven't seen you in here in a few. What happened, find a new place to hang out?" Melissa asked, showing very little respect.

"Mellie, I hate to tell you this, but you sure do have a big mouth, and a smart one, too. You and me, we're overdue to have a talk about showing a little more respect."

"That right? Consider yourself lucky that I haven't finished adding up that mysterious tab you keep mentioning."

Nick took this banter to be a joking routine and smiled as he ate his pie and pretended to read the newspaper as he listened. The waitress seemed to be holding her own with the sheriff. No doubt she knew everyone in town, what they liked to eat, and a whole lot more. This sheriff didn't look anything like Mayberry's Andy Griffin-type sheriff he'd been thinking about lately.

"I should warn you, mister that there are other places to eat in this town besides this place," Sheriff Billy said to Nick without any introduction.

"That right? Well this one suits me just fine." Nick winked at Melissa. She smiled in return.

"So what is it that we need to talk about, Billy?" Melissa deliberately didn't use his title. She did walk down the counter so she could lean over and talk to him directly while wiping her hands on her apron.

"I thought we had agreed you'd stop providing information to the TBI agents and direct them to me. I'm responsible for all the investigations in this county. You don't need to be sending them all over on wild goose chases, causing trouble and…."

"And what?"

"And pissing me off. You've been doing that a lot lately. It's time you stopped. I don't want to have this conversation again, hear?" He got up, dropped two quarters on the counter and walked out, adjusting his hat as he left.

"He calls that a conversation. I call it an ultimatum, or maybe a threat, I don't know and I guess I don't care. At least he's paying for his coffee for a change," Melissa appeared to be talking to herself.

"What did he do before, charge it?" Nick asked, still curious about the exchange he'd just overheard.

"Always told me to put it on his tab, except he never had a tab. Just expected me to write it off, I guess. Finally one day I just got tired of hearing it and reminded him in front of a few customers. I guess I embarrassed him and its been eating away at him ever since."

"He said something about TBI agents," Nick said.

"Yeah, we had three agents nosing around here for a few days last week. For a minute there, I thought maybe you were another one."

"What made you change your mind?" Nick got up, paid his bill leaving a dollar tip. He kept the newspaper to read later.

"Well now that you put it that way, I'm not sure I have. Are you a TBI agent from Chattanooga?"

"I'm not from Chattanooga, and I won't tell, if you promise not to," Nick winked again and left. He let the implication hang in the air. It wasn't quite a lie.

Melissa thought about that for a few moments. The sheriff had hinted that they might come back, and it appeared he was right. This one acted friendlier and certainly did remind her of Frank. She hoped he'd be in town for a while. Peeking out the window she watched him cross the square and drive off in a dark blue Ford Crown Victoria 4-door. It was enough to confirm her suspicion that he too was a special agent, even though he never actually said he was, but didn't deny it, either.

149

Nick stopped at the Exxon station for gas. Inside, he overheard some people talking about Bovis's barn burning down, and how they hoped it would not affect the price of his shine. It was amazing what you could learn in a short period, if you just took the time to listen, Nick thought, waiting to pay for the gas. His impression of the town was becoming slightly tarnished by what he'd recently seen and heard. He didn't care much for the sheriff, or the way he treated a local business owner. Nick assumed the waitress behind the counter at the café, was also the owner. She acted like it.

He also sensed a slight flirtation. There was a time when Nick might have probed the situation a little. Now that he and Carol were close friends, he put aside any impulse to jump in the sack with another woman. It was a sure sign he was getting older and hopefully wiser. Sex didn't have the same priority it once had. It was still important to him, but it didn't cause him to do impulsive things any more. As a consequence his libido had gone from full race to cruise to slow over the past three years. If he and Carol spent more time together, he might get back to cruise.

Nick saw the sheriff's white Bronco parked at the curb in front of the office. Nick parked in an open space next to it, easily seen from inside the sheriff's office by anyone looking out the window.

This time Nick didn't have to ask if the sheriff was in, he saw him sitting behind his desk reading the newspaper. He still had his Stetson hat on his head. Nick wondered if he also slept in it? As soon as Eulla saw Nick arrive, she realized that she'd forgotten to mention his earlier visit to the office. It was too late now. Billy wouldn't be too happy about that.

"Hello Sheriff, you got a minute to spare?" Nick asked.

"I guess. Didn't I just see you over at the café?"

"Same person. You have a good memory."

"Was that meant to be funny? 'Cause if it was, I'm not real partial to strangers who come in here trying to act smart. So what is it you want to talk to me about?"

"I left my card with your assistant over there a few days ago when I stopped in to see you. You were busy with the TBI boys I guess. Anyway, I'm trying to re-establish an incident that happened here a few weeks ago."

"What kind of incident?"

"A young girl was arrested for speeding and held over-night in your jail. I'd like to see the arrest report."

"You would, would you? You some kind of lawyer?"

"No, I represent the girl's family. I'm a private investi-gator. The girl's name was Cindy Stevens. She was driving an older model Mustang convertible."

"Is that right? And why would I want to show you the arrest report? You want to know how fast she was going?"

"That among other things." Nick continued to stand, not having been invited to take a seat. He stood by the counter looking down at the sheriff, noting the shined cowboy boots.

"Such as?" Sheriff Billy didn't like where this was go-ing. He was also annoyed that he hadn't been warned earlier about this man's prior visit. He'd have to have a talk with Eulla about that.

"How much was the fine she paid, and did you give her a receipt?"

"Uh huh, and just what did this young lady tell you?"

"She said she spent the night here in one of your jail cells and you released her the next morning."

"Sounds 'bout right. She got off lucky if you want to know the truth. She had two prior arrests for speeding. One more and she would have lost her license," Billy was looking up at the ceiling while pretending to be remembering. "She also had an open bottle of whiskey in her car. The kid had quite an attitude as I recall, which is why I decided to let her spend a few hours contemplating her situation in a different atmosphere. I hope she learned a lesson. Anything else you'd like to know?"

"Yes, how much was her fine for speeding?"

"We let her off easy I seem to recall. Eulla, you got that receipt book over there?"

"It was fifty dollars, Sheriff," Eulla answered a little too quickly, and without looking it up. Nick didn't miss this. He didn't see her refer to any paperwork, or files.

"And may I see a copy of the receipt?" Nick asked.

"No, you may not. Now I've indulged your nosey questions, gave the kid a break and I'm not interested in discussing it any further. That's about as plain as I can be. Anything more, go get a court order. Otherwise you've wasted enough of my time." The sheriff returned to his newspaper ignoring Nick. It was a rude dismissal. Nick smiled at Eulla turned and left.

"Thanks for your time, Sheriff," Nick wanted to add, and all your hospitality, but bit his tongue. There was no point to be gained by antagonizing the man... at least not yet. That might happen later.

He had confirmed that Cindy was held overnight in jail. He also learned she might not have been too cooperative, hence a little time in a cell to teach her a lesson. As far as the rape went, that was going to be real difficult to prove, particularly since there was another woman working in the office. So far, Nick and Carol only had Cindy's version of what happened. If she was spoiled, as Carol had indicated, and had a bad attitude, what the sheriff did wasn't that far out of line.

The rest of the story could have been made up, fantasized or lied about to cover up having had a sexual experience elsewhere. Anything was possible. Nick didn't know the young lady, so he had to keep an open mind, even though he was a bit skeptical that the rape ever happened. Yes the sheriff was a bit rough, and abrupt, but he didn't appear to be stupid.

Nick called Carol at work to see if she wanted to go out somewhere for dinner. He'd give her his observations and what he'd learned later. He was unaware of being observed as he left town.

* * *

"Eulla, did you happen to forget to tell me that I had a visitor a few days ago?" Sheriff Billy hated surprises.

"Yes, Sheriff, I completely forgot and I'm sorry. You were all tied up with those TBI fellas and I didn't want to bother you then. Then I guess I just plumb forgot all about it until he showed up again. I think you handled the situation real well."

"Hmmm. Don't be making those kinds of mistakes again. I don't like surprises, you know that." Billy was wondering if the girl recalled anything else, or suggested anything else happened?

The PI didn't bring it up. And the man seemed to have too much confidence. Billy decided he didn't like the man. Eulla found Nick's business card and gave it to Billy who studied it for a long time. How was it that someone from up in Michigan was down here in little old Paradise Valley investigating a $50 speeding ticket? That just didn't compute.

The man was definitely a Yankee. That was obvious enough by the way he talked. Didn't seem to show a lot of respect either, now that Billy reflected back on the brief encounter. He also wondered how much Melissa might have blabbed, not that she knew all that much.

If the man showed up in town again, it would be a tell-tale sign that there was more going on. The sheriff put Nick's card in the middle drawer of his desk.

Returning to the newspaper, the sheriff re-read the front page editorial again, for the third time. The way it was written told Billy that Edgar had an ax to grind with the way the sheriff's office was handling things in Harmon County. Billy didn't like that one damned bit and decided that sooner or later he'd make his feelings known to Edgar; another man he never cared much for.

When they attended high school together, Billy never really liked Edgar much, mainly because he seemed so much smarter than the other students. Here he was years later, with that same smarter than you attitude, and using his newspaper to tell the world that he didn't think Sheriff Billy Hargis was doing a very good job. He was making a big mistake intruding on Billy's domain.

There was a time, years ago, when Billy and Harvey would have waited after school for Edgar. A bloody nose and a black eye would be enough to tell everyone that Edgar had made a big mistake saying anything nasty about the Hargis boys. Anyone at school, including some of the teachers, knew better than that.

Now Billy had to think of a different way to give Edgar a bloody nose. He had to be careful because Bovis was fond of Edgar for some reason. The threat would have to be disguised.

Then Billy thought about re-election time, when he'd need Edgar's support, or at least have him write something positive about the progress being made in the sheriff's office. Deputy Willoughby Jones was already spreading a rumor that maybe he'd run against the sheriff in the next election. Yes, there was a lot to consider in how he approached Edgar Ames. Newspaper people had the power of the pen, known to bring down some very important people in the past. Just look at what happened to President Nixon, he thought.

Chapter 12

Over dinner at Frankie's, Nick's favorite restaurant in Cookeville, Nick gave Carol a summary of his visit to Paradise Valley. He admitted he was still skeptical about the rape. The sheriff was a tough bird, but didn't appear to be overly concerned with Nick's questions, any more than he'd be with any other stranger.

"I appreciate you're taking the time to at least explore it the way you did," Carol said. "It's quite possible Cindy made up the rest of the story, but I just can't comprehend why she'd do it? Maybe she'd lie to her mother, but not to me. I know she hasn't had a lot of good parental supervision. That's why she has that smart attitude you mentioned. I believe that part."

"Too bad she didn't think to go to a clinic and get checked. They might have been able to corroborate her story with some evidence," Nick said.

"She told me she thought he used a condom. Wouldn't that eliminate any evidence?"

"Not necessarily. A doctor could determine that she'd had sex recently and might find trace elements." As soon as Nick said this he doubted a small, local clinic would find anything. It would take a forensic specialist to find what he was mentioning, and then it would most likely involve a corpse. If the clinic were in Paradise Valley, the sheriff would probably have some influence there. Nick was aware that Erlanger Hospital was a big facility in Chattanooga and would have the capability to do a variety of tests. That's where Cindy should have gone, he told Carol.

Back at Carol's place, Nick and Carol sat on the sofa watching the news on TV. Nick wasn't too interested in the local items being covered and picked up the newspaper he'd brought from Paradise Valley. He hadn't taken the time to read it until now. He was amused by Edgar Ames's editorial. It was obvious the man wasn't one of the sheriff's fans. Nick wondered if the man had any additional background on the sheriff, or if similar rape incidents had ever been known or reported? He should have checked on that while he was there.

Monday morning early, Nick said goodbye to Carol. They had a cup of coffee together in the kitchen then she had to leave for work and Nick wanted to get an early start back to Detroit. He liked driving early in the morning before there was a lot of traffic on the road. For a small town Cookeville seemed to have a lot traffic at all hours. Carol mentioned that she could remember when there were only a dozen traffic lights in the entire town.

As Nick approached Route 111 to go north just outside of town, he abruptly got on the highway going south instead. It would take him an hour and a half, perhaps a little less, to get to Paradise Valley. He'd have breakfast there and talk with that newspaper editor. Then he could file away any doubts he had and forget everything. Curiosity and chasing down miniscule items had been responsible for Nick's past success as a homicide detective. Those traits didn't disappear when he retired from the force. If Cindy were his daughter he'd want to know the truth about what happened.

* * *

"Well hello there," Melissa said giving Nick her best smile. She was obviously pleased to see Nick appear back at her café. "You got that hungry look," she said trying to tease him.

"You are one observant lady." Nick said. After eating a large breakfast that included grits, he lingered over a second cup of coffee, waiting for the last customers to leave. "I'd like to ask you a few questions about the sheriff." He looked toward the dishwasher and lowered his voice. "Maybe this isn't the best place...."

"That certainly is a new approach. If you were thinking of buying me a drink later, you're out of luck. This is a dry county. However, I might have something back at my place. If you're interested in taking me to dinner, there's a place outside of town that's nice. Or, if you just want to talk, we can do that at my place. It won't ruin my reputation."

"Let's see, you gave me an A, B or C choice there. How about all of the above?"

"I had a hunch you were going to say that. Tell you what; I've got to clean up around here before I close. That's going to take me, and Maria back there, a half hour or so after I close. I'll tell you how to find my place. You can just meet me there around four." Melissa gave him her address and directions. She needed to buy some time to look more presentable. She wasn't sending this one over to see Happy Harry first, like she had done with poor Frank.

Nick hadn't planned on spending that much time in this town. On the other hand, Melissa appeared friendly enough. He felt pretty sure he was being picked up. He'd had a lot of experience with waitresses, most of them from Michigan, and most of them a little younger. He reminded himself that he was doing this as a favor for his friend, Carol.

Fortunately, Melissa was still an attractive woman about Carol's age. Nick had made the observation several times recently to himself that his selection of female companions were getting older, not younger... just as he too was getting older. Fifty-six wasn't all that old, but there were days when he was aware of new aches and pains. And, he needed a full night's sleep rather than just a few hours. Having a young mind and an aging body was a bit frustrating. He wondered how he'd feel when he hit 65. That was less than 10 years away!

While still at Carol's place, Nick had Carol call her niece in Knoxville. He wanted Cindy's Social Security number, license plate number and her driver's license number. Later, he'd run the numbers and see what offenses were listed. He doubted that her recent speeding ticket would appear, but he wanted to be certain. The sheriff had mentioned two prior tickets. Nick needed to confirm that as well. Too much speculation could get you into trouble. Nick wanted to have as many facts as possible before filing it away in his Forget About It file in the back of his head.

Now that Nick had plenty of time to kill, he decided his next stop was at the newspaper to speak with Edgar Ames. This was his intended objective earlier.

The Bugler's office was on a side street a block away from the town square. It was in an old building with high glass windows in the front. The newspaper's name was painted on the plate glass in gold old-style lettering. Below the newspaper's name, Edgar was shown as Publisher and Editor. So he owned the business, Nick made that observation as he walked in. Unlike the exterior, inside he saw a modern office complete with computer equipment.

"How can I help you? The man wearing a bow tie said.

"Hello. My name is Nick Alexander and obviously I'm not from around here." Nick handed the man his card. "I read your recent editorial on the barn that was torched. You had some great photos. I was impressed."

"Well thanks. Not too many people appreciate good photo journalism these days, especially in a small town weekly." He looked at Nick's card with a puzzled expression. "What's your interest in Bovis Tinch's barn burning?"

"Don't have any, my interest is in the sheriff."

"Hmmm. What exactly are you looking for Mr. Alexander?"

"Call me Nick, please." Nick explained that he'd had a brief encounter with the sheriff and felt the man was a bit too testy and wondered if perhaps there was more going on in this small town than the average visitor might recognize?

"Well of course there is. That's true for every small town. We're no different. One thing that is different, we don't have a police department or a police chief. The county sheriff handles those duties. It saves the taxpayers money. We're basically a rural community and not a wealthy one, except for the scenery. That you can't beat." The man was giving a chamber of commerce pitch and avoiding talking about the sheriff.

"I agree with you. It's very pleasant here, no pun meant. I guess that's the reason for the town's name." The man nodded. "I also see where the TBI had a few agents here investigating a car that was burned and an insurance investigator that disappeared. Anything you can tell me about that?"

"Nick, we're treading on some dangerous ground. Most of what I know is pure speculation, or third-hand commentary. The sheriff doesn't seek publicity; therefore, he doesn't openly share much with me, or anyone else for that matter."

"And here I thought it was because I was from out of town," Nick joked.

"He doesn't care much for strangers either. He's your basic suspicious type. If you're not from here, he doesn't feel the need to be real friendly. You can't vote for him," Edgar said.

"Is he competent as a sheriff? I realize that may be an unfair question to ask. I promise not to quote you," Nick said, hoping that the journalistic expression might be caught.

"Considering where we are, and what he has to work with, I suppose you could say he's doing a reasonable job."

"You're being a bit generous I think," Nick said.

"Yes I am. And cautious, too. I live here don't forget. You don't. A run in with our sheriff isn't pleasant."

"I understand. I used to be a police detective before I took an early retirement and do what I do now. I've interviewed a lot of people who were reluctant to say anything negative about a suspect we were investigating."

"You're looking for something. What is it?"

"If I knew I'd tell you. I don't know if the sheriff here is corrupt, and I'm not sure that I care if he is. I'm trying to learn if he's abusing his office with some of the people he takes into custody."

"You must be talking about our famous speed trap out on the by-pass."

"So it's a well-known secret?" Nick asked surprised that the editor was suddenly so open.

"Well put. The sheriff catches a lot of unknowing motorists on that stretch of road. Mostly people traveling between Knoxville and Chattanooga."

"And who holds the sheriff accountable?"

"He answers to the county commissioners, but primarily it would be Bovis Tinch."

"The man whose barn was recently torched?"

"Yes. Where's this going?"

"Like I said, I wish I knew. Does the sheriff make it a habit of keeping violators overnight in his jail?"

"I really can't answer that, but it is an interesting question. I should probably ask him sometime. Might make a good story."

"When you do, ask to see a list of those detained and see how many are young single women. It would be interesting to know if any have filed a complaint against the sheriff later for improper behavior."

"Ah. At last I see what it is you're digging for. You have a client who was detained overnight, is that it?"

"Yes and there might be more to it, but I'd rather not speculate. My information may not be correct and I don't want to insinuate anything that's unsubstantiated."

"You sound like a lawyer. But you suspect old Billy is doing the nasty with young girls he keeps locked up overnight."

"Something like that, but I didn't say it, you did."

"No, you just planted the seed and pointed me in that direction. The problem is, it would be almost impossible to prove. You'd have to have several different people come forward with the same, or similar experience, and I doubt many would."

"I guess you see the problem and why I'm being a little vague." Nick said. "Tell me, did the sheriff invite the TBI guys in to help investigate the car burning and the disappearance of that insurance investigator?"

"I don't think so. Someone tipped them off and they came on their own. Sheriff Billy would never ask for outside help. He was on his best behavior while they were here sniffing around I heard."

"Well you have my card. If anything should develop that you want to share, call me, send me a fax or do the e-mail thing."

"I just realized why you look so familiar to me. I took your picture leaving the sheriff's office. I thought you were one of the TBI agents."

"Yeah I know. That's been happening a lot lately."

Nick left feeling he had made his first ally in this small town. Melissa might become number two. She was sure to know some good gossip, but how much she'd reveal was something else.

Nick managed to kill some additional time window shopping and walking around the town square and adjacent streets with shops, many of which had been upgraded with attractive awnings and new entrances. All the commercial establishments appeared to be occupied, no vacant buildings. He did notice an abundance of antiques shops. Neither he nor Carol was into antiques, so there was little point in attempting to buy something for her.

With a few more hours to kill and no place interesting to visit, Nick decided to get a trim at the barbershop he spotted.

"You got business here in town, or just passing through?" Lou asked, draping Nick with a cotton cover.

"You sound just like the sheriff," Nick said chuckling.

"Well that's a new one on me. How is it you know the sheriff?" Lou's curiosity was instantly high.

"Oh I've met him a few times in the café down the street. He has a unique way of greeting strangers."

"You got that right. Sheriff Billy, he's one suspicious character all right. He's been busy lately."

"Yeah, I read in the paper about that car getting burned up at the quarry. Then some old guy was found murdered, then that barn got burned down. That's a lot of criminal activity for a small town to have."

"Yep. I reckon you're with the TBI bunch. Had three in town last week. That was before Bovis's barn burned. Is that what brought you boys back?"

"Not exactly. I'm more interested in the speed trap out on the by-pass." Nick decided not to correct the man.

"Oh hell, that's been goin' on for years. Everybody around here knows about that. Just don't go over fifty-five and you'll be fine."

"I doubt they'd stop me any way. I'm not a young female. I heard the sheriff likes 'em young and single."

"Don't know where you heard that. That's a new one to me, but I guess anything is possible." The rest of Nick's session went quietly. His trim looked more like a military haircut. He hadn't lost that much hair in a barbershop in over 25 years.

"I guess I won't be needing another haircut for a month," Nick said digging out his wallet. He wasn't happy with the trim. It looked more like a military haircut.

"Guess not." Lou took the money, made change, accepted the tip and walked over to the window to look outside. No 'goodbye', 'stop back' or 'have a nice day'.

One more seed had been planted. It wouldn't be long before the word would spread that the sheriff's behavior was being noticed beyond the local community. Nick still had some time so he asked directions to the Tinch farm. Nick drove by slowly taking notice of the charred remains of the barn. The blackened steel bleachers were a sharp contrast to the surroundings. A patrol car was sitting in the driveway as Nick passed.

The deputy in the car watched Nick pass by, turn around and later pass by again. The deputy noticed Michigan plates on the car and wondered why any out of state visitor would be interested in Bovis's place? He called Eulla to report what he'd just seen. Eulla would be sure to report this important bit of information to Billy as soon as he returned. She also knew he wouldn't be happy about it.

Melissa's small house was on a side street. Like all the other houses, it was old, yet neat. It looked to be about a 1930s story and a half bungalow. The shingle roof had been replaced with the new style painted metal. As he pulled into the gravel drive, he could see part of a flower garden in the back yard. Even though she lived alone and ran a business, she still had time for a garden. It told Nick something about

Melissa and the kind of person she really was, when she wasn't behind the counter at the café.

Seeing a person outside their element was always an interesting experience for Nick. Right now he was somewhat outside his element, never having spent time in a small community like Paradise Valley, where everyone knew everyone else.

"Now I want you to know I have some reservations about offering you some of our famous Pee Vee syrup. The last gentleman I went out to dinner with had some, and later had an unpleasant experience," Melissa said pouring a small amount in a glass for Nick.

"Is that right? What exactly is Pee Vee syrup? I never heard of it." He had an idea what it might be.

"Since you're not from around here, I'm not surprised. It's a local product. Some of the smoothest moonshine you'll ever taste, if you like moonshine that is. We call it syrup around here, and the Pee Vee stands for Paradise Valley of course."

"Of course. Well you've warned me. I'll try a little." Nick took a sip of the chilled liquid and felt it working its way slowly down this throat. He knew it was potent. "A little of this goes a long way."

"Glad you like it. Don't have anything else to offer you except a beer."

"A beer would be good!" Nick didn't want to hurt her feelings, but the syrup would take some getting used to. And since Melissa said it was a local product. That meant there was a moonshine operation of some sort nearby. The fact that she was so open about it also meant that all the locals knew about it, and that had to include the sheriff.

Melissa brought him a beer and sat down next to him on the couch, but not close enough to be touching. It was a small couch in a small living room with everything neat and orderly.

"So now that I've corrupted a TBI agent by serving him moonshine, what was it you wanted to ask me?"

"What can you tell me about the sheriff? I met him last week in your café, but only spoke to him briefly. I got the opinion he was the boss in this town, or at least thought of himself that way."

"You pegged him pretty well. Billy Hargis can be a charmer when he wants to be. Most of the folks around here like him and think he's doing a good job. He won't have any trouble getting re-elected."

"But there's more to him than that, right?"

"Billy's hard to figure out. He expects everyone to respect him, but sometimes that's a hard thing to do, especially for me."

"You mean because of the tab thing?"

"Oh he's cheap alright. Never leaves a tip, just expects people to go along with whatever he wants. I've gotten tired of it."

"Is he married?"

"No. Never has been."

"How about a girlfriend, then?"

"Well now that's the puzzler. For a little while, about three years ago, I went with him, but not for very long. When I found out how cheap he was, I lost interest. He was just looking for someone to do his laundry and fix all his meals... with me buying all the groceries! Uh unh. Playing house has to have some romance and other benefits, or it just isn't any fun."

"I agree with you. So what do you suppose he does for ....?" Nick was trying to be careful how he phrased what he was about to say. He arched his eyebrows and smiled.

"Getting any? There's a rumor that his assistant, Eulla may be giving him some, but I sort of doubt it. One look at her and you'll understand," she winked as she said this. "I think he may have somebody stashed away someplace that he sees once in a while. Probably some married woman whose old man is gone a lot, that would be more his style."

"Dangerous if he got caught though."

"Danger doesn't bother Billy Hargis. It's part of his mean disposition."

"I heard a rumor about him. Tell me what you think. I heard that maybe he was getting it on with some of the women they haul into jail for speeding. Keep them a few hours, or overnight, then let them go."

"I wouldn't put it past him. He's not beyond doing something like that. Of course he'd deny any charges and Eulla would back him up."

"I understand there's a fairly well known speed trap on the by-pass."

"Oh yeah. We got us a good one out there. You go over fifty-five, and you got out of county plates on your vehicle, they'll get you." She and the barber had confirmed part of Cindy's scenario.

"So how do I go about buying some of that Pee Vee syrup? I'd like to take some back with me. I've got a few friends who might appreciate it," Nick asked. He took another sip of beer.

"Bovis Tinch would sell you some, if he knew you. Since he doesn't, you'd have to get someone else to buy it for you. He's real careful about who he deals with. Has to be. He's been doing it for a long time without anyone ever complaining."

"I'll bet he's careful. So how would I go about it, any suggestions?"

"You being a TBI agent and all, you have to be extra careful. Bovis is a powerful man in this county. If he shot you, nothing would ever come of it, and it wouldn't make any difference who you are. He's a friend of the former governor."

"So you're saying the sheriff would protect him?"

"You got it, Honey. Bovis is a county commissioner and carries a big stick in this county. Sheriff Billy reports to him, so what does that tell you?"

"Bovis has a big stick, therefore Billy has a big stick. I guess I get the picture."

"Good. Now do you have any more questions, or did you want to go someplace to eat? I'm not trying to rush you, you understand."

"No, no, that's fine. Let's find a place to eat where you'll feel comfortable."

"Oh don't worry about that. Any rumors you hear floating around about me are just bull duty. I went out with this one fella from Atlanta who was here looking for a missing truck, and that caused a few tongues to start waggling. He got burned up in a car fire just outside of town."

Nick decided to wait until after dinner to pursue that event. He'd read the newspaper account and since Edgar had filled him in, the picture was coming into focus. Edgar hadn't mentioned the moonshine. He had to know about it. Nick wondered what else Edgar might know? Talking with Melissa away from the café proved to be the right move to get some additional background information.

Nick also had the feeling that it was going to be a long evening. While Melissa was talking, he became aware that she had turned just enough so that her knee was pressing against his. Another time and he might have forgotten about dinner and moved the interrogation into the bedroom. Now he was hungry and being careful not to suggest a romantic wresting match later. That might be a problem. Carol would just have to trust his good judgment, whatever that was.

Since Nick wasn't planning to spend the night, he hadn't bothered to check into a motel. Now it appeared that he'd be sticking around part of another day. During dinner Melissa asked him where he was staying? He told her he hadn't made any arrangements yet, but could use a good suggestion on which of the motels would be best?

"And you're expecting me to know?" She asked giving him a big grin.

"Not necessarily. Being in business here, surely you know the owners of these other establishments and know something about their reputations. After all, it's a small town isn't it?" She was quick, and had a good sense of humor. He enjoyed that.

On the way to the restaurant, Melissa sat on the passenger side of the split seat. On the way back to her place, she was sitting much closer to Nick and casually dropped her hand onto his thigh. A jolt of electricity shot through him. Most of the women he knew weren't this aggressive, at least not on the first date. He was enjoying the sexual teasing and knew it wouldn't go any further.

Suddenly Nick was back to when he was a horny teen-aged kid in his dad's car. It would be easy to let the flirtation go into high gear, but he didn't feel right about it. A lot of things had changed since he'd met Carol. They weren't exactly engaged, but he felt he owed Carol some fidelity. There was a time, after his divorce, when he felt differently. He'd had his fair share of waitresses, nurses, receptionists and secretaries. There were even a few real estate sales-women and two bar maids. Now they were all faded memo-ries and most of their names forgotten.

"Listen, I don't want you to take this the wrong way, but I'm involved with someone right now and that's not fair to her, or to you. So I don't want you to think this is going to lead where you want it to," Nick said, gently removing Melissa's hand from his thigh. It was a delicate situation and he didn't want to hurt her feelings.

"Well I'll be. A real honest to goodness true blue fella who wants to remain faithful to his sweetie. I didn't think there were any of those around anymore."

"Yeah, well I'm not sure I measure up to what you call a true blue, but I'm trying, and you're not making it easy for me."

"Honey I promise I won't tell, or make any trouble for you. You don't have to worry."

"Melissa, I think you need more than just a one-night stand. You need a good man who will stick around and treat you with respect. I'll be gone in the morning and I doubt that I'll be back this way anytime soon. So let's not start something, okay?"

"I'm not believing this. But I'll tell you what. I sure wish I was the lady you're so sweet on. She must be something special. I never met a man who turned down an opportunity for some strange."

"It wasn't always like that. I've had my fair share. My girlfriend is a special lady and I don't want to hate myself later that's all. I hope you understand." Nick felt foolish having to explain his new attitude. It also confirmed an old observation he'd made that whenever you're not looking for it, it jumps out and hits you by surprise, just like tonight. It would be easy to feel 19 again and guilty tomorrow, regretting the indiscretion as he had so many other times.

Nick drove Melissa home. Neither said another word.

"Come on in for a little while," Carol said when they pulled into her driveway. "I've got some homemade peach pie left. I promise not to try to jump your bones."

"Won't your neighbors wonder about a strange car parked in your driveway?"

"Only if it's still here in the morning."

Nick accepted the offer. Over pie and coffee they talked about the town, the people and how all the younger kids left once they graduated from high school. There wasn't enough excitement to hold them. Then she told Nick about Frank Gibson.

"You sure do remind me of him. I can't get over the way he just disappeared like that. I guess I blame myself for telling him about Dent's junkyard across the river."

"He was just doing his job. Don't beat yourself up over it. When you're investigating a strange situation in a strange place, you need to be extra careful," Nick said. Then he realized that the same thought applied to him. Paradise Valley was still a strange place, even though he'd spent a little time here.

"Now don't take this the wrong way, but why don't you just spend the night here? I'm enjoying your company and you can sleep on the couch if you want. It'll save you driving halfway back to Chattanooga tonight. You can leave early."

"Are you sure you don't mind? I can get a motel room."

"No. I like the idea of giving my neighbors something to talk about. They all think I'm becoming an old maid." For once Melissa didn't care what the neighbors, or anyone else thought about her. It was time to find someone like Nick to fill the void in her life.

The couch was comfortable and Nick never heard another thing until 4:30, when Melissa's alarm woke him. It was still dark outside.

"You want the shower first, or do you want me to wash your back?" Melissa decided to try one more time just in case he changed his mind. She'd left her bedroom door ajar, hoping he might come in later, but he didn't. She heard him snoring and knew it was a hopeless wish. She liked his integrity and the way he handled himself. She wished she could get to know him better.

"Are you still trying to get into my pants?" Nick asked.

" If you wear pants in the shower, I'll think you're one strange dude. Go on in, I'll have some coffee ready soon."

Nick could smell the aroma of coffee as soon as he opened the bathroom door. Melissa had a cup poured and waiting for him when he walked into the small kitchen.

"I could sure get used to this," he said.

"Yeah, I'll bet you say that to all your girlfriends." Melissa allowed her bathrobe to open enough to reveal a lot of skin. She was being shameless and flirty knowing he'd have a difficult time trying to resist.

"You're a trip alright. I meant what I said last night. If I wasn't involved right now, we'd still be in the sack burning the sheets."

"I guess I deserve that for acting like a whore."

"No, you're not following me. I think you're a very nice lady in need of some romantic attention. I'm sorry I couldn't be that person for you. That doesn't mean you didn't make me feel horny, you did and still do."

"Well thanks. I was beginning to really feel old."

"Nah, you've got a lot of miles left."

"But I'm way past the warranty period." With that she left the room.

Chapter 13

Nick was eating a hearty, but early breakfast at the café when the sheriff walked in. There was no point in having Melissa fix breakfast for him at her place. For Melissa, it was déjà vu. She had a difficult time remaining calm. Thoughts of Frank kept running through her head. And there was Nick sitting at the counter in the very same place Frank had sat not long before.

"Morning, Mellie, morning everyone," the sheriff said nodding to all the customers before sitting at the counter in his usual spot. He was earlier than usual.

"It's not re-election time yet Sheriff, why so polite?" Melissa asked pouring him a cup of coffee. "You eating anything?"

"Guess I better. Got a big day ahead of me. Coupla eggs, hash browns, bacon and toast... and a big smile there Mellie."

"I'll smile after you pay the bill, not until then." She turned to the grill and started preparing his order.

"See, that's what I mean about you, Mellie, you gotta lose that attitude. Pretend you're glad to see me when I walk in. Did we have an argument that I don't know about?" He laughed, and so did several others listening to their banter.

"Well I'll say this for you, Sheriff. You seem to be in exceptionally high spirits this morning. Must have a new girlfriend," Melissa said without turning around.

"You know I wouldn't cheat on you, Mellie."

His last remark was sufficient for Melissa's face to turn pink, which several customers noticed, including Nick. The teasing was becoming personal.

"I believe I saw you in town last week didn't I?" The sheriff turned his attention to Nick.

"You've still got a good memory." Nick nodded, then held up his cup for a refill.

"Is that your Crown Vic I see parked out there with Michigan tags?"

"Yep." Nick planned to let the sheriff pull it out slowly. He wasn't going to offer any additional information.

"You some distant relative to Mellie here?"

"Nope." Nick wondered where this was going.

"Didn't think so. How is it then I saw your car parked in her driveway earlier this morning around two O'clock?"

"I guess that's none of your business, Sheriff."

"Son, let me tell you something. Everything that goes on in this fine community of ours is my business, whether you like it, or not! So what's your business in Paradise Valley this time? You just here to sample some of our sweet commodities?" Billy already knew about Nick driving by Bovis's place yesterday.

"Well since you want to conduct this interrogation in public, I'll give you an answer, but you might regret having asked the question."

"I'm still listening, city boy."

"On the side, I sell Mason jars to moonshiners. Is your boss needing any?" Nick had a nasty smirk on his face. He couldn't see the surprised look on Melissa's, face but he was sure it was there. An instant hush enveloped the café.

"That's not funny, Slick. Just who the hell do you think you're talking to?" Sheriff Billy was red in the face.

"Look, you started this conversation. I'm just pulling your chain a little because you're being nosier than you have any right to be. You seem to be awfully curious about strangers visiting, or passing through."

"I'll show you how curious I am. When you're done there, let's take a little walk across the street to my office and we'll have us a nice little chat, and get to know one another real good."

"Now just so I understand you, is that an invitation, or an order?" Nick asked. Everyone was listening. The suspense was like static electricity.

"Why don't we leave it as an invitation for now."

"Then thanks for the invite, but I'm busy." Nick knew the sheriff's temperature was rising rapidly. He was baiting the man and it was working.

"Guess I changed my mind then about the invitation. It's an order. So move your ass out of here... now!" The sheriff got up and walked toward Nick who was giving everyone a casual, unconcerned look as he pulled out a $ 5 dollar bill and left it for Melissa. Nick gave her a big smile.

"I'm not buying your breakfast, Sheriff in case you thought I was." Nick stood there waiting until the sheriff reached into his pocket and threw a $ 5 dollar bill on the counter as well. One of the customers snickered, knowing this was unusual for the sheriff.

"Let's go," the sheriff grabbed Nick by the arm. Nick shook off his hold.

"Unless you're arresting me for something, take your hands off me!" Nick was a good six inches taller than the sheriff and wasn't displaying any fear, causing the sheriff to back off slightly. They walked across the square together to the sheriff's office. Eulla was there and Nick shot her a wink. He sat down before being told. He crossed his legs, folded his hands over his knee and waited. He was aware that Eulla was giving him an appraising once over and not hiding her smile.

"Okay, mister smart guy, I already have your phony business card, now let's see some real identification."

"My name happens to be Nick Alexander and I'm from St. Clair Shores, Michigan. Here's my PI license and permit to carry." Nick took the items from his wallet.

"I said I wanted to see some eye dee. Are you deliberately trying to piss me off?" The sheriff wanted to see his driver's license. Technically any photo identification was sufficient as long as he wasn't driving. So he had already complied with the sheriff's request. And he hadn't lied about who he was.

"No, but I seem to be doing a pretty good job of it, don't I?" Nick said chuckling to let Eulla know he wasn't being intimidated. "See Sheriff, I haven't done anything wrong here except jay walk across the street with you. A stop and search isn't warranted. You don't have any right to force me to come to your office and there were a few witnesses back there that heard your little speech. I'm not a fugitive, don't have a police record, just a law-abiding, tax paying citizen who happens to know all his rights, some of which you've violated."

"How about I throw your smart ass behind bars for a while, and you stick those rights up your ass? And you sure enough don't pay any taxes here in Harmon County."

"Whatever makes you happy, and makes me rich later."

The sheriff examined Nick's license. "So, you're really a private investigator? That's like being a wanna be cop, but not quite. I thought we saw the last of you last week. What brings you back? You just looking for a little strange pussy? Melissa take good care of you last night? She used to be pretty wild, I seem to recall."

"Is that right? She was wondering if you turned gay. Said you never were much fun in the sack."

"You shut your foul mouth, or...."

"Or what? You gonna try to lay a hurt on me big guy? If so, you better get a couple of your deputies in here to help you. I guess you don't like it when somebody gives you some of your own trash talk right back."

"I guess it's time I remind you that you're not in Michigan. You are in my jurisdiction right now. I make the rules around here and I enforce them, too! Anybody breaks them, I use whatever means suits me to make the point I want made. You gettin' any of this, city boy?" The sheriff was irritated that he wasn't intimidating Nick.

"Oh I hear you alright, I'm just having a hard time believing what I'm hearing. You making the law and all. You got another brother who's a judge or magistrate to keep you out of prison? I never thought moonshine was that big of a business to have influence all the way to the top."

"Just shows how much you don't know." Billy's mind was racing through all his options. He didn't have anything he could hold this dude on, but he was itching to throw his ass behind bars anyway. He had to be careful though. Bovis would be upset if he knew about this slicker running his mouth the way he'd done at the café in front of all those customers, most of whom were also voters.

"Uh huh, that still doesn't explain how you happened to be shacked up with Melissa last night."

"No it doesn't." Nick hadn't moved in his chair.

"So what's so special about Melissa? I don't recall her ever being all that good in bed."

"She's a friend of a friend. And that's all you need to know. I'd be a little careful about defaming her character though. If she knew what you were saying about her, she might take a notion to sue your ass. Of course the way things look around here, she might have to stand in line."

"You just love to run that smart mouth don't you?"

"It all depends on where I am, and who I'm talking to."

"Yeah? Well someone needs to teach you to have more respect for the law."

"Oh believe me, I have a lot of respect for the law. What I don't respect are people who abuse their authority and try to intimidate people just because they know they can. Sooner or later, they get in trouble. It's just a matter of time. You might keep that in mind, Sheriff." Nick got up and started to leave.

"Sit down. I'm not through with you yet. And when I am, I want you to make tracks out of town."

"Now it's my turn to teach you something. I'm leaving, but if I decide to stick around, there's not much you can do about it, unless I happen to break the law, which I'm not inclined to do. So, either you keep me here by putting me under arrest and reading me my rights, or I'm out of here. It's the law. You ought to read up on it sometime." Nick waved to Eulla and walked out the door, leaving the sheriff red in the face and Eulla giggling.

"Shut up!" was all Nick heard as he closed the door. He assumed the sheriff was addressing his plump assistant. Nick made a point of crossing the street properly as he made his way back to the café. He was ready for another cup of Melissa's good coffee. He also wanted to reassure her that he was okay. She looked worried when he left.

"I'm surprised you're not behind bars." Melissa said when he walked in the door.

"I am too. He got pretty worked up, but he didn't have any grounds to hold me."

"He doesn't need any. He puts folks back there in one of his cells whenever anyone gives him a hard time."

"A good lawyer could teach him an expensive lesson about doing that."

"Maybe that's our problem. We ain't got any good lawyers around here. We got a few bad ones though."

"I think your old beau is a bit jealous of my being at your place last night."

"What did you tell him?"

"I said you were a friend of a friend and left it at that. It's none of his business anyway, which is what I told him earlier."

"Yeah, we all heard you. You should have seen all the snickers I got after you two left here. I'll be a tarnished lady for a long while now."

"Or, very popular." They both laughed at that one.

* * *

Nick drove around the town for a few minutes, then out to the by-pass, just to get a better sense of the surrounding area. When he drove back into town, the sheriff's white Bronco was gone. Nick found a convenient place to park and walked back into the sheriff's office.

"Back again so soon?" Eulla was pleasantly surprised to see him.

"Yes, I forgot to ask the sheriff where I should go, to get that court order he said I needed, before I could look at the arrest report on Cindy Stevens. You know, the young lady you folks kept in jail overnight without proper cause. When her lawyer sues the town and the commissioners, I suspect everyone here will be looking for work." Nick hoped to scare the woman.

"The sheriff ain't going to help you any. You got him plenty mad right now. If I was you, I'd get out of town fast while you still can."

"How long has this speed trap scam been going on?" Nick asked, ignoring her warning.

"Mister, you got more nerve than brains." Eulla was beginning to sweat. She sensed trouble and didn't know what exactly to do. She had the feeling this man knew more than he was letting on. And Bovis would be upset when he heard about what went on between the two men. She knew

Billy was worried by the way he stomped out of the office without saying where he was going. Usually he told her.

"Tell you what. Why don't you call the deputy who made the arrest? Tell him I want to ask him a few questions, that's all. Then I'll be on my way."

"As long as you're not plannin' on makin' trouble. I believe it was Deputy Terry Wolfe. We call him Deputy Dog, ha ha hah." It was a nervous laugh to relieve some of the tension.

"Thank you. Is he out on patrol today?"

"Yeah, you want me to call him?"

"Sure. Tell him if he wants to take a coffee break, to meet me at the café on the square. I'll buy him a cup of coffee, and send one over for you, too." He winked at her and left. He needed a little more information. Maybe the arrest was never recorded.

Nick moved his car back across the square, went into the café and waited. He was still a little tired. Melissa was busy with customers. In about 15 minutes, Deputy Wolfe appeared. He looked around then approached Nick.

"You the one wants to see me?"

"Yes, have a seat Deputy. Melissa will bring you a cup of coffee in a minute. Name's Nick Alexander, from the Detroit area." Nick shook hands with the man who had a frown on his face and was reluctant to sit.

"Just what is it you want, Mr. Alexander?" The sheriff hadn't warned him not to talk to anyone and Eulla was acting very nervous when she mentioned what happened earlier.

"Do you recall stopping a young lady in an older Mustang convertible for speeding a few weeks ago?"

"Sure do. She was zippin' right along, radio blarin' so loud she didn't even hear my siren. Pretty girl though."

"And you gave her a ticket, right?"

"Are you her uncle or something?"

"That's really beside the point. You either gave her a ticket, or you didn't."

"I believe the sheriff gave her a reduced fine and let her go." Deputy Wolfe was trying to avoid the question.

"Was this before, or after she went before a magistrate?"

"I think the sheriff was doing her a favor. She had a couple of other speeding tickets I seem to recall. One more and she was in big trouble, so he gave her a break."

"Uh huh, but he put her in a cell for a while, didn't he?"

"If you know this girl, then you know she has a smart mouth and a bad attitude. The sheriff was just trying to make a point. It worked, too. When we let her out, she was real polite and appreciated what the sheriff did for her. I watched her leave. She drove off nice and slow, obeying the speed limit, so maybe she learned a good lesson."

"So what happened to the ticket you wrote?"

"I guess we probably tore it up, why?"

"I didn't realize the sheriff was such a nice guy. I must have misjudged him."

"Well I need to get back out on the road. Thanks for the coffee. You want me to take a cup back for Eulla? She said something about you buying her a cup."

"Sure if you don't mind. Save me a trip."

Nick's next stop was the county court house where he learned from the clerk that court was in session for local violations every Thursday morning, unless there wasn't anything on the docket.

"Does the magistrate hear cases any other time?" Nick asked.

"He can, provided there's a special request made by the sheriff."

"Can you tell me when was the last time that happened?"

"Oh it's been a while. Maybe once last year. Do you need the date?"

"No, I was just curious. Where are the traffic fines paid?"

"Right here, unless it's after hours, then the sheriff's office collects them."

"Did you receive anything from the sheriff recently for a speeding ticket issued to a Cindy Stevens?"

"Not that I recall, let me look." The woman disappeared behind the counter and checked a register she had on her desk. Nick knew the answer before she even looked up. "No, nothing's been registered here in the past few weeks. Are you sure he wrote a ticket? Sometimes he lets people go with just a warning."

"That's probably what it was then. Thank you for your time." Nick had a pretty good picture of how the sheriff was circumventing the system. He had proof that Cindy was held in a cell for a few hours, but beyond that, he doubted anyone would confirm the sheriff visited her in her cell while either sleeping, or drugged. If he did it once, there was a good chance he did it other times as well. Three or four similar complaints would attract enough attention and create enough doubt to put the sheriff in the spotlight. However, getting that type of information would be difficult.

As Nick was leaving the courthouse, he spotted the reward notice on the bulletin board in the hallway. The name, Bovis Tinch jumped out at him. He'd learned from Melissa that Bovis was a local moonshiner, a county commissioner and Sheriff Billy Hargis's superior to whom he reported.

It was time to call a TBI agent Nick knew. They had worked on a case together in Cookeville last year and had become friendly. Nick sat in his car and used his cell phone. He had just finished putting notes into his laptop for recall later. His TBI friend was interested in what Nick told him and asked Nick to fax, or email his notes so he could review them with agents in that jurisdiction who might have some additional information.

He also warned Nick to be careful, and not do anything foolish. It was easy to have high visibility in a small town, particularly when you started asking a lot of questions that involved the sheriff.

* * *

"Sheriff, we just might have a little problem on our hands," Deputy Wolfe said.

"Like what?"

"That fellow that's been driving around town in that Crown Vic with the Michigan plates? He's asking a lot of questions about that girl I stopped a few weeks ago. You remember the cute one in that Mustang convertible?"

"Yeah, what about her?"

"He wanted to know if I gave her a ticket? Wanted to see a copy."

"What'd you tell him?"

"I told him we tore up the ticket and you let her off with a warning."

"Good thinking."

"I also told him you only kept her in the cell for a few hours until she adjusted her attitude a little and showed some respect."

"What! Why'd you tell him that? I knew he was sniffing around for something and not just passing through, looking around. Hah, the man must think I'm a fool. You didn't need to mention anything about the cell though."

"He already knew about it. Saw him walking out of the courthouse a little while ago, too. I figure he's checking on all the past fines on file." He'd asked the clerk after Nick left.

"Okay. It's time we did a little checking on him. I got his license plate number and his business card. Let's just see who we're really dealing with." He gave Nick's card to Eulla and told her to use her computer magic.

A few minutes later he knew a little more about Nick Alexander, retired police lieutenant and now private investigator. At least the man hadn't lied about his name. Now the sheriff was about to teach Nick a lesson. The fact that the man was a former police officer didn't matter. He'd embarrassed the sheriff, showing no respect.

Sheriff Billy called Special Agent Greg Mathews at the TBI office in Chattanooga. The sheriff still had his card.

"What can I do for you, Sheriff?" Agent Mathews asked, curious that a corrupt sheriff would ever ask for any TBI assistance.

"Well we got an interesting situation going on here. There's a fellow pretending to be a TBI agent that's been asking a lot of questions."

"What's his name?"

"Says his name is Nick Alexander. You got anybody working for the TBI by that name?"

Chapter 14

Nick was sitting in Edgar Ames's newspaper office. They were drinking coffee. Nick had asked to use a free desk and telephone line for his modem. He had his laptop out and had just finished using the modem. He was sending his friend at the TBI office in Cookeville the notes he had compiled on Cindy Stevens' arrest and retention. He also sent the notes he'd taken of Cindy's account of that afternoon, evening and the following morning.

She'd been held for at least 12 hours and hadn't spoken to anyone on the phone. Several attempts were allegedly made to her friend in Chattanooga, and to her aunt in Cookeville. A check of the phone records would reveal if those calls were actually made. Nick wasn't in a position to do that, but his agent friend was.

Edgar had just ordered a pizza when the office door opened. Nick was just closing his laptop and finishing his coffee when the two deputies walked in.

"Looks like we'd better order two large pizzas," Edgar said.

"No need. We're here to arrest Nick Alexander for impersonating a TBI agent." They handcuffed him, read him his rights and escorted him out of the office to the waiting patrol car. Nick gave Edgar the phone number of his TBI agent friend to whom he'd just sent the notes and asked Edgar to call him and explain what was happening.

"You'd best just stay out of it, Edgar." The deputy said. "This man is an imposter. We've got a cozy cell for him until the TBI boys come and get him. Sheriff Billy told them there was no hurry. Next week would be fine, ha, ha, hah. I guess Melissa won't be getting any tonight and neither will you," one deputy said to Nick. "I sure hate to see her feeling so lonely lately. Maybe I'll go over to her place later and check on her for the sheriff. He seems to be worried about her and the company she's been keeping lately, know what I mean? A good ole country boy knows what a country girl needs better'n a city boy, any day of the week." The deputy sounded like a clone of the sheriff, Nick thought.

Nick was glad he'd finally gotten around to correcting Melissa when she had referred to him as a TBI agent. He explained that she had assumed he was an agent and that he hadn't bothered to correct that impression at first because it seemed to work to his advantage. Finally, when she said something about his Michigan license plate, he felt it was time to tell her who he was, and why he was in Paradise Valley. Now two people here knew, Edgar Ames and Melissa and his TBI friend in Cookeville.

As soon as the two deputies left with Nick in handcuffs, Edgar picked up the phone and called the number Nick had given to him. Edgar knew Nick was in for a nasty time with Billy. He also had to be careful not to get overly involved where things could reflect badly on him. Billy still had a lot of friends, including Mr. Bovis Tinch, who just happened to own the building Edgar used for his office. Tinch was his landlord.

"Well now, Mr. Private Investigator, let's see how you like our accommodations." The sheriff seemed to be in a joyous mood.

"Could I have the cell where you do the young women?" Nick asked, hoping to break the euphoric spell.

"You keep talking like that, and maybe you won't be in such good shape by the time they come to get you."

"Do whatever you feel makes you happy, Sport. I keep thinking about how rich I'm going to be when I'm done with you. It's one thing to play little king in a small community, but you've gone too far, breaking so many rules."

"Shut up! I'm tired of hearing you run that smart mouth of yours. Lock him up back there," the sheriff ordered.

Nick was put in a cell, but not the Honey Hole. Nick didn't know which cell it had been where Cindy was held, nor did he know they had a special name for it. An hour passed before Eulla came back to Nick's cell and asked if she could get him anything to drink? Without thinking, Nick said he'd take a soft drink. Eulla brought a can of Dr. Pepper, popped the top and poured the contents into a large plastic glass, which she passed to him through the bars.

"You need to be more careful speaking to the sheriff. He likes it when folks show him a little respect. I swear, I've never seen anyone piss him off the way you've done," she said.

"He'll get over it." Nick started to take a sip of his drink then remembered that Cindy thought she might have been drugged. Would they try something like that with him? He pretended to take some, tasting it with his tongue. It tasted okay, but he wasn't about to take any chances. He'd pour the contents into the toilet later then use the glass to drink some tap water. "Were you here when the sheriff raped that young girl?"

"I don't know nothing about that. She never said she'd been raped when she left here. She's making up a story, that's what I think."

191

Nick yawned and feigned sleepiness. A few minutes later he flopped over on the bunk and closed his eyes. He'd pretend to be asleep. And, he'd listen carefully to whatever was going on.

"Mr. Nick, are you falling asleep on me, Sugar?"

"Mmmm." He sighed. It would be easy enough to fall asleep since he didn't get a lot of sleep last night on Melissa's couch waking up at 4:30. That left him two hours short of his normal sleep, of which he needed more lately. He had to be careful not to doze off now. It would be easy to do except for all the caffeine he'd had earlier.

"Well you just sleep tight, Sugar Buns and I'll check in on you later."

Whatever was going on around here, it was a safe bet she was in on it. So much for trying to solicit her help. As soon as Eulla left, Nick poured the contents of the cup into the sink.

Meanwhile Melissa heard that Nick had been arrested and walked over to the sheriff's office to see him. He might need some help, she thought.

"I'm sorry, Honey. The sheriff left specific instructions that the prisoner wasn't to see anyone except those TBI agents you've been so friendly with lately. I guess you'll get a chance to see them again real soon." Eulla was taking pleasure in reciting all this. She wanted Melissa gone so she could check on the prisoner.

After calling the TBI agent in Chattanooga and arresting Nick at Edgar Ames's office, Sheriff Billy walked over to Lou's barbershop for a trim and to load up on some local gossip.

"Ya think Bovis is gonna' rebuild his barn soon?" Someone asked, when Billy sat down to wait his turn.

"Don't know. You'll have to ask Bovis."

"There's a rumor going around that Melissa has a new boyfriend. Any truth to that?" Another regular asked, hoping to get a rise out of the sheriff.

"Oh I doubt that he'll be sticking around very long. Right now, I got him locked up, so Melissa won't be getting any tonight." That produced a few chuckles.

"What's he in for?" Lou asked, listening to all the comments with great interest.

"Can't discuss it. TBI agents are on their way here to pick him up. I keep telling everybody not to be so trusting with the strangers that visit here. They bring trouble. Look at that one fella got burned up at the dump. He had no business here. And that fugitive that jumped off the train here, then hid out up by Ely's place. Poor old Ely learned a lesson that cost him his life. No, Sir, I just don't trust strangers who come around asking a lot of questions. I remind everyone to direct those visitors to my office." The sheriff made that same speech several other places earlier.

"Lou, I didn't shave this morning. Been up all night. How about giving my whiskers a whack?" Lou heard this same statement at least twice a month from the sheriff.

"You want the lilac water, or the witch hazel?" Lou asked when he was finished. The sheriff always paid him $5 for the haircut, but never gave him a tip, and always forgot to pay the extra buck for the shave. Like Melissa, it annoyed Lou that the sheriff took so much for granted without ever asking. It was supposed to be understood.

* * *

Nick succeeded in falling asleep despite his efforts to stay awake. He heard his cell door open and almost opened his eyes before he remembered he wanted to appear drugged. He felt Eulla sit on the bunk and heard the springs protest the added weight.

"I'm back Sugar Buns. You awake?"

This was truly a strange experience for Nick. He didn't know what to expect. He didn't know how long he'd been sleeping, or what time it was. He felt her hands rubbing his buttocks. Now she was unbuckling his belt and unzipping his fly. She was tugging on his trousers, pulling them down. Against his will, he was getting aroused. The woman was fondling him in a gentle manner that wasn't unpleasant. He was wondering how far she would go? And, how far would he let her go?

Eulla was attempting to roll Nick over onto his back. He'd been lying on his side when she came in. She was having some difficulty because Nick wasn't helping. He heard her heavy breathing and exasperated sigh. She was hovering over him now.

"Too bad you're not awake to enjoy this, Sugar Buns," she whispered in his ear. She was attempting to straddle him.

Nick hated having to hit her. His fist caught her on the chin knocking her back without a sound. He'd managed to put her lights out. His hand hurt from the blow. Nick managed to get out from under her weight, pushed her aside and pulled up his pants. He took his handkerchief and stuffed it in her mouth. There was a little blood around her mouth and her chin had broken skin with some swelling. Nick pulled off his belt and pushed Eulla face down on the bunk pulling her arms behind her. He used the belt to secure her arms together behind her back. Then he listened for any sounds in the office area. He didn't hear anything.

Being as quiet as possible, Nick walked slowly down the hall and into the empty office. He found the bathroom and searched the medicine cabinet for something to put on his sore knuckles. He saw an open bottle of aspirin. The cap was off and lying beside the plastic bottle. Nick shook out a few and was surprised when he saw they were capsules not tablets. They weren't aspirin tablets as he was expecting. It dawned on him that this must be what they were using to drug prisoners. Nick put a tablet into a glass of water and carried it back to his cell. He'd test his theory on Eulla once she was awake.

Nick made it back before she came to. He unfastened his belt, removed the handkerchief and pulled her into a sitting position.

"What? What happened?" She groaned.

"I think you fell and hit the floor. Here, drink this, it's just water." Nick held the glass to her mouth.

Eulla was still groggy. She took the glass from Nick and gulped the contents. "Thanks," she mumbled. "Did you hit me?" She asked falling over onto the bunk. Nick took the glass from her hand and put it on the floor. Then he pulled her off the bunk and left her lying face down on the floor. He had to stage the scene just right. He wasn't sure how much time he'd have. Moments later he heard the office door open.

"Hey Eulla, You back there molesting our prisoner?" Sheriff Billy yelled. Nick heard him laugh.

"Back here, hurry!" Nick yelled leaning over Eulla.

"What happened?" The sheriff asked stepping into the cell, seeing Eulla lying on the floor with Nick hovering over her. "Step back," he ordered.

"I think she may have had a heart attack," Nick said standing up and moving back so the sheriff could get a closer look.

"Maybe we should call the EMS," Nick suggested.

"Hey Eulla? You okay?" Billy asked trying to turn her over. He was leaning over her prone body. The next moment he was lying on top of her.

Nick came down on the back of the sheriff's neck with a hammer blow that flattened him instantly. Now he had to act fast before anyone else arrived. He pulled the sheriff's limp body onto the bunk. Nick removed his gun and handcuffs, just in case he came too suddenly. Nick ran back to the bathroom, shook out another capsule, put the sheriff's gun in the desk and returned to the cell. He filled the same glass again and waited for the sheriff to come to. When he did, Nick held the glass for him to take a drink.

"Drink this, you'll feel better," Nick said standing in front of the man sitting on the bunk. Eulla was still out cold on the floor behind him.

"Is she dead?" Sheriff Billy asked taking the glass and drinking it all, just as Eulla had done. It didn't take long for Billy to slump back onto the bunk.

Now Nick had to hurry in case someone else arrived. He pushed the sheriff's body up against the cell wall, unbuckled his belt and pulled down his pants until they reached the tops of his cowboy boots. Next, he had to struggle with Eulla, lifting her dead weight onto the bunk beside Billy. He adjusted her body so she was facing the sheriff. They barely fit together on the narrow bunk, each lying on their sides.

196

Nick lifted Eulla's dress, exposing fat legs and thighs. She was wearing blue cotton panties with a day of the week sewn onto the side. No lace. Nick stepped back to admire his creative efforts. He had no desire to take things to the next level. Any onlooker would get the message instantly. Nick removed the glass, picked up the sheriff's hat and closed the cell door, making sure it locked. He'd taken the keys.

Nick walked back into the office and sat at the sheriff's desk, rummaging through the drawers. It no longer mattered who arrived. He found a Polaroid camera and that gave him an idea. It had several frames left. Nick walked back to the cell, unlocked the door and took several shots from various angles. He couldn't have planned this event any better. Eulla and Sheriff Billy were victims of their own wicked medicine. Nick had to smile about how strange justice was. It looks a little kinky, but what the hell, Nick thought. The pictures would serve as his *Get Out of Jail Free* card. Back in the office Nick called Melissa.

"Why don't you come over to the sheriff's office? They're allowing me to have as many visitors as I want. In fact, they're giving a tour of the jail while I'm still here, so bring along a few people who might be interested in seeing the sheriff in an entirely new light," Nick was having fun and couldn't pass up the pun.

"So they're letting you go?"

"In a manner of speaking. Which of the deputies around here do you think can be trusted?"

"That would be Deputy Willoughby Jones. He's a bit of a straight arrow. Doesn't get along too well with Billy."

"He's the man I need to talk to then."

"What's this all about, Nick?"

197

"I'll tell you when you get here. Bring some friends along for the tour of the jail. I'm exposing the deplorable condition it's in. I'm also trying to reach Edgar Ames. He needs to be here."

"Nick have you been drinking?"

"Not me, but somebody else has. Hurry on over, Melissa. I've got your ex-boyfriend in a compromising situation here."

Next, he called Edgar Ames. He got the answering machine. Apparently Edgar had left for the day. Nick left a message. "There's an interesting photo opportunity over at the sheriff's office if you hurry," Nick said without explaining anything.

While waiting for Melissa and Edgar to show up, Nick walked back to the cell to check on Eulla, who was still out. The sheriff hadn't moved either. Nick now knew that two swallows was more than enough to do the trick.

Melissa walked into the office dragging along Mary Lou Haslette, the librarian.

"Hello... anyone here?" Melissa called out.

"Back here." Nick returned.

"Oh my God! I don't believe this." Melissa's hands went to her cheeks as she stared at the couple huddled together on the bunk, the sheriff's left arm lying on Eulla's thigh. Nick thought that was a nice touch in case anyone had doubts.

"Are they dead?" The librarian asked, not taking her eyes off the prone couple on the bunk bed.

"No, I think they're just wore out," Nick replied. "They put on quite a performance earlier."

"So who let you out?" Melissa asked, still confused by what she was seeing and hearing.

"I let myself out. And since I was entitled to one phone call, I called you. Stick around for a minute, will you ladies? I've got another call to make. Nick paged Deputy Willoughby over the special channel.

"What's up?" The deputy asked.

"You need to get back to the office pronto. The sheriff needs your help."

"Who's this? Where's Eulla?"

"I think she's sick." Nick didn't bother to respond further. People were starting to crowd around the doorway, peeking in and wondering what all the commotion was. Deputy Wolfe arrived just ahead of Deputy Willoughby and they forced their way through the crowd into the office. Nick pointed toward the cells and they ran back, ordering everyone to clear the area. Just then Edgar Ames arrived, asking anyone and everyone what was going on.

"I think they committed suicide." Someone exclaimed.

As soon as Melissa reappeared, Nick took her hand and led her out of the office. He already had his personal items that were in a big brown envelope in the sheriff's desk. "Time for us to leave. Come on, I'll drop you off at your place." Nick said, walking to his car with Melissa in tow.

"Now I know you had to have had something to do with all that back there. It shows on your face. You look like the cat that ate the mockingbird."

"It was a canary," Nick corrected.

"Down here it's a mockingbird. That's our state bird in case you didn't know. And why are you taking me home?"

"I'll tell you all about it later. Right now you don't need to be there when the sheriff wakes up. It will be one of those Kodak moments he'll never forget."

Chapter 15

Ralph Goodwin spent three days roaming all over Harmon County, being careful not to be seen. Not having his rifle with him when he chanced upon the sheriff and the plump woman still angered him. It was the only time he had a good chance of shooting the sheriff without anyone else being around. He'd seen the sheriff's Bronco a few times cruising around, but never within range. Ralph knew he had to be patient. Another opportunity would present itself, and he'd be ready.

The area by the old abandoned farmhouse had proven to be a good spot to camp undetected. Being alone, and not having anyone to talk to, Ralph carried on a few conversations with himself.

"Maybe if I kidnapped someone and left a ransom note stating that the sheriff should be the one to drop off the money, I'd get another chance at him." Then he answered, "No, that would bring in the Feds and limit my chance for escape. That was a stupid idea." Yet the idea lingered. He was beginning to think the sheriff was in constant motion, going here then there, and then back to his office, never remaining anyplace very long.

Ralph had yet to discover where the sheriff lived, which was a small, two-story house in town about three blocks from his office. He and his brother, Harvey grew up in that house. The two brothers now owned it jointly, but only Billy lived there, since Harvey had a larger home and family several blocks away. Not too many people were even aware that Billy lived there because he always came and went through the back door, crossing the back yard, which was surrounded by tall, untrimmed bushes. The back yard opened onto a small alleyway that he used to cut across to the square.

By leaving his Bronco outside the office, most people thought he was on duty, even when he was home sleeping. A kid in the neighborhood cut the grass. The blinds were always closed, and the sheriff got all his mail at a box at the post office. Few neighbors even knew the house was occupied. The only clue was a light on at night occasionally.

* * *

Billy woke up while Deputy Wolfe was covering him with a blanket. He thought his head was about to explode. He tried to sit up and had some difficulty. "What happened here?" he asked.

"I don't have a clue, Sheriff. It sort of looked like you and Eulla were getting it on, then fell asleep. You caused quite a stir, I can tell you that."

"Where's Eulla?"

"She's in the bathroom. Won't come out until everyone leaves. I've tried to talk to her, but she won't say anything, just cries and tells me to leave her alone," Deputy Wolfe said.

When the sheriff managed to stand up, he pulled up his pants and tried unsuccessfully to buckle his belt. The deputy got a good look at his puffy face. "Jesus, did you and Eulla have a fight? Looks like she beat the shit out of you."

It was coming back to him now. "It wasn't Eulla, it was that smart mouth prisoner we were holding. Where is he?"

"Don't know Sheriff. When Willoughby and me arrived, there was a big crowd of people trying to jamb into the office. I was busy trying to clear everyone out, then we found you and Eulla back here laying together and well."

"Okay, I get the picture. We've got an escaped prisoner on our hands who might be dangerous. Did he take my gun?"

"No, it's in your desk drawer. There's a big envelope on your desk with you're name on it. It's marked confidential. You want me to get it?"

The sheriff sat down on the bunk. His legs wouldn't support him and he still felt groggy. He couldn't remember all the events just prior to passing out. He seemed to recall being hit from behind. Deputy Wolfe brought him a glass of water and handed him the brown envelope that had previously contained Nick's personal items. Nick's name was printed on one end. The sheriff opened the envelope and stared at the Polaroid picture. He felt sick. The note taped to the bottom said:

> *Now you know how it feels to be drugged and raped, you sick, sorry piece of shit. This isn't the only photo. Any more attempts on anyone, or on me, will cost you dearly. Think about it because I'll be your worst nightmare!*

The note sent a chill through him. The sheriff didn't doubt the threat for a single moment. What the man knew, along with the photo, would cost him his career and any respect anyone ever had for him. I'll kill the son-of-a-bitch, he thought. He slid the photo and the note back into the envelope and tried to stand up.

"I'll put out an all points BOLO on him, sheriff," Deputy Wolfe said.

"No, we'll let the TBI guys handle it whenever they get here. Tell Eulla to go home and get some rest. I'm going to do the same. You stay here at the office and catch the phone. Don't call me, even if it's an emergency."

"Why don't you let me take you over to the clinic? You don't look so hot."

"I'll be okay in a day or two. You hold the fort."

"Let me at least drive you home. You'll never make it."

"Okay. We'll take my Bronco, then you can drive it for a few days while I'm taking a little time off."

"What do you want me to do if I find this slicker?"

"Keep an eye on where he's going, but don't apprehend him. That's an order, understand?"

"Yes, Sir, I copy, but I'm not sure why you don't want me to pick him up, if I see him."

"Because I said so! The son-of-a-bitch knows too much. He knows about the girl we held. He could sue you, the town, and me. Now do you understand? He knows about the Honey Hole."

"Holy shit! So he's blackmailing us?"

"Something like that. I need him dead, but I'm not in a position right now to do anything about it, so we'll just wait. Maybe he'll leave now that he's embarrassed me." The sheriff was still holding the envelope as he got into the passenger side of his Bronco. For the first time in years, Billy wondered what he'd do, if he weren't the sheriff. Deputy Jones was sitting at his desk smiling when they left. For an instant, the sheriff wondered if Willoughby had played any part in all this? Was it some sort of conspiracy? Surely

Bovis wouldn't let that happen, and without Bovis's support, Deputy Jones didn't stand much of a chance getting elected as sheriff.

* * *

It wasn't often that Deputy Wolfe got an opportunity to drive the sheriff's Bronco. He planned on using it for the next few days while the sheriff recuperated. When he arrived back at the office, Deputy Willoughby was answering the phone. Eulla had left for the day, saying she wasn't sure when she'd be returning.

"This is the craziest mess I've ever seen. The sheriff is acting sort of strange. And that guy we were holding? The sheriff said to let him be, so he doesn't cause more trouble. How's that for a strange turn of events?" Deputy Wolfe asked. The sheriff had left explicit instructions and Deputy Wolfe was the only other person who knew the real reason why. He also knew he wasn't about to become the fall guy for the sheriff's weird peccadilloes.

From now on, the sheriff could catch his own pussy. The TBI agents had everyone acting nervous and sooner or later, there would be hell to pay. Deputy Wolfe decided that putting a little distance between himself and the sheriff might be a good survival tactic. It was time to become friendly with Deputy Willoughby Jones, who might become his next boss.

Meanwhile Eulla unplugged the ringing phone at her mother's house and went to bed. She tried to block out the image of all those people staring at her lying on the bunk beside Billie, with his pants down and her dress up, exposing everything for the world to see. Her chin still ached and her face was swollen. It was the first time a man had ever struck her. She couldn't imagine the sheriff allowing something like this to ever happen. She was mortified and humiliated. Tomorrow, she'd call in sick then maybe take some vacation time. She wasn't about to show her face outside for a while.

Her mother was curious about why she was home so early? And what had happened to her daughter's face? Eulla used being sick as her excuse. Sooner, or later the truth would come out. The prisoner they were holding was the one responsible for everything that had happened. How he managed to find her special pills she kept hidden in that aspirin bottle was a real mind boggler. How the sheriff wound up next to her on the bunk was another puzzle. Maybe she'd quit and look for another job that was less dangerous. That would probably mean moving to Chattanooga.

* * *

That evening, Ralph was restless. His supplies were low. He decided to drive into the far edge of town and get a few items. Maybe get a six-pack of beer. He parked his Jeep in the Mini-Mart parking lot and went inside.

When he came out, he spotted the sheriff's Bronco parked up the street. A young black girl was hanging halfway inside the driver's window. A minute later, she ran around to the other side and hopped in. Ralph watched the Bronco pass by and continue on the road away from town. Ralph jumped into his Jeep and followed them. He hung back far enough so that he wouldn't be noticed. In another few minutes, it would be totally dark outside, so he had to watch for taillights.

The road ran parallel to the railroad tracks. On one straight stretch, Ralph turned off his headlights because there wasn't any other traffic in this remote area. He saw the lights ahead cross over the tracks then disappear. Now he had to be extra careful not to be seen following.

This was only the second time Deputy Wolfe had taken Reba for a ride, and the first time in the Bronco, which was roomier. He left word with Willoughby that he was patrolling out in this quadrant, just in case he was needed. He thought a car was following him and slowed down, checking his side and rearview mirrors, then it disappeared in the dust he was creating. When he crossed over the railroad tracks, he checked again and didn't see anything.

Deputy Wolfe turned into a dirt drive that ran beside a stand of Sycamore trees. The farmhouse at the far end of the drive had burned down years ago. The tobacco field beside the drive was still used. Halfway up the dirt drive, he parked, lowered the window so he could hear the night sounds, particularly the frogs and crickets. He also heard a car in the distance but was distracted by Reba.

"Whatchoo so jumpy 'bout?" Reba asked.

"Nothin' that concerns you, Sweetie." He was jumpy, but he wasn't about to admit it to a young girl eager to please him. The sheriff's situation still played on him, so he was being extra careful. He pushed his seat back and he pulled her to him in a tight embrace. Because he was nervous, he needed a little time to get into a relaxed mood.

Ralph knew he was getting pretty close and didn't want to attempt driving any farther. He parked the Jeep just before the railroad crossing, which rose higher than the surrounding ground. Taking out his rifle and binoculars he was careful to close the door quietly. Every little noise seemed to be amplified out here, even his breathing. Gravel crunched under his feet as he walked beside the road, crossing the tracks. He couldn't see the white Bronco anywhere. It was too early for the moon to rise, so it was totally black except for an occasional firefly. Several times Ralph stumbled over small rocks. He felt like a blind man walking around in a strange room.

It took him five minutes to reach the drive with the Sycamores. He couldn't see the Bronco parked farther up the drive, hidden by darkness. Suddenly the stoplights flashed for just a second, revealing its position. The sheriff must have hit the brake pedal by accident while shifting around inside, he thought. That brief flash of red light was like a beacon for Ralph. Now he knew exactly where his prey was parked.

Rather than walk up the drive and risk being seen, or heard, Ralph moved from tree trunk to tree trunk slowly remaining hidden from the Bronco. It was if he were stalking a deer. He already chambered a bullet and had the safety off, so no clicking sounds would be heard, giving away his position. Every step was cautiously slow as he drew within 40 feet of the Bronco. He could hear them now, but he couldn't see them, so he waited beside a large tree, big enough to hide him completely from view.

Ralph heard the girl laugh, heard a seat being adjusted, then the engine started and the brake lights flashed again. Ralph aimed, trying to get his scope focused for the distance. Then the headlights came on as well as the instrument panel lights, providing just enough illumination to see the sheriff's silhouette.

Just as the Bronco was about to pull forward, Ralph squeezed the trigger. Pow! The quiet night was filled with the blast, followed by a high scream and the horn sounding as the driver's body slumped forward onto the steering wheel. Deputy Wolfe was dead before the horn blew. The windshield shattered as the exiting bullet continued. Reba jumped out of the Bronco and started running down the drive still screaming, not hearing the radio call to Deputy Wolfe from Deputy Willoughby Jones.

Ralph bent down and felt around the ground for the spent shell casing. It was still hot when he picked it up.

Before leaving, he walked to the Bronco, reached through the side window, pulled the slumped body back, away from the horn. He turned off the ignition and lights, using a dirty handkerchief.

That done, Ralph started jogging back to his Jeep, hoping the girl wouldn't see him or his parked vehicle. He congratulated himself on remaining patient. It had paid off. All that remained was to dismantle his campsite and disappear back to his other life at the warehouse, with no one the wiser. This was exactly how assassins worked, without the slightest bit of remorse over their kill. In this case, he had some personal satisfaction of taking revenge on someone who deserved to die. He had been tempted to leave a note.

* * *

The TBI agents arrived. They came prepared to investigate why the sheriff and a private investigator were squaring off on one another. Agent Mathews suspected the sheriff was fabricating the whole incident. He'd also heard from another agent who knew Nick Alexander and vouched for his credentials and capability. It was difficult to keep an open mind when a corrupt sheriff was involved. The same trio of agents made the café their first stop, knowing that Melissa might be able to add something useful.

"Well talk about a sight for sore eyes, I sure am glad to see you gentlemen." Melissa said, seeing the trio arrive.

"That's nice to hear. How are things going?" Agent Gregg Mathews asked.

"How much time do you have?" She told them that Nick was staying at the same motel where Frank had stayed. Nick knew he had to stick around and wasn't about to stay at her place, waiting for someone from TBI to arrive. He didn't want to leave the area and be considered a fugitive. She told them about Nick being arrested and put in jail.

She also said that Nick had sent some notes to a friend who was with the TBI in Cookeville. The notes were part of his effort to determine what had happened to a young girl that had been illegally detained and raped. All three agents at the table were taking notes. Greg was glad Nick had the good sense to stick around and not leave. It was added proof the man knew what he was doing, even though he was up against a corrupt, redneck sheriff who had a lot to hide. It made for an explosive situation.

Two TBI agents went to the motel to talk to Nick, while Greg walked over to the sheriff's office. Deputy Willoughby Jones looked exhausted from being on duty for a double shift. He knew something was wrong when Deputy Wolfe did not report in, or answer any of his calls. He had another deputy out looking for the sheriff's Bronco. Eulla refused to come into the office, and the sheriff had left strict instructions not to be disturbed, regardless of circumstances. One other deputy was on vacation. So he was the only one tending the office.

"We need to organize a volunteer search party for Deputy Wolfe, and put a BOLO on the sheriff's white Bronco." Deputy Willoughby said. No accidents had been reported.

"Okay, I'm going over to see the sheriff, whether he likes it, or not. We'll have somebody here to take over within the next hour, so hang in there until then." Agent Greg was given directions on how to find the sheriff's house. Before he left, he called the motel and had one of the agents meet him. The other agent was to help Deputy Willoughby arrange the search party.

Sheriff Billy took a long time to answer his front door. He wasn't happy to see the TBI agent, or be seen in his present condition.

"Oh Boy, now I know why you're not on duty over at the office. You look like hell, Sheriff." Greg pushed his way inside without waiting to be asked. Greg still didn't have the entire story of what happened earlier.

Sheriff Billy was standing in the middle of the room, wearing a white tee shirt, plaid boxer shorts and his cowboy boots. His face looked pale. To Agent Greg, the man looked pathetic.

"We're here to investigate the charges you've made against Nick Alexander posing as a TBI agent, but right now there's another matter that is more urgent. Get dressed. We need your help trying to locate your Bronco and your deputy who was last seen driving it. He isn't answering his calls."

"Shit! I swear that man is worthless sometimes. He's probably drunk and sleeping it off somewhere. I find him, he's fired!"

"Let's find him first."

"You think that private dick, Nick Alexander had anything to do with this?" Sheriff Billy asked.

"I doubt it. He's been hanging around, waiting for us to show up." It seemed the sheriff was hell bent on pinning anything and everything on Nick, which made the whole accusation smell.

"Good, 'cause I owe him a big knuckle sandwich." Maybe brass knuckles, he was thinking, or a sap behind the ear. That would give him a good goose egg to nurse for a while. Not unlike the sore neck he had.

"Judging from the way you look, you might need some help."

"You don't know the half of it. I caught him messing around with Eulla in his cell. Before I can do anything, he gets the jump on me. Locks us both in the cell, then starts calling people to come take a looksee. You shoulda seen 'em, all those people curious about what was going on. It was embarrassing being caught like that." He neglected to say anything about his pants being down, or how Eulla appeared, with her big butt exposed.

"We'll get it all sorted out, and Nick isn't going anywhere. Let's find your missing deputy first. Get dressed."

While the sheriff was getting dressed in his bedroom, Greg looked around the living room and the kitchen. He spotted a big brown envelope on the kitchen table and looked at the contents. After reading the note and seeing the Polaroid picture, he was able to put it all together. He had a hard time stifling a laugh. He'd have to ask Nick about it later, how he managed to stage the shot like that?

Just before Sheriff Billy appeared, Agent Greg managed to hide the note and photo in his pocket, leaving the empty envelope on the table. In time, the sheriff would know he'd seen everything. Right now it was just one more piece of evidence against the sorry man.

"Let's go out the back way," Sheriff Billy said starting for the door.

"No, I've got a car waiting out front." It was the first time Billy was seen walking out his front door in ages. He was wearing a fresh uniform and appeared normal... from a distance.

A group of volunteers found the Bronco and Deputy Wolfe, an hour later. The news of the bizarre discovery spread quickly throughout the community. Everyone was asking, who would do such a thing? It was the third murder in less than a month. Surely the fugitive wasn't involved in this one.

The TBI agent was still with Nick when they got word that the Bronco and the missing deputy had been found. It took them 10 minutes to arrive at the scene. They left their car at the base of the gravel drive and walked to the Bronco, being careful to stay on the gravel. Nick was with them. Agent Mathews and the sheriff arrived a few minutes earlier.

"Oh Jesus," Sheriff Billy yelled seeing what happened.

"Looks like he might have been meeting someone," Agent Greg said. He pulled on latex gloves and started examining the interior of the Bronco. He noticed the victim's fly was unzipped, but didn't comment on it. The deputy's gun was still holstered, so whoever shot him, took him by surprise.

Agent Cody was taking pictures from every possible angle. Nick watched the way the three men worked the scene. They were a good team, each knowing what to do without being told.

As Nick watched, Sheriff Billy came over and stood close, turning to Nick so as not to be heard by the others. "I'm not through with you. You got lucky once, but it'll never happen that way again, no, Sir. Nobody sucker punches me and gets away with it."

"You're right, it won't ever happen again. You're not worth the effort. I'd be real careful what I said, or did, if I were you. You could end up in prison before all this is over," Nick said.

"That'll never happen. You're forgetting this is a small community here, and I've been the sheriff for quite a while, keeping things peaceful. The folks appreciate me and what I've done for them."

"Well there's at least one citizen around here that doesn't appreciate you, Sheriff. He may well have thought that was you in the Bronco when he took that shot. It was probably dark and he didn't notice that it was your deputy, and not you. Think about that. There's someone out there gunning for you, and when they find out you're still alive, they'll no doubt keep trying."

"Are you threatening me?" Suddenly the sheriff looked very tired and worried. Nick's speculation was just now getting through to him. His deputy may have been mistaken for him in the dark. His stomach tightened into a knot.

"I wouldn't waste my time. You got any vacation time coming? Now would be a good time to use it... and not come back." Nick hadn't meant to verbalize his thoughts, they just slipped out. The sheriff nodded that he understood the message and walked away. He wasn't in charge of this investigation. He had nothing to do, making his presence awkward. He stood a distance away and toed the gravel, deep in thought.

Nick watched him. He'd planted a seed. He wasn't sure if the sheriff was thinking about who the shooter might be, or if he was thinking about where to take a long vacation? Either way, the man was no longer a threat to Nick. He'd lost most of his bully attitude. His focus was elsewhere.

When Nick walked behind a big Tulip Poplar to take a leak, he saw fresh footprints and called Agent Greg to take a look.

"Let's hit these trees with a spray job and see if there are any traces of gun powder." Greg said. "No shell casings, he cleaned up after he was done. It tells me he wasn't in any hurry."

Sheriff Billy waited for Harvey to arrive with the tow truck. An ambulance had already removed the deputy's body. Billy rode back into town with his brother. Neither said anything until they arrived at the storage yard.

"I'm thinking about taking a little time off," Billy said.

"I'd say you could use a rest right about now. Where are you planning to go?"

"That's a tough one, Harv. I thought about Florida, but I don't know a soul down there. Only place I know real well outside of here is Chattanooga."

"Well it would be a change of scenery for you at least. They got some good places to eat down there. Stay a few days, then go on down to Atlanta and look around. Don't forget to send Eulla a postcard, or she'll be pissed."

"The way she's acting, she might as well find herself another job. That's another thing, I'm not sure if I want to be sheriff much longer."

"Look, just because that Yankee rang your bell and got away with it doesn't mean you need to go into hiding. You want me to take care of him for you?"

"No, don't mess with him. And I'm not going to hide! I'm just trying to decide what to do with the rest of my life, what's left of it, and I'm wore out. There's just too much happening here all at once. Bovis sure won't be happy about any of it."

"Jesus, Billy, this is beginning to sound like one of the mid-life crisis things. When was the last time you got laid?"

"Hmm? I don't...." he was about to say it was a long time, but it wasn't. The last young lady he had in the Honey Hole was the last time and the lack of any sexual response from the women was starting to turn him off. The women didn't resist him, but they didn't respond either. It hardly seemed natural. And with all the hoopla going on, the Honey Hole would soon be a thing of the past.

"I'd make that my number one priority when you get to Chattanooga, if I was you." Harvey couldn't remember when he'd seen his younger brother so depressed. "When are you leaving?"

"Right after Terry's funeral. I gotta stick around for that. It wouldn't look right to leave before then. And I gotta get some replacements lined up." He hated to think about the next few days. Deputy Willoughby Jones could fill in for him. Normally Billy wouldn't consider Jones knowing the man wanted his job. Now it didn't make any difference. A strange turn of events was taking place rapidly and Billy didn't see himself in the picture. He tried to think who might want him dead.

* * *

Melissa's living room became an informal meeting room with all three TBI agents and Nick. Melissa enjoyed being a hostess to so many nice men, serving pie and coffee. She didn't care what the neighbors thought, or saw. For her, it was more like a party.

The sheriff was back in his office catching the phone calls. It gave him something to do. Most of the calls were from friends asking what happened. Most were surprised when Billy answered the phone instead of Eulla. It was the first signal that something was definitely wrong. Eulla always answered the phone.

"It's like a crime spree suddenly erupted in this peaceful little town," Agent Greg said. He now had Nick's version of what happened earlier in the cell. Everyone thought it was a hoot that he had managed to pull off such an incongruous stunt. The Polaroid photos were on the coffee table, along with Nick's note to the sheriff.

"You sure you didn't plan it that way?" Agent Cody asked.

"That's not something you can plan. The thought of being sexually molested by Eulla had me terrified. Probably got me pumped enough to clock her the way I did. The corruption has been going on for some time," Nick said. "I think things got out of hand here. If the sheriff could get away with doing whatever he wanted, sooner or later, you know someone is going to seek revenge.

"I did it my way, by exposing the sheriff to the local community who elected him. Somebody else is out there gunning for him. That's my guess. If he raped Cindy Stevens, how many others did he rape? Some enraged parent may have decided to stop him." Nick was speculating and the agents were nodding in agreement. It was a pretty good summation of the situation.

"So you think someone may have thought it was the sheriff in the Bronco and shot him?" Greg asked, mulling it over. "That's possible, particularly if it was dark. But why was he parked way out there alone?"

"Who said he was alone?" Nick asked.

"Why would the shooter leave a witness?" Greg asked.

"Maybe the shooter didn't see anyone else, or didn't care, if it was dark enough. It would be impossible to identify someone who shot at you from any distance in the dark, from behind a tree. He had to be an experienced marksman to make that shot."

The group spent an hour discussing all the possible reasons why the deputy would be at that isolated spot, where nobody saw, or heard anything. Finally Greg offered his view, mentioning the man's unzipped fly. He waited until Melissa was in the kitchen and couldn't overhear. Still he lowered his voice.

"Whoever was with him, is too scared to say anything. It had to be a horrifying experience, not knowing if you were next." Agent Mathews said. "Why don't we start asking around? We might turn up a witness."

They asked Melissa where they should start looking. She wasn't any help. So they went over to the sheriff's office and asked him the same question.

"Go over to the Mini-Mart by the low-rent area. Lots of young black girls hang out at the market. One of them might know something, but you have to pull it out of them, they don't volunteer anything."

"Sounds like maybe you've been there a few times." Greg said.

"Yeah, but not to mess with any of them, if that's what you're thinking." He wasn't surprised, when Greg told him his theory on what was going on out there in the dark. He thought about little Rita and how she'd taken Bobby Lee's money. "Did you check his wallet?"

"Nothing appears to be taken. Something you're not telling me, Sheriff? You think the witness is a hooker?"

"No, they're just a bunch of young girls doing silly things when they should be home. I've checked on 'em a few times. Ask around, if you don't believe me. You want hookers, you'll have to go to Chattanooga."

"Can't imagine why I wouldn't believe you, Sheriff." Greg flashed back to the photo he'd snatched from the envelope on the table. Somehow this last shooting left the sheriff in a very subdued mood. He'd had time to reflect on the entire episode. Perhaps he was feeling guilty. After all, it was his vehicle the deputy was in, and he was using it only because the sheriff was in bad shape.

"I don't have to listen to any insults. Since I'm short-handed here, why don't you highly intelligent fellas go out and find the shooter who killed my deputy," Billy said in a lower than normal voice.

Billy hoped they would find him, but doubted they would. The shooter wasn't someone from Paradise Valley. The thought of someone stalking him made Billy feel uneasy. Like that PI said, it could happen again, any time, anywhere. The man could be a sniper on a rooftop looking through a scope at him right now, while he was sitting at his desk.

"In Africa, when the natives hunt lions, they use a baby goat staked out as bait. Then they wait, hidden close by, for the lion to catch the scent and come charging out of the brush. Maybe that would work here." Greg was actually being serious, even though Nick thought he was trying to goad the sheriff.

"Yeah well, I don't plan on being your goat. You need me, I'll be right here in this office, catching the phone calls."

As far as Nick was concerned, he'd done as much as he possibly could. The sheriff wasn't about to make any confession about molesting female inmates. However, his future didn't look too promising. The TBI guys didn't need Nick's help so he was free to go. He gave them a formal statement. The sheriff probably wouldn't get re-elected, he thought. Especially, if someone decent were to run against him, like Deputy Willoughby Jones.

Edgar Ames had enough material to fill several editions of *The Bugler.*

Cindy Stevens might not appreciate Nick's efforts, but her Aunt Carol certainly would. And, Melissa had been a most gracious hostess. While she was still at work at the cafe, Nick found a florist and bought a huge flower arrangement. He took it back to her house and left it by the back door, along with a note expressing his thanks for all she'd done.

Nick also promised to return someday, on his way down to Atlanta, just to see how things were going in Paradise Valley. He had no way of knowing the events that would follow. His actions had put it all into motion and it would play out over time.

The café was the busiest it had ever been in Melissa's memory. For the first time ever, she ran out of pie. Edgar Ames stopped by to interview her and she put him off until after she closed. She was too busy to talk with anyone.

. Lou's barbershop was also busier than normal with speculation about whether the sheriff would be foolish enough to run for re-election after the folly at the jail. Edgar Ames stopped by for a trim and to register some of the comments he overheard. It was always a good source for gossip, unless you were a stranger just passing through.

Everyone wondered what Bovis Tinch made of the recent events. He'd been keeping a low profile lately.

* * *

"Ashes to ashes, and dust to dust," The minister finished his brief sermon and remarks at the gravesite.

Deputy Terry's sister arrived from Spring City. Eulla cried during the entire ceremony, annoying Billy. She still hadn't bothered to return to work. He couldn't fire her because she knew too much. It also bothered him that Bovis hadn't spoken to him lately. In fact, people seemed to be avoiding him, just nodding to him from a distance.

Chapter 16

Nick didn't stop in Cookeville on his way back to Detroit. He took a more direct route going up Interstate 75 through Knoxville. There still wasn't any proof that Cindy Stevens was actually raped and the sheriff wasn't about to satisfy that question. He doubted that Eulla would say anything to corroborate the story because it might implicate her as well. Nick felt she was in on it, but proving it was another matter. He'd call Carol when he got home and tell her about his recent adventure in Paradise Valley. The name was sure a real disguise for unsuspecting visitors, he thought.

He wondered if Edgar Ames would send him a copy of the next issue of *The Bugler*. Nick knew the situation in Paradise Valley was still under investigation with three unsolved murders and a corrupt sheriff who was being stalked. The TBI agents had Nick's statement and knew how to reach him. He doubted they'd have any reason to call unless there was a trial.

* * *

Sheriff Billy was looking forward to getting out of town. Since the shooting, he'd been keeping a low profile. He'd worn large, dark sunglasses to the funeral and waved off anyone approaching him with questions. Most of the citizens thought he was mourning, and a little surprised at how close he must have been with Deputy Terry. They were wrong. Sheriff Billy just didn't want to talk to anyone about anything. He was just going through the motions, and keeping some distance.

Edgar Ames, Editor of *The Bugler,* wanted to run the story about the sheriff being caught with his pants down, locked in one of his jail cells with Eulla, but the recent death of Deputy Terry Wolfe took a higher priority. If his readers only knew the truth about their sheriff, they'd be shocked. He'd never written anything of a sensational nature, although it was a fantasy he harbored.

He had taken some good photos, as proof, but they weren't appropriate for a small town newspaper. He considered sending them to one of the supermarket tabloids, like *The National Inquirer*, along with a feature story, using a pseudonym. He thought about it for a full day. It was so tempting. He would be part of a new committee to get Deputy Willoughby Jones elected.

Finally, the urge was too great to resist. Once the story was published, the sheriff would be ruined. Meanwhile, Edgar worked on an editorial about all the violence that had suddenly swept through peaceful Paradise Valley. In the article, he even included Bovis's barn being burned to the ground. He used the same photos of the barn burning with the bleacher seats in dramatic silhouette. It produced an unusual effect.

The piece had all the elements of an award-winning journalistic effort. The article ended with the suggestion that perhaps it was time local law enforcement in the valley, became more involved, than just giving out speeding tickets at a speed trap, known to just about everyone who traveled on the by-pass. What the town needed was more tourists. Setting up speed traps didn't encourage travelers to come back.

The Bugler wasn't big enough to have access to the wire services. The only way for Edgar to have anything picked-up, was to send it to the Chattanooga newspaper. He had a friend working there who could get it processed. Rather than fax all the material, some of the photos were in color, he decided to hand carry the package. He could drive there in an hour, have lunch with his friend, tour the facilities and be back by dinnertime. The trip would expedite his efforts, and take a big step toward his dream of becoming a feature writer for a large newspaper.

Edgar's long-standing dislike for Sheriff Billie was finally being satisfied. In Edgar's opinion, the sheriff was too arrogant, too lazy and too pre-occupied to be effective. The recent scandal provided the perfect opportunity to expose the sheriff for what he truly was... worthless. Edgar was unaware of the sheriff's plans to take a vacation.

* * *

"Harry, while my Bronco is in the garage being repaired, why don't you lend me something to drive for a few weeks?" Sheriff Billy asked Happy Harry. Everything his brother had was older and had some damage.

"A few weeks? It won't take more than two days to have your Bronco repaired and ready. It's just the windshield that needs to be replaced and a good clean up job."

"Yeah I know, but I'm thinking of taking a little time off. Take an overdue vacation. They need the Bronco here. It doesn't belong to me you know. It belongs to the county."

"Had me fooled. I never thought I'd hear you ever say something like that, Billy. You've always treated that Bronco like it was your personal property. Of course it's sort of tainted now, isn't it?" Harry noticed the sheriff wince. He'd hit a raw nerve there. However, Harry was always free with his observations and opinions. And he was usually right.

"You gonna lend me something, or not?"

"Of course I'll lend you something. Got to stay on the right side of the law, don't I? I just got to get my digs in a little, to pay you back for all the shit I've had to take from you."

"You're still pissed that I won twenty dollars from you at that last cockfight aren't you?"

"Damned right I am. You rigged that fight."

"I didn't have to rig the fight. Just switched birds, that's all." Sheriff Billy couldn't believe that Harry would be upset over losing $20. He was the second richest man in the county, Bovis being the richest.

"How long you plan to keep it?"

"I don't know, maybe two weeks. Don't worry, I'll stand good for any damage."

"Okay, I've got a Chevy pickup I just finished putting in a good engine and transmission, that should get you down the road nicely. I'll put some temporary tags on it and let you try it out. You don't like it, I'll find something else."

"No, the Chevy will do fine. Thanks, Harry. I owe you one."

"You owe me a lot more than that, Billy Hargis. Just bring it back in one piece. Oh, and try to stay out of trouble, too." He handed the keys to Billy, put a temporary tag on the back and filled out a temporary registration in Billy's name. That would alleviate any liability to him, in case Billy did get into an accident. "You break it, you pay for it," Harry said with a smile.

Sheriff Billy was never one to be shy about asking for a favor. Harry had known him a long time, never trusted the man, but maintained a good relationship out of necessity.

Harry did business with Billy's brother, Harvey, and Harvey's friend, Dent. To get crosswise with one, was to get crosswise with all of them. That was a small town businessman's dilemma.

Harry knew that Billy's reputation had taken a big hit lately. Deputy Willoughby Jones would make a good candidate to run against him in the next election. Harry would put his money behind Willoughby. Bovis would no doubt continue to back Billy, so it might be an interesting race. Bovis's two illegal enterprises had taken a hit recently, so Billy's usefulness wasn't as important as before, there was that to consider. He knew Bovis was looking around for an available barn to rent.

It was another day before Sheriff Billy could get away. The white Bronco remained parked outside the sheriff's office while Billy drove the Chevy pickup. He had half decided he might buy it, if Harry would make him a decent deal. Eulla returned to the office reluctantly. Sheriff Billy noticed that she hadn't giggled once.

"You planning on checking in while you're gone?" She asked.

"Don't know what good it would do, but I might, just in case you need to get in touch with me."

"You going to send me a postcard from Rock City?"

"I doubt that I'll be visiting Rock City. I've already been there, years ago. I'm sure none of it has changed any."

"What about Ruby Falls? Have you been there, too?"

"Yeah, I've done all that tourist stuff. This is strictly a vacation." He hadn't taken a real vacation in years.

"How come you didn't ask me to go along with you?"

The question stunned him. He hadn't realized that she was expecting him to ask her to go along with him. "Well... for one thing, I need you here to keep an eye on things. And how would it look? You and me going on a vacation together, the whole town would be talking."

"Oh shit, Billy. Wake up. The whole town has been talking. You just haven't been paying attention. I don't know what's got into you lately. You sure aren't your old self. You hardly ever leave the office."

"And that's exactly why I need to get away for a while. In a couple weeks the old Billy will be back on the job, kicking ass."

"Uh huh. Just be sure you don't get yours kicked again. I swear, I never saw a man move so fast as that Nick fella you had locked up."

"Can we not talk about him? He's gone, outta here. I told him never to come back this way again. It was because I was concerned about you, that he got the drop on me. I would have paid him back in spades, but he kept hanging around with those TBI agents for protection. So I couldn't do anything."

Eulla didn't see it quite that way, but there was no point in arguing over something they couldn't change. She figured she had a job until the next election then things would surely change. She could tell by the way people were avoiding her. Even Deputy Willoughby was polite in a formal way, but distant. Like the other deputies, he too, refused to drive the Bronco. So it remained parked in front. Eventually Billy would move it to the parking lot next door, when he was tired of looking at it.

Billy Hargis was packed and ready to leave early Saturday morning. He stopped by Melissa's café for a cup of coffee and put a dollar on the counter when he left. That was a startling change, alerting Melissa that something was going on with Sheriff Billy. He hadn't asked any questions, or engaged her in any conversation. When he left, he just nodded to the people in the café. It was as if he was leaving, and not coming back. That thought stayed with her the rest of the day. She knew the TBI boys were still trying to make a case against him, and they were still looking into Deputy Wolfe's murder. So far, nobody was admitting to being with him that night.

Meanwhile, Deputy Willoughby Jones was temporarily in charge. He had three new deputies to work with. The highway department had trimmed the trees along the by-pass so the half-hidden sign indicating the reduced speed limit was now prominent. Motorists could see it and heed it.

Once on the road, Billy felt like a new man, free from all the problems he'd just left. He still had the $ 2,000 he'd confiscated from Jerome, plus another $ 15,000 from his secret stash. His Master Card had a low balance and for the first time he thought about maybe driving across the state and visiting Tunica, just south of Memphis, where all the big casinos were. He hadn't made any plans or reservations, just pointed the truck south to Chattanooga. Running next to him was a freight train, going in the same direction, causing Billy to wonder about the fugitive Darius was supposedly tracking.

Think about someone for a while, and like magic, they somehow get the message and call you, or you run into them by accident. That's what happened to Billy. He drove around the city for a few hours, watching all the tourists. Finally he was ready for a drink. Billy selected a bar that had a convenient parking lot across the street. It was late afternoon so the bar wasn't too busy.

Billy sat at the bar, ordered a beer and looked around. He noticed a couple sitting in a booth at the rear, their backs to him. The man was big and bald. The woman had dark hair and was sitting very close. The big man put his arm around her displaying a series of tattoos and looked over his shoulder to see if anyone was watching him. It was almost a sixth sense that he knew Billy was looking his way.

"Well I'll be damned! Is that you, Billy Hargis?" Darius yelled, then waved for him to come over to the booth.

"Hey Darius, didn't expect to find you here."

"Well that's good to know. It must mean you're not looking for me. Say hello to Melody. Mel, this here is the badass sheriff of Harmon County. Sit down and have a drink with us, Billy." Darius was being very friendly.

For the first time in ages, Billy didn't have someplace else to go, or something to do, so he sat down, nodding to the middle-aged woman called Melody. She had some miles on her, but she had a pleasant smile and seemed attracted to Darius, sitting very close. Black roots were showing through her bleached blond hair.

"Ever catch your man?" Billy asked.

"Which one?" Darius smiled. "I prefer catching women, ain't that right Mel-oh-dee?" She nodded and gave him a kiss.

"You know, the guy who set fire to the car and burned up that insurance investigator."

"Nah, he's not worth chasing. If they put up a decent reward, I may get interested again. Right now I got me a hostage to deal with."

"What the hell you talking about a hostage?"

"Melody is my hostage. Her old man owes me some money, and until he pays me, he's cut off." Billy didn't quite understand the logic of what he was hearing. The woman didn't seem to mind being with Darius, so how could she be a hostage?

"You don't get it, do you, Billy? Melody's old man, sorry her husband, owns this pawnshop here in town. I do business with him sometimes. That's how me and Melody met."

"She doesn't appear to be trying to get away...."

"That's because she ain't. She's been staying with me for the past three days. I put her husband in touch with a guy I know who has a fortune in old coins. Melody's husband deals in old and rare coins, so he gets excited. Almost peed his pants when he actually saw the collection. I told him he had to pay me a finder's fee. I told him I wanted ten percent, and he agreed."

"So what's the problem?"

"Just shut up and just listen. You're interrupting my story. You want to hear this, or not?" Darius waved to the bartender for another round. "So her old man buys the collection. This is about a week ago. Then he sells part of it to some guy in St. Louis, sells part to a collector in Atlanta, and the rest of it to a guy right here. The shithead tells me he made fifteen hundred dollars on the deal. I asked Melody here how much he really made, and guess what?"

"He made a lot more?"

"You got it! Damn you're one smart fella, Billy. Shithead made five thousand bucks on that collection, and wants to give me a hundred and fifty. I don't think so!"

"Darius, are you serious? You're holding her for the three hundred and fifty dollars he owes you?"

"You better believe it, Billy boy. Nobody fucks with Darius, particularly when it comes to money."

"Know what I think?"

"Tell me, I'm dying to hear it, not that I give a shit you understand."

"I think you were looking for an excuse to screw around with his wife and used the money he owed you, as your excuse. How come he hasn't paid you yet?" Billy had a better chance to look her over and decided she was on the plus side of attractive and sexy, also on the plus side of forty.

"Because he doesn't know where to find me. I haven't told him. We're having too much fun."

"So what happens when she goes back to her old man?"

"She acts pissed at him for taking so long to pay me. We got it all figured out, don't we, Melody?" She nodded and kissed him again, longer this time.

Billy felt uncomfortable sitting across from these two lovebirds. They'd been shacked up for three days and still acted like they couldn't keep their hands off one another. Billy got up and started to leave.

"Hey, Billy, where you going? Stick around. I'll have Melody call one of her friends, get you fixed up."

"Sounds great. Why don't I meet you guys somewhere, later? I've got a few things to do right now. Where are you staying?"

"Staying right here. Ha, ha, hah. Hey, don't look so serious all the time, Billy. I'm at the Day's Inn around the corner. Room two-fourteen. If the blinds are closed, keep knocking. We'll probably be busy, know what I mean?" Darius pulled her to him with a gentle hug.

Melody had to be a few years older than Darius, so any girlfriends she'd have would be about the same age. And that would be the same age as Billy. He wished he hadn't run into Darius. The man imposed himself on everyone he met. Billy was surprised he didn't get stuck for the drinks, but that was because he left first.

Chapter 17

A week earlier, Edgar Ames had passed the same bar where Billy and Darius were drinking. Edgar was on his way to the Chattanooga newspaper with a story sure to shock all the residents of Harmon County. Edgar's friend at the newspaper reviewed the material and hinted that the newspaper would also be interested in the scandalous story. The paper would have a one-day advance, before putting it out to the wire services. He also agreed that it was a perfect story for one of the tabloids.

They discussed the possibilities over lunch. It would be a few days before the story would run because the newspaper would want to confirm some of the incidents with the TBI agents and the sheriff's office. Edgar's credibility wasn't being questioned; it was just a policy of the newspaper to follow-up any story involving scandal and get quotes and opinions from other third parties. It also helped make the story even more credible to readers.

Driving back to Paradise Valley that afternoon, Edgar was pleased with himself. The first step in the sheriff's destruction had been put into motion. *The Chattanooga Times Free Press* would print the story, using one of their reporter's byline, so nothing would reflect back on him. He wanted to remain behind the scene for as long as possible. The story, *Trouble in Paradise Valley*, appeared the same day Sheriff Billy left for Chattanooga.

The Chattanooga newspaper had limited circulation in Harmon County. Requests for additional copies started coming in soon after the paper was distributed. Bovis Tinch read his copy while finishing his breakfast. He wondered how the story managed to have so much detail. He knew that Billy would be gone for a few days and considered the irony of that, leaving poor Eulla to face an onslaught of phone calls and questions. Like so many others, Bovis wondered if perhaps Deputy Wolfe had been mistaken for Billy, since he was in the sheriff's Bronco. If so, Billy had plenty to be worried about in addition to this scandal. Maybe it was time to start thinking about his replacement.

Soon after Sheriff Billy left Melissa's café, that morning, the Chattanooga newspapers arrived, along with a string of gossip. Melissa had never heard so much buzzing from all her customers. Everyone had an opinion about the sheriff's relationship with Eulla. Everyone also had an opinion about what Deputy Wolfe was doing out on that remote stretch of driveway outside of town. Most thought he might be involved with drugs and he was meeting somebody.

Another rumor was that he knew too much and perhaps knew who killed poor old Ely Slocum. Blackmail was even suggested by a few. Once it was learned that Sheriff Billy had chosen this very day to depart Paradise Valley, other suspicions started to evolve. It was Melissa's busiest day ever at the café.

The same was true at Lou's barbershop, a few doors down the block. It was another common gathering area where customers could voice their opinions and learn a few new rumors. Today they were flying freely.

For Eulla, the phone never stopped ringing. After the tenth call that morning, she refused to discuss anything about the newspaper article, which she still hadn't seen. It was lunchtime before she found a copy and read the story twice. Everyone was asking her why the sheriff had left town? And why she hadn't left with him? There was no question that she and Billy would be out of a job soon. Like Bovis Tinch, she too wondered who could have given so many facts to the newspaper reporter who wrote the scandalous account, which she had to admit was fairly accurate. She hadn't spoken to the reporter, but the story hinted that she had, making her seem like she may have been a source of information.

Happy Harry sat back, put his feet up on the desk, and reviewed the newspaper, skipping over items that didn't interest him. When he came to the article about Paradise Valley, his feet hit the floor and he sat up reading the story with intense interest. Billy had told him that he might be gone for a couple weeks. Now Harry wondered if he would even bother to come back. He dug out his insurance policy and read it carefully, thinking there was a good possibility that he might not get his truck back.

While residents of Paradise Valley were speculating on Billy's future, he was enjoying a long walk, something he seldom did. The downtown area was conducive for walking and browsing. The waterfront park had benches where one could watch the passing yachts as well as work boats. Since his future looked doubtful, Chattanooga, with its many fine restaurants and good drinking establishments, was looking like a suitable alternate home.

He also thought about Darius' offer to fix him up later. Billy decided he should be resourceful enough to handle his evening's entertainment, without Darius' help. Failing that, he had a fallback consolation with one of Melody's available friends, so he couldn't lose. With that thought lingering, Billy considered getting a room at the same motel where Darius was staying.

* * *

Melissa had Nick's business card. After she closed the café, she went over to the library and used the copying machine and made several copies of the newspaper story. She was sure Nick would be one of the few people who would actually enjoy reading the account.

Ralph Goodwin didn't read the story until later that afternoon when it became apparent that he'd killed the wrong man, and the sheriff was still alive! While the article would serve to embarrass the sheriff, that wasn't sufficient for Ralph. He hoped that Marsha, his fiancée, didn't see the story. Not only would it bring back the trauma she suffered, it might also arouse her curiosity about his sudden trip out of town. It was likely she'd suspect him of doing something rash in an act of revenge. He had to be careful what he told her. She'd never appreciate what he had tried to do, or that he'd done it for her.

The more he thought about the mistake he'd made, the more intense his rage became. He'd followed the white Bronco, thinking it was the sheriff he was following. He wouldn't make that mistake again.

By now the sheriff had to know someone was out there trying to kill him, Ralph thought to himself. That meant the sheriff would be more alert, and aware of dangerous situations. Ralph thought about sending a threatening letter to the sheriff. That would cost the son-of-a-bitch a few sleepless nights. He'd have to be careful not to leave any fingerprints on the letter, or the envelope. Then in a flash of genius, he considered the postmark. There was no sense letting anyone know that it came from Chattanooga. He'd mail the letter in Paradise Valley. That should cause the sheriff to look over his shoulder every few minutes.

Ralph devised a plan to mail the letter then he'd wait a week before proceeding to stalk his prey again. Ralph was getting excited, thinking about how nervous the sheriff would be. Would he go into hiding, or just wait? It didn't really matter since Ralph already knew the town well enough. This next trip, he'd make an effort to learn where the sheriff lived. Maybe sneak into his house when nobody was home and leave a surprise in the refrigerator. Or, put some poison in an open box of cereal. Ralph tried to imagine what kind of house the sheriff lived in. Hopefully he lived alone and didn't have a dog.

While everyone in Paradise Valley was reading about him, Billy spent the afternoon unaware of the newspaper article. He spotted a few black hookers on the edge of town in the warehouse district. They held no appeal. He had a lot of money with him and didn't plan on having it stolen. Just thinking about that possibility caused him to stop, pull over and take a wad of hundred-dollar bills from his wallet and stuff them inside his boot. He decided to check into a motel and take a nap. Maybe call Eulla to see how things were going without him being there?

Since Darius' room number was 214, Billy asked to be separated by several rooms, so that any noise coming from Darius' room wouldn't disturb him. As Billy passed room 214, he noticed the door was ajar and could hear the TV. Curious, he pushed the door open and found Melody sitting on the bed, legs crossed, revealing blue underpants. She was polishing her nails and watching a television program.

"Hi there, come on in." Melody motioned for him to come inside.

"Where's Darius?"

"He had to go out. He gets antsy all cooped up in this small room."

"So he just leaves you here?"

"Sure. I'm not going anywhere, at least not for a while. We'll go out and get something to eat later. Want a beer?"

"Okay, if you don't mind me being here."

"Oh don't be silly. Besides Darius isn't the jealous type, know what I mean?"

"All the same, he's not someone you ever want to have pissed at you."

"Are you afraid of him?"

"No. I'm not afraid of anyone, but I also don't like to get into a fight unless it's absolutely necessary."

"Have you ever shot anyone?"

"Sure. When you're a sheriff, you run up against all kinds. It's part of the job."

"Ever kill anyone?"

"Yeah, but I don't like to talk about it," he lied. "Has Darius contacted your husband yet?" Billy wanted to change the subject. He was sitting in one of the two chairs in the room with his boots on the bed, fairly close to Melody's bare foot with a good view of her legs and where they stopped.

"I think that's what he's doing now. Benjamin hates for anyone to get the best of him. He's so cheap, you wouldn't believe."

"How long you been married to him?"

"Too long, you ask me. We're going on twenty-five years next month." She finished her toenails and rubbed her foot against Billy's boot. He knew she was flirting with him. He liked it, but he didn't want it to go much further and have Darius walk in on them. Jealous, or not, Billy did not want to tangle with Darius. Only a fool would even consider it.

"That's a long time to be married to the same person. What are you going to do after he pays Darius the money?"

"I guess I'll go back home. Maybe this will teach that cheapskate a good lesson."

"Won't he be angry that you've been messing around with Darius for the past few days?"

"Honey, he's sixty-five years old. He can't do the tango anymore. All he can do is count his money and complain about the weather. It's either too hot, or too cold. I'm tired of being his nursemaid, cook and housekeeper. These past few days have been like a dream vacation, so I'm not in a big hurry to go back there."

"Is your husband in poor health?"

"Not poor enough. My luck, he'll live another ten years. Are you married?"

"No, never have been and probably won't be now. It's a little late for me to start that shit."

"So what do you do for fun? You like to fish?"

"You know, it's funny you'd say that. I don't really have any hobbies. I've gone fishing a few times, but couldn't get into it. I spend most of my time being the sheriff, making sure things don't get out of line. Sometimes when I can't sleep, I get up and cruise around the town, making sure everything's okay. You'd be surprised what goes on at two in the morning."

"Honey, you need a girlfriend. You wake up at two, she'll give you something to do, or give you something to make you go back to sleep. Darius doesn't sleep too good, either."

"How long have you known Darius?"

"Oh it's been maybe a year now. First time I met him he came in looking to buy an expensive used watch. I think he looked at every watch we had before he asked me out."

"What took him so long?"

"He was waiting for my husband to leave. He overheard Benjamin say he was going to the bank and the post office, so he waited until he left."

"So did he buy a watch?"

"No. But I gave him one later that he particularly liked. So where are you staying?"

"Right here. I'm just a couple of rooms down from you."

"Really? Well why don't we go down and check out your room? Make sure everything is nice and comfy."

"Melody, I know where this is leading, and believe me I'm really tempted. I've never been one to turn down free pussy, but this isn't a good idea."

"You're not gay or anything like that are you?"

"No, I'm your normal, like to get laid kind of guy. I thought you were going to fix me up with one of your girl-friends."

"Yeah, well, see all my girlfriends are married, or living with someone. I can call one of them and ask her to meet us for drinks and dinner and tell her about you, but…."

"But what? I'm not their type?"

"No, it's just they're gonna ask me if I checked you out. And what am I gonna say? No he's saving it all for you? It'd be better if I could tell them you're a real stud and raring to go."

"So tell them that, you won't be too far off the mark."

"Yeah, but I'd be telling a lie. How do I know you're a stud? I keep making suggestions, and you keep putting me off like I smell bad or something. I just took a shower a little while ago, and I used deodorant, too." She had her arm raised, offering to let him take a sniff. It was a crude gesture and he momentarily turned away. The lady could use a bit more class, he thought.

The news was on TV and Billy just caught a glimpse of a reporter standing in front of the Harmon County courthouse. He wanted to turn up the sound, which Melody had turned down. Just then Darius appeared in the still open doorway. Billy was thankful he still had his clothes on and wasn't sitting too close to Melody. Another 10 minutes and he and Melody could have been burning the sheets in his room. He wasn't sure how long Darius might have been standing outside, watching and listening.

"So, did he give you the money?" Melody jumped off the bed and ran to Darius, pretending to be glad to see him.

"He said to tell you that he didn't care if you came back or not. You want to come by the house to pick up your things, that's okay, too. I think he's throwing you out, Melody. I didn't figure him for that."

"That bastard! That's all he cares about me? What did you tell him?"

"I said I'd give you the message."

"And what about the money? Did he pay you? Remember, I'm supposed to get half."

"I don't believe the two of you. Trying to pull a scam for a lousy three hundred and fifty dollars." Billy said, shaking his head.

"That's what he owes me for the rest of my finder's fee. He has to pay another ten grand, if he wants Melody back. I probably forgot to mention that."

"Holy shit! That's serious stuff, Darius. He could bring in the Feds and you'd be doing time for kidnapping. You better hope he doesn't call someone."

"Billy, do you think I'm stupid? He isn't calling anyone. It took a while, but he finally coughed up the three-fifty he owed me. He's going to have the ten grand ready in the morning. I told him no checks, it has to be cash."

"Then what? He's just going to wait for you to show up and collect? The cops will be waiting for you, take my word."

"Don't worry about it. I got a plan. Come on, let's go get something to eat, I'm starving." Billy caught Melody shooting him a wink. He made a mental note to catch the 11:00 news later. He was curious about what was going on at the Harmon County courthouse.

Chapter 18

They were back at the same bar around the corner from the motel. Billy was glad he didn't have to drive anywhere and worry about getting stopped. He could drink as much as he pleased, and if Melody wanted to flirt with him, he'd let her.

"I thought you said you were starving," Billy said after they had consumed three rounds.

"Yeah, we'd better think about eating. First I want to ask a favor, Billy. We been friends for a while, isn't that right?"

"That's true." Billy was apprehensive about what was coming next.

"I ever give you any shit?"

"No, you've always been straight up with me."

"Never cheated you, or anything?"

"No. Of course there wasn't any reason for you to."

"Okay, then listen up. Here's the plan. Tomorrow, you're going to go over to Melody's place, show old Benjamin your badge and pretend you're looking for me. You see anything that looks suspicious, be cool. Stick around for a few minutes, chat him up then leave. Nobody's going to think anything of it. Now, if everything looks okay to you, just drive off. I'll be sitting at the end of the street. You just nod to me and I'll go in and pick up the money. See, that way if there is somebody else there looking for me, you showing up won't raise any red flags. Pretty good plan, huh?

"Uh huh, and tell me why I should be jumping up and down glad to be doing this for you?" They were sitting in a booth. Darius and Melody on one side, Billy across from Melody who was starting to blow kisses his way while Darius was laying out the plan. Billy was aware of Melody's bare foot working into his crotch. She'd slipped her shoe off.

"Way I have it figured, you're here with not much to do, just sort of bumming around for a few days. Melody is in no big hurry to get home, and her old man doesn't seem to want her back, but that's just a temporary situation that will change. Meanwhile, she needs someone to keep her company. I can tell by the way she's acting that she wants to get in your pants and I got to tell you, she's a damned good ride. So what do you say?"

"Let me see if I understand this. You two are gonna split ten grand, which her old man has already agreed to pay, and I all gotta do is check out the place to see if anyone is there watching? I'm pretending that I'm looking for you. So why am I looking?"

"Okay, good point. I'm supposed to be helping you look for a fugitive who killed somebody back in Harmon County, which is true, right?"

"Yes, but how is it that I'm looking for you at her old man's house? He's gonna wonder why I'm there looking for you. How am I supposed to know the two of you even know each other?" Billy had doubts about Darius' plan.

"I can see you've been giving this some thought. That's good. Okay, you ran into me in a bar today and we were suppose to get together, but I didn't show up. You remember hearing me say that I had to collect some money from this guy in Garden Hills who's a pawnbroker. So you start asking around and learn that Benjamin Wasslemann is a pawnbroker and the phonebook shows his address. You're just wondering if he's seen me, and if so where you might find me?"

"I don't know, that sounds a bit much. Maybe you just mentioned that you were meeting this guy and told me where. I don't like long bullshit stories. What if he asks me about his wife?"

"You don't know anything about her, you never met her. Anyone else is there, and they start asking questions, you dummy up."

"Okay, so where is Melody gonna be, while you're making the grab from her old man? She gonna be in the car with you?" Melody was wiggling her toes and he was having a hard time trying to concentrate.

"Hell no! How would that look? No, she'll be in your room at the motel waiting. That way, in case anyone should start looking around, or follow me back there, they won't find Melody, or any trace of her."

The drinks were starting to affect Billy's thinking. He knew Darius could consume more alcohol because of his massive body, so while he too was showing some signs of getting drunk, he wasn't there yet. Melody was almost out. Billy persuaded Darius to guide them to a restaurant that was close. Billy didn't want to be seen weaving and swaying while walking down the street. He knew he'd start sobering up once he ate and had some fresh air.. He had several more questions he wanted to ask, but couldn't think of them. Everything was a bit fuzzy, except for Melody's foot.

The Waffle House was the closest place, so they settled on it, finding a vacant booth with dirty dishes waiting to be removed.

"Somebody better get their ass over here and clean this table... now!" Darius yelled, causing everyone in the restaurant to turn and take notice of the huge man standing by the table.

"Sorry 'bout that," the manager said, hurrying over to clear and wipe the table. He kept his head down, not looking at Darius.

Billy ordered a pecan waffle with a side of bacon and coffee. Darius took his time examining every item on the menu, making the waitress wait. Having heard his earlier outburst, she wasn't about to leave, or wait on anyone else until she had his order. Finally he ordered scrambled eggs for Melody, and a double order of what Billy was having.

"Tell me something, Darius. You like being the center of attention, don't you?" Billy asked, stirring his coffee.

"When you're as big as I am, you are the center of attention, like it or not. Look at Jesse Ventura. He walks into a strange place, people stop what they're doing and look at him. After a while you get used to it."

"You remind me a lot of Jesse Ventura, now that you mention it."

"Yeah? Well thanks. He's my hero. I appreciate the compliment."

Their orders arrived in record time, and everyone started eating. After three cups of coffee, Billy remembered what he wanted to ask.

"If I hadn't showed up today, how were you going to do this payoff thing? You had an alternate plan didn't you?"

"Of course I had another plan, but this one's better, thanks to you showing up."

"You never did get around to telling me what's in it for me, helping you out with your plan and all," Billy said feeling better now that he had some food.

"Tell me something, Billy. You got any real friends?"

"Of course I do, why?"

"I'm beginning to wonder about that. Tell you why. Because real friends do favors for their friends and they don't expect anything in return. They do it because they want to. Not because they expect something in return. The fact that you have to ask me that question, tells me a lot about you and I'm a little disappointed."

"Really? Why is that?"

"You grew up in a small town and you live in a small town. You think the way small town people think. Being sheriff, you've had your hand out for a long time, expecting everybody to do whatever it is you want done. I've seen it. Then you step out of that picture and into a strange place and all of a sudden, you're not that important person anymore. That must be a difficult transition for someone like you, Billy."

"Why is it you never call me, Sheriff Billy like everyone else?" Billy heard Darius' observation and tried not to wince. The day would come when he wouldn't be Sheriff Billy, and he wondered how he'd handle that. Right now, he didn't appreciate Darius holding a verbal mirror to his face. He didn't like the reflection he was seeing. Part of what

Darius said was true, about having a small town mentality. He planned to change that.

"Consider yourself lucky that I don't call you something more disrespectful. If I call you Sheriff Billy, or say, Sir, that means I'm putting you above me, and I ain't never done that, except to a judge once. If you were six feet, eight I might change my mind, but you ain't. Does that answer your question?" Billy just nodded and in a strange way, he understood.

It was all about respect, or the lack of it. Not being tall was the other part. That had been a problem for him since he was a teenager. Consequently he'd displayed a mean disposition as compensation. With his brother Harvey to back him up, Billy picked fights just to assert himself. If he moved away from Paradise Valley, Billy wouldn't have the benefit of Harvey's presence.

They walked back to the motel together. Melody had been noticeably quiet. They stopped by Darius' room and a long silence hung between them. Billy wanted to ask Darius where Melody was going to sleep then felt it didn't really matter. He was too drunk and too tired to care. He'd wanted to watch the news, but it was now midnight.

"So what time do I go see old man Benjamin?" Billy asked.

"We'll go over it one more time in the morning, over breakfast." Darius and Melody disappeared and Billy walked to his room wondering why he was there. This was supposed to be a vacation away from trouble. He reminded himself that he didn't actually like, or trust, Darius. Despite the suggestion, Darius wasn't his friend and Billy didn't owe him anything.

* * *

Ralph Goodwin carefully composed his warning note to the sheriff, wearing latex gloves:

Sorry I missed you the first time. I won't make that mistake again. You won't know when, or where it will happen, but it will. Then young women won't have to suffer the indignities you imposed upon them.

Ralph used a wet sponge to seal the envelope to avoid any DNA testing that might identify him as the sender. He'd left word with his supervisor at work that there was a death in the family and that he'd be gone just a few days. Once again, he packed all the items he thought he might need, including a box of rat poison he'd found in the warehouse. Being careful not to exceed the speed limit and risk being stopped, he made the trip to Paradise Valley in just over an hour. There was a mailbox outside the post office where he deposited his note addressed to the sheriff. Now it would have a local cancellation mark on the envelope.

Earlier, Ralph caught the 6:00 O'clock news and saw a TV field reporter doing a standup news item in front of the courthouse. It was a brief recap of what had appeared in the newspaper. There was an attempt to interview a deputy who refused to make any comments. Then the reporter said something about the sheriff being unavailable. Ralph wondered what that meant? Was he hiding, or just avoiding cameras and reporters?

Ralph cruised around the town hoping to see something, or someone who could tell him where the sheriff lived. After making a circuit around the square, finding all the shops closed, he drove down some side streets and discovered a TV news van sitting by the curb on a street of small houses. This had to be where the sheriff lived. They had to be watching for him.

While their presence helped Ralph zero-in on the sheriff's house, it also presented a new problem. Anything he did was liable to be seen with so much attention being focused here. Ralph decided to take a chance regardless. He parked behind the TV van and walked up to the cab. The driver was talking on a cell phone and smoking a cigarette. Ralph waited patiently. He could tell it was a personal conversation.

"Excuse me, I saw your earlier news coverage here. Why wasn't the sheriff at his office? His white Bronco is still parked over there." Ralph wanted the man to think he was someone local.

"I'm not the person to ask that question. I just drive the van and keep on eye on things. Right now we're watching his house, but it doesn't look like anybody's home," the driver said.

"Maybe you're watching the wrong house. Which one are you keeping an eye on?"

"That one across the street with no lights on. No vehicles in the drive, either." He sees this TV news van sitting here, he'll keep going, Ralph thought.

"Yeah, you're right about nobody home. Why don't you park down the street where you're not so obvious? You can still see if any lights come on in the house."

"You live around here?" The driver asked.

"Yes, the next street over," Ralph lied.

"Can you tell me where I can get a cup of coffee at this hour? The town rolls up the sidewalks pretty early."

250

"There's a Hardee's out where the by-pass ends, or you can try the Mini-Mart." Ralph gave him directions to the Mini-Mart and watched as the van drove away.

Now Ralph knew which house the sheriff lived in. He also knew that nobody was home. That was two good pieces of information attained by his bold move. Getting the driver to leave for a few minutes was also a bit of good luck. Ralph drove around the block and found an alley running behind the sheriff's house. He drove slowly past the back yard of the sheriff's house and saw a convenient place to walk through.

He parked his car on another street and walked back, carrying a small backpack. Going through the alley, then between tall bushes, Ralph was at the back door without being seen. He doubted there would be an alarm system, but he did a quick search just to be sure. The back door was old and so was the lock and handle. A flat bladed scraper was all it took to force the bolt back, while leaning against the door. It opened easily. No dead bolt to fuss with.

He figured he had 10 minutes in the house before the van would be back. Hopefully the driver would take his advice and park farther up the street. Meanwhile Ralph used his penlight, being careful not to trip over any of the furniture. Ralph was thankful he hadn't heard any dog bark. He resisted opening the refrigerator door because of the light. He opened all the kitchen cabinets carefully and found what he was looking for. The opened box of cereal was in an upper cabinet near the sink.

The Wheaties box wasn't open., but a box of Granola was. That was even better because of the composition of the contents. Taking his time, Ralph emptied the small box of rat poison into the cereal box. Then he closed the lid and shook the contents to mix it in with the cereal. He still had five minutes to look around. He headed for the downstairs bedroom and saw the unmade bed. The closet door was open. Ralph saw the uniforms hanging, several pairs of shoes and boots. On the shelf he saw a shoebox. When he opened it, he found 38-caliber, 45-caliber and 9mm bullets, suggesting the sheriff had several different handguns. It would take too long to explore the entire house to find where the guns were kept.

Before leaving, Ralph took the brief note he'd written earlier, and pinned it onto the breast pocket of one of the hanging uniform shirts: It was covering the spot where a badge would be affixed. The sheriff couldn't miss it.

Think about it, if I can plant a message here, then you're not really safe anywhere, are you?

Ralph left the same way he came in, being sure the back door was locked. He walked between two tall bushes, came out onto the alley and walked back to his car, walking casually in case anyone should notice him. A hurrying figure might be noticed and remembered. As he pulled away from the curb, he saw the TV van return, parking a block farther away, just as he'd suggested.

So far, Ralph's plan was working better than he had anticipated. There was no need to camp out in the woods again. He drove back to Chattanooga, pleased with his subtle attempt at terror. He had wanted to put the note inside the shirt pocket, but there was always a chance the sheriff would never see it.

* * *

Billy woke to the sound of thunder. Outside it was pouring. It was only 6:30 in the morning and he had a terrible hangover. He rummaged through his shaving kit looking for some aspirin. He had to be careful because one aspirin bottle, taken from the office, contained several Ecstasy tablets. He'd brought them along to remove them as evidence. How that private investigator had found them was still a mystery.

Billy sat on the edge of the bed, his head bent over, and wondered again, why was he helping Darius? Maybe if he got dressed and checked out early, he could avoid Darius and his stupid plan to extort ransom money from some old fart. With that thought in mind, Billy hurriedly shaved, dressed and gathered his stuff together. He noticed that his boots were scuffed. He'd get them shined later, but it annoyed him that they weren't highly polished. He used the bedspread to wipe them off and buff them.

He had to run ran across the parking lot to the office, getting wet. Billy put his key on the counter and told the sleepy clerk he was checking out.

"You got any coffee made?" Billy asked.

"Over there," he pointed and Billy turned around.

"Well look who's up early. Better cancel that checkout, Billy. That's not part of the plan, remember?" Darius was sitting on a sofa, drinking coffee and reading yesterday's newspaper.

"I need to get back to Paradise Valley."

"You better give that some thought, Billy. Your name's in the newspaper, and it says you've been a bad boy. They probably have a lynching party waiting for you back there, or some tar and feathers," Darius was chuckling at his own comment.

"What are you talking about? Let me see that paper." Billy took the newspaper, scanned the page then sat down to read the article in detail. "Oh Jesus, you're right, I must have just missed that reporter I saw on TV last night. I wonder how they got all this information?" Billy wasn't talking to anyone in particular, just voicing his thoughts.

"People like to talk, don't you know that?"

"Yeah, but who? There aren't too many people who know all the details mentioned here." He thought about Eulla. Would she have betrayed him? He'd call her later at home. She didn't work on Sundays.

"You ready for some breakfast? Don't forget your key on the counter. You're going to need it later. I told the clerk that you'd probably be checking out tomorrow. Give you a little time with Melody."

Over breakfast at the Waffle House, which Billy was beginning to hate, they went over Darius' plan again. Darius drew Billy a map with directions on how to find the man's house. Darius would be following him most of the way.

"Is Melody still sleeping?" Billy asked.

"Yeah, she had a rough night and little too much to drink. We'll give her your key and she can move her stuff into your room while we're gone. I'll wake her up and take her a cup of coffee when we get back to the room."

"We never talked about what we'd do if something goes wrong with your little caper."

"That's because nothing will go wrong. Just stick with the plan. Trust me, it's going to work out just fine."

"Okay, then I come back to my motel room, then what? We just sit around and wait for you to show up, is that it?"

"Yeah, unless the two of you want to get cozy. Melody will be up for it by then. And in case you're wondering, it's okay with me, so stop worrying. It's not like she's my wife. She thinks she's my girlfriend, which in a way she is I guess. I don't like to get too tied up with any of them. You know the old saying, anyone can be nice for a long weekend."

"So are you checking out of your room, or continuing to stay here?"

"Billy, Billy, what's with all these worried questions? Relax will you. I'm coming back to pick up Melody. If she wants to go back to her old man, which she'll eventually have to do, I'll send her home in a cab with her half of the ten grand. Then I'm off to Atlanta. Got a man to find down there. I think I know where he's hiding out."

By the time they were finished eating, the rain was just a light drizzle. They walked back to the motel office. Billy paid the clerk for another night's stay, picked up the key, while Darius got some coffee for Melody. Together they crossed the parking lot, climbed the stairs and walked back to their respective rooms. All of Billy's things were packed and he'd leave them that way. Except for a quick romp with Melody, there really wasn't any reason for him to stay. Breakfast had helped his headache disappear, but the newspaper article was still haunting him. He called his office.

"What the hell is going on? I just read yesterday's newspaper...."

"Well, if you'd been here, you probably would have been on TV. There were several reporters here, asking all sorts of questions." Deputy Willoughby said. "You missed a good photo opportunity." It was meant as a dig.

"What kind of questions?"

"Mostly they wanted to know where you were. I told them you were on vacation and couldn't be reached. They thought that was sort of convenient on your part. Bovis wants you to call him. He's called here several times."

"Great. I try to take a few days off and the fucking roof caves in on me. Where did all that stuff in the newspaper come from, you have any idea?"

"No idea, Billy. Eulla seems to think Melissa might have called the newspaper and told them." Eulla was worried that Sheriff Billy suspected her of leaking the information. Also she didn't really like Melissa, so she was a convenient scapegoat.

"I guess it's possible. She was sure cozy with all those TBI agents. Maybe they put the idea in her head?" The more he thought about it, the more it made sense to him. She'd been acting a little strange ever since that insurance investigator got burned up.

Maybe Melissa thought he had something to do with it? When he got back, they would definitely have to have a long, private talk.

Chapter 19

Billy followed Darius' instructions and found the house. It was much larger than he expected, in a nice development of upscale homes, paved streets and nice lawns. Billy wasn't all that good at estimating what the house was worth, but it had to be in excess of $250,000, maybe more than that. He pulled in the wide concrete driveway that led up to a three-car garage. He wondered why a 65-year old man needed three vehicles, unless one was a boat.

An older gentleman answered the door. He had a puzzled look on his face. The first thing Billy noticed was the cast on the man's left hand. Billy flashed his badge and asked the man if he by any chance knew Darius? The man nodded he did, and invited Billy inside. It was the biggest entryway and living room Billy had ever seen. He immediately revised his estimate of the house's value.

"I'm expecting Darius to show up sometime this morning. We have a business arrangement to conclude," Benjamin said.

"Does this have anything to do with your wife?"

"Yes, as a matter of fact it does. How is it you know about my wife?"

"Is her name Melody?"

"No, it's Gertrude. Melody used to work for me. I fired her a few weeks ago. Is she in some kind of trouble?"

"I'm not sure. Is Darius posing some sort of threat to you?"

"How do you know about that? He's a very violent man. Look, he broke my hand a few days ago. He wants fifty thousand dollars, or he's going to expose me for a stupid indiscretion. He's threatening to tell my wife."

"Does this indiscretion have anything to do with this Melody?"

"Yes. We had a brief affair. She was always very flirty with the customers, and that was good for business. Then I did a very foolish thing, I believed she was interested in me. We went back to her place a few times after work. Then I started to worry that Gertrude might suspect something. I gave her some money and told her it was over. Then Darius suddenly appeared. He knew all about it, so I can only assume Melody told him. Can I get you something?"

"Sure. Any kind of cola would be nice." Billy had been suspicious of Darius' scam all along. It wasn't $ 10,000 it was $ 50,000 he planned to collect! And Melody wasn't this gentleman's wife. She probably baited him. When the older man returned from the kitchen with his drink, Billy asked, "So where is your wife right now?"

"She's visiting her sister in Naples, Florida. She'll be back next week. That's why I want to get this over with now."

"Have you spoken with the police about this extortion?"

"No, Darius said that if anything went wrong, he'd break a few more bones. Right now, I'm in enough pain."

"Okay, do you have the money ready to give to him?"

"Yes, I have it."

"Then this is what we're going to do. I can't arrest him until he actually takes possession of the money. You can file an assault charge against him later. Give me the money, I'll deliver it to Darius and he'll have it just long enough to start counting it when I arrest him. Then you'll get the money back, but it may be a few weeks, you understand that?"

"Where will you find him to give him the money?"

"I have a feeling he'll show up here pretty soon. When he does, tell him that you gave me the money to deliver to him, and that he's to meet me at the Day's Inn, where I'm currently staying. I'll wait for him there."

"Then why not just arrest him here when he shows up?"

"Because it will take a few extra men to help me subdue him. You know how big he is, and how violent he can be."

"Yes, of course." Benjamin got up, left the room and returned with a blue nylon gym bag, handing it to Billy.

"After we have him in custody, I'll bring you a receipt for the bag and the money." Billy was eager to look inside and count the money, however he allowed restraint to control his rising anxiety.

"Thank you. I appreciate all your help Sheriff."

"By the way, do you own a gun?"

"Of course I own a gun. I own a pawnshop. I own lots of guns, why?"

"I suggest you keep one handy, just in case Darius decides he wants to break some more bones before I get him locked up."

"Yes, I suppose that's good advice. I've never been a violent man, and I've never shot anyone although I've been robbed a few times."

"There's always a first time for everything. I'd appreci-ate it if you'd keep the advice I gave you quiet. I'm out of my jurisdiction here, but there won't be any problems."

Billy tried to appear casual as he peeked out the door be-fore leaving. He didn't see any evidence of cops, or Darius. He knew Darius was supposed to be parked near the entrance to the subdivision, and by now was wondering what was taking Billy so long?

As Billy approached the entrance to the subdivision, he saw Darius sitting in a red Dodge Durango, drumming his fingers on the steering wheel. Billy pulled up beside him and lowered the window.

"What took you so long? You two have a long talk?"

"You said there wouldn't be any cops."

"I said I didn't think there'd be any cops, you're suppose to check it out. What's going on?"

"Well the cops are there alright...."

"Shit. I get my hands on that old fart, I'll break...."

"I don't think you'll get close enough to break anything. There are two cops inside, waiting for you to show up. They grilled me pretty good. Wanted to know if I knew where you were staying. They're also looking for Melody on some other charge. I didn't get into it with them. They're after you for assault as well as extortion. You're on your own, pal. Keep me out of the rest of it. I doubt you'll get any money from him now, but you can try."

"Let's go back to the motel and rethink this."

"Count me out. From here on, it's between you and old man, Benjamin. If you talk to him on the phone, I'd be care-ful. I think they got a wire tap on the phone."

"He sure moved fast. You sure they're cops, not just some hired muscle?"

"No, they're cops, no doubt about that."

"Come on, let's go get Melody, then we'll get something to eat and figure out our next move."

"Nah, I'm outta here. I'm on my way back to Paradise Valley to find whoever is causing me all this grief. Be careful, Darius."

Billy drove away, making sure he didn't take off too fast. He wasn't sure if Darius bought his bullshit story, but he wasn't about to spend any more time talking and slip up. He had to buy some time. His jump on Darius was limited to a few hours at most. Sooner or later, he'd learn that Billy did an end run around him, and would come looking for the money. By then, Billy didn't plan to be anywhere Darius would find him.

The way things were shaping up, Billy knew he needed to disappear... fast. Billy still had a few things to get from his house, talk to his brother, Harvey and get out of Dodge. He'd wait until it was dark, sneak back into town and be gone. His career as sheriff was certainly over. Bovis no doubt wanted to explain that to him.

With $ 50,000 in a gym bag sitting on the floor of the truck, Billy was extra careful not to run a stop sign, or forget to signal when he turned. This was the most money he'd ever had in his possession. And, he'd never get another chance like this. Driving back toward Paradise Valley, Billy passed the Days Inn and wondered if Melody was there waiting. Darius had used her as bait, teasing him. He wondered if Darius ever planned to split any of the money with her, or would he just split... like Billy was doing now? His suitcase was still in the room but it wasn't worth going back for. Darius might show up while he was there.

Not many people would recognize Billy driving the Chevy pickup. They always saw him driving the Bronco. Thinking about that, Billy removed his Stetson and put it on the seat beside him. Another familiar item changed. He had just a few hours in which to plan his future. He thought back to what Darius said about friends, and how many did he have?

Other than his brother, Harvey, and maybe Eulla, there wasn't anyone who would really miss him. Willoughby Jones sure wouldn't. He'd always been a bit standoffish, never going along with anything Billy was involved with. He'd be Mister Clean in the next election. Billy decided that he'd write a brief resignation letter, leaving it on his desk for Eulla to find in the morning. By then, he'd be long gone and halfway to somewhere. What scared him the most was he didn't have any idea of where that would be. Chattanooga was no longer a consideration.

Billy remembered a side road that crossed the river and went up to a small cemetery. He parked and counted the money twice. He put half into a plastic bag he had just as a precaution. With both windows down to capture a breeze, Billy put the gym bag on the seat and used it as a pillow so he could take a nap. In a short time he was dreaming about Darius chasing him down the alley behind his house. Just as he was about to enter his house a sniper took a shot at him, splintering the doorjamb beside his head.

He woke with his shirt, soaking wet. He thought about the dream he'd just had and remembered there was still someone else looking for him, wanting to kill him. It was one more good reason to leave town and disappear. His newly gained wealth would help finance a trip and a new start... somewhere.

* * *

"Do you know who this is?" The voice asked cautiously over the phone.

"Yes, I recognize your voice, Darius."

"Don't mention my name, you idiot. Are the cops still there?"

"What cops are you talking about? The one who came looking for you?"

"I already know about him. What about the others?"

"There are no others. Have you met with the sheriff yet?"

"Briefly. Now let's talk about the money and how you're going to deliver it."

"That's already been taken care of. The sheriff has the money. He said he'd give it to you when you two got to-gether back at his motel. I believe he said it was the Day's Inn."

"That son-of-a-bitch! He scammed me. I'll kill him when I catch up with him." Darius was furious. Until now he thought Billy wasn't all that bright. Somehow he'd underestimated the man. And now he had the money, which belonged to Darius. The sheriff was nothing more than a common thief, he thought.

"Don't bother trying to reach my wife. I've already met your request. I don't plan to pay another cent, do you under-stand that?"

"Have you got a tap on this phone line?"

"I'm not going to answer that. Stay away from me, or I promise I'll make trouble for you." Click. Benjamin hung up.

"Honey, what's wrong?" Melody asked getting up from the bed. It was noon and she hadn't bothered to get dressed yet. The maid had been by several times to make the bed and change towels.

"That stupid SOB, Billy, told Benjamin where we're staying. Come on, get dressed, we're getting out of here." He knew Billy had already paid for the room earlier, and Darius had already checked out of his room, in the event someone started checking registration records.

"What about the money?"

"Our little friend, the one you thought was really dumb? Well guess what? He made the pickup. Something must have tipped him off. Now he knows we were playing a game with him, but I'll get the money, and then make him feel sorry he ever tried cheating his old buddy. He's headed back to Paradise Valley. He probably didn't think I'd find out for a while. So we got to move fast. Catch up with him before he suspects we're on to him."

"So we're going after him?"

"You bet your boobies."

"It's booties, not boobies," she giggled, unconcerned about his growing anger.

"Whatever. Come on move your ass." The maid was knocking on the door again.

* * *

Billy had one distinct advantage over Darius, and anyone else who might come looking for him. He knew every inch, ditch and driveway in town. He knew places where he could hide that even the kids didn't know about. The TV van had since left, so he didn't see anything suspicious when he drove around his block. He pulled into the alley and left the truck there. He didn't plan to be more than an hour packing a few important items he'd need. Everything was quiet. He entered through the back door as he always did. Even with the shades down there was sufficient light to move around without knocking over anything.

Out of habit, he opened the refrigerator door, took out a cold beer and carried it into the bedroom. He took a suitcase from under the bed and started filling it with clothes from his dresser. In the closet, he lifted a piece of loose carpet, pulling it back far enough to allow him to lift the flooring. In the small space under the floor he had several small boxes. In one, he had his emergency stash money he'd earned from Bovis, $13,200. In another box he withdrew a vintage Colt 45 handgun, the deed to the house, his birth certificate and his discharge papers from the Army. He'd leave the deed with his brother.

He replaced the flooring, took a few items hanging in the closet, but not the uniforms. He'd have no need for them. Everything he was taking fit into the one suitcase. He grabbed another beer from the refrigerator, looked around the only house he'd ever known. He grew up here. His folks had owned it. When they died, they left it to Harvey and Billy. Now, for the first time, he was leaving. He shook his head and walked out the back door unnoticed.

His next stop was his office to leave his resignation. He also had a spare pistol in his desk he thought he might need. Willoughby Jones was sitting at Billy's desk when he walked in.

"That was a short, but well-timed vacation," the deputy said, not getting up. It was just one more sign of disrespect. The sarcastic remark wasn't lost on Billy.

"I'm still on vacation. I just stopped by to see how things were going, and to leave a note for Bovis."

"He's called a few times wanting to talk to you. And there's a letter here for you marked personal."

Billy opened the envelope and read the threatening note. He wondered who could have sent it and checked the postmark on the envelope. He noticed that it was sent from someone in Paradise Valley. He showed the note to the deputy, watching his surprised expression.

"I guess someone really is gunning for you, Sheriff. I'm glad he isn't after me. We need to turn this over to the TBI guys."

"Yeah, you do that. Make sure they check it out. I need to get a few things out of my desk."

The deputy stood up and moved out of the way. He found a big manila envelope and put both the cancelled envelope and the note inside.

"Is this note the real reason for the sudden vacation plans?"

"What would you do? Stick around like a tethered baby goat and wait for the lion to strike? That's what that one TBI agent suggested."

"I don't know, Sheriff, this sounds like some kind of whacko to me. If he had a daughter, or a girlfriend, locked up here, we'd have a record of who they were, wouldn't we?"

"Not necessarily. I let a lot of them go with just a warning, so there aren't too many available records." He could see the logic of what Willoughby was suggesting and had to agree it would be a good place to start looking for the whacko. It was probably someone he did recently. He was trying to remember the young girl's name driving the Mustang convertible. Would she have a boyfriend capable of this? It was doubtful. This was the work of an older, confident person. An angry man certainly.

"Uh huh, I knew that Honey Hole routine you and Wolfe were working would come back to bite you in the ass someday. This crazy is related to one of them, I'd be willing to bet on it."

"You could be right, Will. But that means he's not from this county, because we never held any women here from this county."

"Do you realize what that really means? Look at the postmark again. He mailed it from here. He's here right now, watching and waiting for another chance."

Billy felt a sudden urge to use the toilet. He had to agree with Will's assessment. Someone from another area was here waiting for him with a high-powered rifle, probably with a scope. Billy could be in his crosshairs while waiting for a traffic light to change. He had to get the hell out of Dodge, fast!

Billy left a sealed envelope addressed to Bovis on his desk. He was cautious about opening the office door, looking up and down the street before emerging. He drove over to his brother's house, didn't bother to knock and sat down at the kitchen table, his hands shaking slightly.

"Hey Billy, that was a short vacation. You missed all the action. They had TV people here...."

"Yeah, I know all about it. Read the paper, too. I figure Bovis will be looking to replace me real soon, so I left him my resignation. Save him the bother."

"I thought you might do something like that. What are you going to do now?"

"Harv, I don't have a clue. I do know that if I stick around here much longer, there'll be another funeral, and it'll probably be mine." Billy told him about the threatening note.

He also mentioned that he'd had a little encounter with Darius, who might come around looking for him. Billy didn't mention anything about the money. He didn't want his brother to think of him as a cheap crook after all the years of being sheriff. He gave the deed to the house to his brother. "Rent it out if you want to. I've still got some uniforms hanging in the closet and a little food in the refrigerator, but I've got everything I need."

"Maybe I'll let Bobby Lee stay over there. Give him a place to shack up with Robin until he decides to get married. The kid has been driving me nuts lately. Does your TV work?"

"Yeah everything works." Billy was annoyed that his brother could ask such a question at a time when his life was in peril. So much for concern about his safety, he thought.

"So where are you going?"

"Knoxville, Chattanooga and Atlanta are all too close, and Darius could easily show up there. He knows those three cities very well. I'm thinking maybe Nashville, or Memphis."

"Billy, if I was you, I'd go someplace like New Orleans, or down to the Gulf Shores area where it's nice. You need some money?"

"Not right now, maybe later. I'll let you know. If you see Happy Harry, tell him I still have his truck and it's still in one piece. I'll pay him when I can."

"I got a better idea. This Darius knows you're driving that truck, right? So that's what he'll be looking for. Leave the truck here with me. I'll take it back to Harry. I got a nice Camero in the garage I've been thinking of giving to Bobby Lee, but it's better if you take it."

Billy had to agree. Everyone was thinking more clearly about his situation than he was. By the time he loaded up the Camero and left, it was late afternoon. He left the truck sitting in his brother's driveway. As he left town, he couldn't remember if he'd locked the back door of the house, then decided it no longer mattered. Bobby Lee and Robin would be over there in a hot second. And maybe this would prompt them to get married, not that Billy gave a damn right now. The Camero was fast, but it had one drawback, Billy had to take his Stetson off when he drove. It also kept him from being instantly recognized. Few people knew what he looked like without his Stetson on.

Chapter 20

Ralph Goodwin was with his fiancé, Marsha Lane, watching the news while having a drink at their favorite pub. Ralph was waiting for the sports segment, hoping to learn the outcome of a golf tournament. He almost spilled his drink when the station cut to a reporter at the courthouse in Paradise Valley. He was watching so intently that he didn't hear what Marsha was saying to him.

"They're looking for that sheriff aren't they?" She asked, once she realized what was happening on TV.

"He's hiding somewhere. They're saying he's on vacation, but that's just an excuse." Ralph wondered if the sheriff received his note? Maybe that spooked him. The reporter didn't mention it. Probably didn't know about it yet. Suddenly he realized Marsha had been talking to him again.

"You haven't heard anything I've said."

"Sorry. I was thinking about that sheriff."

"Well he's the last thing I want to think about."

What Marsha didn't know was the sheriff was all Ralph had been thinking about. He'd mailed the one note, and planted the other on a uniform pocket. With the sheriff gone, he might not find that second note for several weeks. And the poisoned box of cereal, well that was just a backup idea in case he didn't get another safe shot at him. After a few minutes, Ralph realized that the TV segment he'd just watched was footage the station had run earlier in the week.

Ralph thought about calling the TV reporter. He could give him a real follow-up story.

"Honey, you look tired. I'll bet you had a hectic day." Ralph wanted some time alone to think of a revised plan.

"Yeah, I am, but I thought we were going to rent a movie...."

"We can do that another time. Why don't I take you home and you get a good night's sleep for a change."

"Well... you don't mind?"

"Honey, you really look tired, so get some rest. We'll rent a movie tomorrow night."

"I can't tomorrow night. I have a staff meeting."

"Okay, no big deal. Then we'll do it the night after that."

"Are you trying to get rid of me? Is something going on, Ralph?"

"No, I'm a little pre-occupied tonight. We had some problems at work, and I've been thinking about that."

"Want to talk about it?"

"Not right now. I'll work it out."

Ever since Marsha had told Ralph about her suspicion that she'd been raped while in that jail cell, he'd been acting strange. He had a distant look in his eyes when she was talking to him. She hoped he wasn't thinking of doing something foolish.

* * *

Darius had a hard time maintaining anything close to the speed limit. Melody kept asking him to slow down. She was working on her nails and having difficulty every time they hit a curve, or a bump. She was still annoyed that Billy hadn't made a pass at her. She'd given him enough signals. Darius told her to flirt with him so he'd become a little distracted. It hadn't worked and she wondered if Darius was upset with her.

Most guys still found her attractive and she wondered if maybe her age was starting to show? It was one of the reasons she liked bars and restaurants with soft lighting. She was also considering a breast enhancement with her share of the money. A girl her age had to think about the future. Right now, a future with Darius didn't look too promising.

Melody also wondered what would happen when Darius finally got the money? Would he giver her half, as planned, or would he take it all and split? She kept mulling over that question. She was still thinking about it when they checked into a motel on the outskirts of town. Darius left her there, explaining that he'd be back in a few hours. It was the same motel where Frank Gibson stayed a month earlier and Nick Alexander had stayed as well.

With Melody deposited someplace where she could watch her TV, Darius was now free to look for Billy. His first stop was the sheriff's office.

"He was here a little while ago. Didn't say where he was going, except that he was still on vacation. Some whacko has him spooked. I sure hope the TBI guys catch him pretty soon," Deputy Willoughby said. "What do you need Billy for on a Sunday?"

"I was hoping he might take a quick trip with me back to Chattanooga. I'm still looking for that fugitive that was here last month."

"And you think he's still hanging around that close?"

"If Billy should stop back, tell him I'm looking for him, and that he owes me. Just give him the message that way, okay?"

Darius drove around the square, through the park and back through the town, looking for the silver Chevy Silverado Billy had been driving.

* * *

Bobby Lee had overheard part of the conversation between his uncle Billy and his father. While he was pissed about not getting the Camero, he was happy about getting the house. Now he and Robin had a private place of their own. No more parking and necking in his truck. They could do some serious love making in bed and really play house.

"Bobby Lee, why don't you drive that Silverado over to the garage and park it there. Get it out of the driveway. Tomorrow you can take it back to Harry," Harvey said.

"Okee dokee. Do you mind if I swing by and take a look at the house first?" Harvey threw him the extra key, thinking how lucky the kid was, and how he would have given anything to be that fortunate, when he was that age.

It was the first time in ages that anyone saw a vehicle parked in the driveway at Billy's house on Maple Avenue.

* * *

Billy adjusted quickly to the Camero. The steering was faster than the pickup truck, and his butt was sitting much closer to the road. He watched the tach jump as the car shifted gears. In no time at all he was doing 80 mph before he realized how fast he was going. He was just slowing to 75 when he approached a curve on the two-lane highway that crossed over the mountain ridge.

The car handled the curve nicely because of its lower center of gravity and the independent suspension. No wonder kids liked to speed in these things, Billy thought to himself with a smile. Once outside Harmon County he'd have to be careful. Even though he still had his badge with him, technically he wasn't sheriff any more. Before he knew it, he was doing 80 again. He liked the sound of the engine.

Suddenly the right front tire blew without any warning. Billy tried to control the car, but he was going too fast. The Camero swerved right, went into a ditch and flipped over several times, finally resting on the passenger side. The seatbelt saved Billy from being thrown out of the vehicle. but he was knocked unconscious. The driver's side front wheel rotated slowly to a stop.

* * *

Bobby Lee was walking around inside the house, raising all the blinds for maximum light and thinking about how he'd arrange a new stereo and get rid of the old carpeting when the phone rang. It was Harvey.

"Get over to the garage and get the wrecker. Billy's had a wreck out on the highway just south of Mill's Gate Rd. I'll meet you later. They've taken Billy to Erlanger hospital, and I'm on my way there now."

Bobby Lee raced out of the house, forgetting to lock the front door, jumped into the truck and roared off. Darius missed seeing Bobby Lee and the Chevy pickup by less than a minute. Darius had driven by the house earlier and noted that all the shades were down. Now they were all open, so Billy was back. Just as Ralph had done on his visit, Darius decided to park his Dodge Durango in a parking lot two blocks away and walk back to the house. No sense scaring Billy off, he thought.

Darius was surprised to find both the front door and the back door unlocked. It told him that Billy went out, but would no doubt be back soon. Darius did a quick walk through, didn't see anything irregular, and didn't see the gym bag that Benjamin described earlier. He found a comfortable chair in the living room and waited. Billy would be surprised when he came back and found him there... waiting patiently for his money.

Opal Pratt lived next door to Billy Hargis for 52 years. Even though Billy was never aware of her, she was well aware of his comings and goings at all odd hours. It was little comfort to live next door to the sheriff when he was hardly ever there. Opal wasn't the town busybody, but she ran a close second place. She knew Billy liked to sneak in the back door and attributed that peculiarity to when he was a youngster sneaking in and out past his bedtime.

While the sheriff certainly kept strange hours, Opal could attest to anyone interested that he never brought any women to the house, for which she was very grateful. She'd also read that horrible piece in the newspaper about the sheriff and didn't believe a word of it, not a single word. Opal was a widow with two cats, Pickle and Petunia, Petunia being the female.

Opal was certain something strange was going on next door. She heard noises in the dark, but when she peeked out her window, she didn't see any lights on next door. She thought she saw some movement in the back yard a few nights ago, so she rechecked all her doors and windows, making sure everything was locked. Then earlier today, she saw Sheriff Billy carry out a suitcase, leaving by the back door.

Later, a strange pickup truck was parked in the driveway and she noticed a young man walking through the house, raising all the blinds. He no sooner left, and in quite a hurry, when another stranger arrived. She didn't recognize him as anyone living in town. He walked all around the outside then entered through the front door. She could only assume that Billy was renting the house. She'd make it a point to find out later.

Darius hadn't eaten anything since breakfast and he felt his stomach reminding him of that fact. He'd been waiting for an hour and thought Billy would have returned by now. Darius opened the refrigerator, checked the milk, it was still fresh. He opened cabinet doors and decided a bowl of cereal would hold him for a while, and since there was milk, he poured out a big dish of Granola, sprinkled it with sugar, added milk and took the bowl back to the living room. The first two spoonfuls tasted slightly bitter and he wondered if the milk was turning sour. He gulped two more spoonfuls and decided he'd had enough.

Darius put the dish in the sink without rinsing it. A few minutes passed before he started feeling sick to his stomach. He started for the bathroom. On his way, he knocked over a kitchen chair. He started vomiting before he made it to the bathroom. It was the most commotion Opal Pratt had heard come from Billy's house in over 15 years. She picked up the phone and called the sheriff's office.

* * *

Bobby Lee arrived at the accident scene in record time. A small crowd of people were standing around, just looking and watching. There were two patrol cars there with deputies directing traffic. One of the deputies motioned for Bobby Lee to pull off the road. The Camero was at least 50 feet on the other side of the ditch. He'd use a cable attaching it to the car's frame to pull it over onto the wheels then drag it to the ditch, where he could hook onto it. Both sides and the top were badly damaged. The windshield and rear window were shattered.

Once Bobby Lee had the Camero righted, he looked inside and saw Billy's suitcase and a gym bag. Bobby Lee knew how fast things could disappear from a crash site, so he forced open the driver side door, reached in and retrieved the two pieces. He carried them back to the wrecker. They belonged to his uncle, so he wasn't stealing anything, which he explained to one of the deputies who gave him a curious look. It took a half hour to get the car hooked to the wrecker and another 15 minutes to get it back to the storage yard.

There was no question that the blown tire was the cause of the accident. Bobby Lee removed the suitcase and the gym bag, putting both in the office. Out of curiosity, he opened the gym bag, thinking it probably held several handguns. Seeing all the money took him by complete surprise. It took him 10 minutes to count it. It was more money than he'd ever seen and he wondered if his uncle had robbed a bank, which would explain his sudden departure, switching vehicles and talking about someone looking for him. It was hard to believe that Billy would rob a bank in Chattanooga. He hadn't seen anything about a robbery on TV.

Whatever trouble his uncle was in, Bobby Lee knew he had to hide the money, so his uncle wouldn't be implicated in anything the TBI agents might suspect. He thought about asking Dent what he should do? Billy's house might be the safest place, he finally concluded. Bobby Lee's mother and Harvey had gone to the hospital to check on Billy's condition. Finally he remembered he hadn't locked the front door when he'd hastily left Billy's house, earlier. He headed back so he could hide the gym bag and lock the house.

When he arrived, there was another small crowd gathered outside. An EMS unit was parked in the drive and the attendants had someone on a stretcher coming out of the front door.

"Looks like the sheriff's stalker finally got him." Bobby Lee was standing next to Melissa. Both turned to the voice they'd just heard behind them. It was a young man neither of them knew. It was Ralph Goodwin, who like Darius, had driven around the block, discovering all the shades were up and the front door standing open. By the time he parked, an EMS ambulance had arrived, along with a few neighbors and some local kids. Bobby Lee was about to correct the man, but decided not to say anything. Melissa recognized Darius on the portable stretcher and tugged on Bobby Lee's sleeve.

"What made him think that was Billy?" She whispered to Bobby Lee.

"Uncle Billy is in Erlanger Hospital in Chattanooga. He was in a bad car wreck about an hour ago. He told Paw that Darius might be looking for him," he whispered back. "I guess he was waiting in Billy's house."

Deputy Willoughby walked out the front door, carrying the bowl from the sink. He had it in a zip-lock bag. He also had the box of Granola and the bottle of milk. Bobby Lee approached him and Melissa was close behind.

"What's going on?" Bobby Lee asked.

"Darius must have been waiting for Billy to return. While he was waiting, he must have helped himself to some cereal and got violently sick. Good thing Billy's neighbor called, or he might be dead. The EMS guys pumped his stomach." Deputy Willoughby told them. "Any word on how your uncle is doing?"

"Paw is at the hospital now. I just towed the wreck back to the yard. Looks like the right front tire blew out on him and he couldn't control it."

"Well, that's two EMS calls in an hour's time, both concerning your uncle. I guess everyone will know where to find him now," the deputy said.

Chapter 21

Melody watched TV and fell asleep waiting for Darius to arrive. It was late when she woke. She knew something must have gone wrong with Darius' plan, or he had the money and took off. Either way, she felt stranded. Sunday night in a hick town where all the restaurants were already closed, and there were no taxis. She had a momentary vision of Darius already on his way to Atlanta with fifty grand, singing some stupid song about being free. If she hadn't told Darius about getting it on with Benjamin, she'd be the one driving to Atlanta with the fifty grand. It was 9:00 P.M. when she called a friend in Chattanooga to come get her.

Ironically, Billy and Darius were at the same hospital in Chattanooga, but in different sections. Billy was in a coma, diagnosed with a concussion and remained on the critical list. A police officer was stationed outside his room as a precaution, since several attempts had been made on his life. Darius was being kept overnight for observation. TBI Agent Noah Cody was patiently waiting for the doctor to finish, so he could ask Darius some questions. The box of cereal, the bowl and the bottle of milk had been sent to a lab for testing. The preliminary conclusion was arsenic poisoning.

"You're lucky Billy has a nosey neighbor, Darius."

"Yeah. Anyone ever find out where Billy is?"

"Yeah. As a matter of fact, he's not far from here. He's on a different floor and in a different wing. He had an accident on the highway. Looks like a front tire blew and flipped the car a few times. He's got a bad concussion. Still in a coma."

"Well I need to talk to him as soon as he's conscious. What room is he in?"

"Uh Unh. You're not going anywhere, yet. And nobody's talking to Billy until we talk to him first. What's so important that you need to see him?"

"He's got some information that I need. I'm tracking a guy...."

"Not now you're not! So how is it Billy would know about a guy you're looking for? Last one I knew about was some fugitive everybody thinks killed those people in Paradise Valley. Is that the same one you're talking about?"

"Yeah. Billy called me. Said he thought he might know where I could find the guy."

"Seems to me Billy should be giving us that information, not you."

"Well, see Billy and I have been pals for a long time."

"Uh huh, and that's why you were in his house?"

"Yeah, waiting for him to come back. He told me to meet him there."

"Uh huh, and you didn't know he had already left town?"

"If I'd known that, why would I be sitting in his kitchen eating a bowl of cereal?"

"I guess that was going to be my next question. Your pal, who has some information for you, leaves town and doesn't bother to mention it to you. Don't you think that's a bit strange?"

"Damned strange if you ask me."

"I just did, Darius. And you're playing games with me. Deputy Willoughby said he talked to you earlier, and you were looking for the sheriff. I guess you thought you'd just wait for him to come home. Was that your plan?"

"Yeah. Something like that."

* * *

Agent Greg Mathews was talking with Deputy Willoughby Jones Monday morning when Bobby Lee called the sheriff's office. He and Robin were at Billy's house and found a note pinned to one of Billy's uniforms hanging in the bedroom closet.

It was as fast to walk over to Billy's house, as it was to get in the car and drive. So they walked, taking a short cut. Bobby Lee and Robin were waiting at the front door when they arrived. Agent Mathews pulled on a pair of latex gloves, removed the note and read it carefully, then held it so that the deputy could read it before putting it into a plastic sandwich bag.

"The guy is certainly persistent, and shows a bit of creativity, too." The TBI agent said. Deputy Willoughby agreed. "And we now know he was in this house recently. We need to ask around about anyone seeing a stranger in the area."

"I saw someone yesterday," Bobby Lee said. "He was standing behind me and Melissa while the EMS guys were here. He said something I thought was strange. Melissa thought so too."

"What did he say?"

"He said, 'looks like the stalker finally got the sheriff'. We both turned around and looked at him. Since he was a total stranger, I wondered how he knew it was Billy's house."

"And how would he know about the sheriff being stalked?" Deputy Willoughby added. "Can you give us a description of this guy?"

Bobby Lee told them what he recalled of the young man standing behind them. When Willoughby and Mathews left, they went over to see Melissa at the café. She confirmed the conversation, and the description Bobby Lee had given them.

"It's possible he'll stop back. Maybe stop in here. Think you might recognize him?" Agent Mathews asked. He and Willoughby sat at the counter and had coffee. Melissa could tell that Will and Greg were working well together. For once it was a cooperative effort, the sheriff's office working with the TBI.

"Oh I'll know him, if I see him again. What should I do, should I call you?"

"Yes, but be careful how you do it. You don't want to arouse any suspicion and spook him. Don't stare at him. Act like you normally do. Then if he should be able to over-hear your phone conversation, say something like you're running low on bread and need more. That way, I'll know he's here and come over. If for any reason, he should leave before anyone gets here, try to see what type vehicle he's driving."

Now they had a fairly good idea of what the young man looked like. He wasn't from Paradise Valley, either Melissa or Bobby Lee would have known him. Between them, they knew everybody in town and the county. Having two eye-witnesses was much better than just one. That would help later, when they had to make the case and present it. Agent Mathews called his partner, Noah Cody at the hospital to give him a heads up, just in case the suspect showed up there. They now knew he was daring enough to try anything.

* * *

Agent Cody received Mathews' phone call while he was still with Darius.

"You didn't happen to leave Billy a note somewhere did you? Maybe pin it on one of his uniforms, so he'd find it later?" Agent Cody asked after the phone conversation.

"I don't know what you're talking about. Billy never mentioned any note to me."

"That's because he hasn't seen this one yet. Somebody went into his house when he wasn't there, like you did. Probably looking for something. Didn't find it, so he left a little surprise behind to let Billy know he was there."

"Hey, the only thing I left in his house was half my guts that I puked out after eating some bad cereal. The doc thinks it had arsenic in it. Surely you don't think I was trying to kill Billy?"

"I can't answer that. It seems there are at least two people who want to get at Billy, and you're one of them. The other one is still loose out there somewhere. He mistook a deputy for the sheriff the first time. It could be that tire blow out Billy had on the road was no accident either." He made a note to check the Camero Billy had been driving. It wouldn't be the first time that an accident was actually a murder attempt.

"And you think that same person might have been in Billy's house and planted poison in the cereal?"

"It's possible. If so, you screwed up his plans. He'll have to try something else next." Having said that, Agent Cody remembered the conversation about killing lions in Africa, using a tethered baby goat as bait. What if he could get the stalker to try again, here at the hospital? He'd discuss his plan with Agent Mathews when he saw him later.

* * *

Bobby Lee still had the gym bag stashed behind the seat in his truck. He was planning on hiding it at Billy's house, but a TBI agent was there along with a deputy. He couldn't think of a safe place to hide it. So far, Billy was still in a coma. Bobby Lee wondered if Billy would ask about the money when he was fully awake, or would he remember it? It was unlikely that Bobby Lee and Robin would move into Billy's house now.

Billy would eventually recover and no doubt move back, and that would be the end of Bobby Lee's plans for the future, unless they ran off and got married somewhere. The more he thought about it, the more the idea appealed to him. It was time he moved out of his parent's house. The money in the gym bag would pay for a nice honeymoon and some new furniture, provided his uncle didn't remember having the money.

Billy woke from the coma. The hospital staff was expecting it to happen. They saw increased brain wave activity on the monitor. When he opened his eyes, he was confused about where he was. Seeing a nurse and intern he was able to guess that he was in a hospital somewhere. He had no idea how he got there, or what had happened. The doctor explained that amnesia was quite common in situations like his, and that recent events, places and names would slowly come back to him.

One of the younger nurses seemed particularly attentive. Her nametag said she was Jenny. Jenny had a nice smile, soft cool hands and a pleasant soothing voice. Billy held her hand and squeezed it lightly. He didn't want her to leave.

"What happened to me?" He asked, not letting go.

"You were in a bad car accident. Do you remember anything about it?"

"No. My mind is totally blank. I think God just erased my data bank. How long do you think it will be before I start remembering things?"

"I don't know, but I wouldn't worry about it. You just relax, it will come back to you in time." She hadn't made any effort to withdraw her hand from his.

"Maybe I don't want it to come back. Be nice to start over with a blank page."

"Do you know who you are? Do you know your name?"

"Ah, let me think. It's Billy. Yeah that's it, Billy. Hey, I'm making a little progress, huh?" He wanted her to stay.

"Yes you are. I'm going to check in on you before I leave. Can I get you anything, Billy?"

"Yeah, could I have a beer?"

"No silly, this is a hospital. They don't allow drinking here." She giggled.

"So how about later?"

"Sure, when you're better and they release you, you can have a beer then."

"No, I mean how about you having a drink with me, when I get better?"

"I'll think about it. Now you get some rest." She winked at him as she left.

Billy watched her leave. Imagine that, he thought, here I am in the hospital, in an oversized bib that wraps around, don't know my last name and I'm getting an erection over a cute young nurse. A few minutes later, a police officer stationed outside his door looked in on him.

"Can I get you anything, Sheriff?"

"Yeah, get me a beer, and bring one for yourself." They both laughed. Billy closed his eyes and tried to recall his former life. The police officer had just called him 'sheriff', that was a start.

An hour later, Deputy Cody walked into his room and sat down. Billy heard him come in and decided to act as though he were still asleep. Maybe he could use his present situation to some advantage. For some strange reason he felt slightly apprehensive around the man who just came in.

"Hey Billy, are you awake? Can you hear me?"

"Mmmm," Billy moaned.

"Your buddy, Darius, is asking about you. He seems to think you can help him. Do you know what he's talking about?"

"Mmmm... Dare-e-us. Who's Darius?"

"He a big bald guy who's been looking all over for you. Says you two are buddies."

"Mmmm… buddies. Don't have any buddies."

"Billy, I think that's the first totally honest thing you've ever said in a long time. The doctor says you're out of the coma and can understand me. So why don't you open your eyes?"

"Because I'm trying to sleep, asshole!"

"Ah, the old Sheriff Billy is back with us. I knew that you'd come around sooner, or later. Do you remember anything about the accident?"

"Nope."

"You were leaving Paradise Valley. Someone was looking for you. Do you remember any of that?"

"Nope."

"Okay. I'll talk to you later. They're not allowing anyone in to see you except family members."

"So what the hell are you doing here then?"

"Still got that smart mouth and bad attitude. You'll be back to your old self in a few days, if not sooner. We've got a lot of questions to ask you."

"What kind of questions?"

"Not now, later. For the time being, just consider yourself to be a baby goat on a long rope. See ya."

As soon as the TBI agent left the room, Billy's eyes popped open, 'a tethered baby goat'? He closed his eyes again and envisioned a lion pacing in the brush. African men with spears were hiding, waiting. The vision of it all scared him. He'd heard all about how they hunted lions sometime in his past.

Billy mulled that over for a few minutes and finally concluded that if someone, whoever they were, was after him and using him as some sort of bait. He hoped Jenny would hurry back. He wanted to tell her that he'd been thinking about her. See if she noticed anything different about him? Maybe notice the bump under the sheet?

Two hours passed. Harvey arrived with Bobby Lee. They sat and waited until Billy woke. An older nurse came in and adjusted his bed so he could sit up comfortably. She gave him some water and left. Not as friendly as Jenny, he thought, and not as cute.

"Hey Billy, I guess that Camero was just too much for you after driving the pickup and the Bronco," Harvey joked.

"I, I don't know... I don't know what you're talking about. I'm sorry. The doctor said my memory will eventually come back to me. So far, I'm drawing a blank."

"Well, I'm just glad you weren't badly hurt. Bobby Lee towed the wreck back to the yard. We have your suitcase at the house. You were leaving for a vacation. Somebody was after you, trying to kill you." Harvey recounted.

"Yeah, and he left a note pinned on one of your uniforms in the closet. Robin and I found it and called Deputy Willoughby." Bobby Lee added. "They think he planted some poison in a box of cereal. Probably wouldn't have discovered it except that Darius helped himself and got sick. Anyone else wouldn't have survived. Lady next door called nine, one, one."

"Mmmm." Billy closed his eyes. He was having a difficult time following what they were saying. He wasn't even sure who these people were, but he didn't want to be impolite in case they were relatives, which they seemed to be.

"I guess we'll check in on you later. Get some rest." Everyone was telling him the same thing. Harvey and Bobby Lee would get something to eat and stop back, before going home.

In the hospital cafeteria, Nurse Jenny was on a break, drinking some juice and talking with her friends. Also sitting at the same table was Nurse Marsha Lane who overheard Jenny talking about the patient with amnesia and a concussion.

"The policeman outside his room told me that he was a sheriff. They think someone is trying to kill him, so they're restricting who can see him. Sounds just something you'd see on TV doesn't it?" Jenny told the small group.

"Where is this sheriff from?" Marsha asked.

"He's from Harmon County, just up the road about an hour from here. It's really pretty in the valley, I've been through there a few times," Jenny said.

"Well I've been through there, too. Make sure you don't speed, because they've got radar traps everywhere, and they're quick to throw you in jail." Marsha stated then wished she hadn't said anything.

"Really? Did they put you in jail?" One of the nurses asked.

"No! But it happened to a friend of mine. She told me all about it. It was a horrible experience." Marsha left before anyone could ask any more questions. The thought that the sheriff who had raped her was right there at the hospital left her shaken. Jenny picked up on Marsha's sudden change and quick departure and wondered if there wasn't more to that story?

* * *

Marsha called her fiancé, Ralph at work to tell him about the sheriff being in the hospital. Ralph had seen the EMS ambulance leave the sheriff's house. He wasn't able to follow the ambulance, and didn't know exactly where they took patient. It hadn't occurred to him that they would take the sheriff to Erlanger, but apparently they had. So now he knew exactly where the sheriff was. Obviously the poison didn't finish him off as he had hoped.

Ralph had been listening for any news report, and hadn't seen anything in the newspaper, but it was still too early. Marsha mentioned that a police officer had been posted outside the sheriff's room because someone was trying to kill him. No kidding, he thought. If only Marsha knew all the details, but he couldn't tell her.

It was ironic that she should be calling him to tell him the sheriff's exact location, which was where she worked... and the sheriff would die. Yes, it would be a fitting end, he thought.

Ralph left work early. He drove to the hospital, parked in the employee lot since he an employee sticker on his windshield. He knew Mrs. Grogan at the information desk. His father had physician privileges here and everyone knew that he and Marsha were engaged. Still, he had to be careful.

"Hi, Mrs. Grogan. The EMS guys from Paradise Valley brought someone in recently who was poisoned. I can't remember the name. Would you happen to know the room number?" He was hoping she wouldn't ask why he was so interested.

Mrs. Grogan checked the computer screen then picked up the phone and spoke to someone. Ralph couldn't hear what she was saying, and thought about leaving.

"He's on the fourth floor, room four-sixteen."

"Great. I just wanted to make sure he was still here and okay. Thanks." Ralph headed for the elevators.

Chapter 22

Harvey and Bobby Lee were waiting for the elevator when the doors opened. Ralph Goodwin stepped out, walking past them into the lobby area.

"That's him! That's the guy we saw outside Uncle Billy's house," Bobby Lee whispered to his father. While Harvey got on the elevator, Bobby Lee followed Ralph out into the parking lot, being careful not to be seen.

Bobby Lee stood behind a concrete pillar and watched as the man got into a camo-painted Jeep Wrangler. The Jeep drove to the employee's entrance and waited a few minutes. A nurse came out and got in. Bobby Lee saw the nurse give the driver a kiss. As they passed by Bobby Lee's observation point, he stepped out to read the license plate number.

A few minutes later, he was back in Billy's room giving Agent Cody a report on what he'd seen.

"That's a real piece of luck," Agent Cody said. "If his wife, or girlfriend works here at the hospital, that poses a new threat for Billy." The TBI agent left. In a few minutes he'd have the name of the Jeep's owner. He called his associates on his cell phone to give them an update. Then they decided on a new plan.

"What's going on?" Billy asked. Two orderlies came into his room and moved him in a wheelchair across the hall to another room. Harvey and Bobby Lee followed. Agent Cody returned once Billy was back in bed.

They were taking a precaution. "You're not in any condition to be released yet, so we had you moved to a more comfortable room with a better view of the parking lot," Agent Cody said trying for some humor.

Billy gave him a curious look. He wasn't entirely buying the agent's story. The police officer was still outside the other room, but was also able to watch the door to Billy's new room, 526A.

The duty nurse, the nurse supervisor and Billy's doctor were the only one's aware of the quick change in rooms. Nurse Jenny had already left for the day. Billy's former room remained listed with the central information desk in case anyone inquired.

Ralph remained unaware of the sheriff's automobile accident. His only interest was in a poisoned victim he still thought was the sheriff. That victim was on a different floor in another section.

$$*\ldots*\ldots*$$

Ralph noticed a young man step out from behind the pillar in his rearview mirror, as he was leaving the parking lot. He didn't recognize Bobby Lee, but his keen sense of caution told him he'd been spotted and was now being watched.

After dropping Marsha at her place, Ralph hurried home. He parked a half block from his building and waited. A half hour later, Ralph saw an unmarked police car drive slowly up his street, turn around and park. Two men got out and walked toward his building. It was enough for Ralph to conclude they were on to him.

After the two men entered his apartment building, Ralph drove away wondering what he'd do next. The future was beginning to look unpredictable, something he hated. Revenge was still an available option, but not for long. Once he got past the police guard, he could kill the sheriff. Later, if they caught him, he'd plead insanity. Fear of capture quickly dissipated once he had a plan of action finalized. In no time he was calm once again. It was this same mental state that made terrorists so formidable and unpredictable.

* * *

Agents Cody and Daniels didn't have a search warrant for Ralph's apartment. They had to be careful not to disturb anything. Once inside, they found the newspaper article, *Trouble in Paradise* on the kitchen table. In the small living room, they found a framed photo of Ralph and Marsh Lane. They took the photo. Their quick search didn't produce a rifle, or any other weapons.

Since it was a small, one-bedroom apartment it had limited storage space. The building superintendent showed them the additional storage locker in the basement reserved for Ralph's apartment. It was completely empty.

The newspaper article, found on the table, wasn't sufficient evidence. They did have reason to hold the young man for questioning, when they found him, since the agents had two reliable eye witnesses who could place him outside the sheriff's house. They still needed more evidence.

* * *

Ralph stopped at his rented storage locker, where he kept all his camping gear and his rifle. He knew he could survive in the woods for weeks without anyone ever seeing him, or knowing where he was. A similar young man, thought to have bombed several abortion clinics, managed to hide out somewhere in the North Carolina wilderness, successfully evading FBI agents for more than five years. That fugitive, Eric Rudolph, was a role model for Ralph, even though he was caught.

He knew that once the TBI agents gained access to his phone records, and learned that Marsha was his fiancé, he'd have to go into hiding. Trying to stay ahead of the agents at this point was difficult. He had to devise a plan of action.

Suddenly it hit him. The TBI agents had no witnesses to his shooting that deputy. Therefore, it would be almost impossible to prove he did it, if they didn't find his rifle. And, he'd been careful not to leave any fingerprints, while at the sheriff's house. All they had were suspicions. Somebody may have seen him in Paradise Valley, but so what? He could easily explain that.

Being seen at the hospital could also be explained. So, he had no reason to run and hide. That would only make him appear guilty. Face them and appear indifferent, he thought. Then, when the appropriate time arrived, he could still finish what he planned to do. Making a hasty plan was stupid. Now that he felt confident again, he was in complete control. He decided to take Marsha to dinner.

"I thought you said you weren't feeling well earlier," Marsha said, surprised to see him.

"My headache's gone." He gave her a kiss.

During dinner, Ralph explained that he thought someone was following him, which was the other reason he'd left her so abruptly.

"Why would you think that?" Marsha asked.

"I don't know, it's just a feeling I've had ever since you mentioned that the sheriff who raped you was in the hospital. I wish I could see him and tell him how much I hate him for what he's done to you... to us. Ralph noticed her wince when he added the 'us'. She knew what he meant. Recently their amorous feelings stopped short of having sex. She was feeling guilty about that, too.

"With a police officer stationed outside his door, I don't see how they'd let you in to see him. Besides, I heard he has amnesia. Jenny said he didn't even know his last name, so he won't recall any of it. Maybe it's better that way."

"What are you talking about? What amnesia? I thought he was in the hospital for some sort of food poisoning."

"Whatever made you think that? He was in some sort of car wreck and got a bad concussion."

"Well I guess I got that confused with a report I over-heard. By the way, you do know that amnesia is just a tem-porary thing. I've heard my dad say that it only lasts a little while, then things start coming back."

So the sheriff wasn't in room 416A after all. That ex-plained why he didn't see a police officer standing outside the door when he passed by earlier. In his haste, he'd made a quick assumption and another mistake. He hated doing stu-pid things like that. He vowed to be more careful.

When Ralph dropped off Marsha, he saw the same un-marked car parked across the street. Later they followed him back to his apartment. He was inside about five minutes when the agents knocked on his door. Ralph invited the two agents in. His plan was to stay cool.

"What were you doing at the hospital today?" Agent Cody asked.

"Let's see, I saw a couple friends, killed a few minutes in the cafeteria, then gave my fiancé a lift home. She works at the hospital. So does my dad. Why?"

"Were you in Paradise Valley recently?"

"Yeah, a couple of times. I was there this weekend as a matter of fact. I've been looking for a small house to buy and fix up. Prices over there are a lot better than here."

"So you made several trips recently?"

"Yes. That's what I just said. It's a nice little town. I like the neat square, all the old buildings, and the people. I also like the nice name of the place. Now, do you mind telling me what this is all about?"

"It seems someone from here has been sending threatening notes to the sheriff in Harmon County. Even tried to poison him. You wouldn't happen to know anything about that would you?"

"As a matter of fact, I do. Marsha mentioned something about a poisoning earlier. She heard about it at work. Is he okay?"

"Yes, the guy who was poisoned is okay. They released him earlier today. The sheriff wasn't home when the man was poisoned. He was in an auto accident and suffered a concussion, but he's in stable condition. They're holding him for a few more days. Tell me something, Ralph, do you happen to know where the sheriff lives?"

"Yeah, I think so. I was in town when the EMS people were taking someone out of his house. I stopped and asked a lady what was going on and she said she thought something happened to the sheriff, so I assumed it was the sheriff they were carrying out." Ralph was being careful what he said. He was pretty sure they already knew he was there.

"Uh huh, what else?"

"Not much. I got some gas and drove home. I still don't know why you're asking me these questions. I don't even know the sheriff. Never met him."

"Well, it seems a little strange, you showing up in both places like that. Small town, people notice strangers, know what I mean?"

"Yeah, I do. It's one of the reasons I like the place. It's quaint and quiet."

"Like I said, the sheriff will be in the hospital for a few more days. They're moving him to a more comfortable room now that he's out of his coma. He'll no doubt have a lot of visitors before they release him."

"I guess you think I'm supposed to care?"

"Just thought I'd mention it. By the way, do you happen to own a rifle?"

"Sure. I use it when I go hunting."

"Do you have it here?"

"No, a friend of mine borrowed it a few months ago. Now that you mention it, I need to get it back from him."

"Your friend got a name?"

"Of course he's got a name, but I'm not giving it to you. And, I'm not interested in continuing this line of questions, gentlemen. If you start asking my friends, and my employer about me, that will cause me some unnecessary embarrassment. Let me give you the name of my father's attorney. He'll be the one you'll want to speak to in the future. Oh, by the way, could I please have my picture back? I doubt you have a search warrant, or you would have shown it to me by now. Good night, gentlemen."

Ralph walked to the door and held it open for them. He closed it softly after they left, then let out his breath. So far he was holding up well. He had to call Marsha and tell her that he'd just been questioned so she'd be prepared.

"What do you think, Cody? The kid's pretty smooth." Agent Williams said.

"Too smooth. Most people would be shitting their pants and looking worried. He knows we've got a witness, so he's being careful not to get caught lying. He had a ready answer, didn't have to think. He's our guy, we just have to prove it."

"Do you think his fiancé might be one of the sheriff's rape victims?"

"Yes I do. Let's go talk to her. We have to keep shaking this tree until something we can use falls out. We're getting close."

* * *

Marsha's father answered the door. He wasn't pleased to have TBI officers arrive at his house, in the evening, asking to talk with his daughter. He insisted on remaining in the room while they talked to her.

"Miss Lane, we have a witness who can identify your fiancé, Ralph Goodwin, at the sheriff's house when the EMS people were removing a poisoning victim. Two people saw him there and heard him say something about the sheriff's stalker finally got him. Do you know why he'd say something like that?"

"I have no idea what you're talking about. I didn't even know Ralph was in Paradise Valley on Sunday. He never mentioned it to me."

"Do you have any idea why he'd be there?"

"None whatsoever. I'm sorry I can't help you. If Ralph was there, I'm sure there's a logical reason. Why don't you ask him?"

"We have. I have a very sensitive question to ask you. It might be best if your father went into the other room."

"You are not talking to my daughter, or asking sensitive questions without me being present! Go ahead and ask your damned question, then I'll ask you to leave. My daughter has done nothing wrong." Mr. Lane was visibly annoyed.

"Okay, whatever you say, Sir. Miss Lane, did you have occasion to be stopped by the sheriff in Harmon County any time in the past few months?" Agent Cody knew the answer by watching the color change in the young woman's face.

"How... I mean why are you asking me that?"

"I think you know where this is leading. The sheriff is suspected of holding female speeding drivers without the benefit of a hearing. Being held in jail can be a terrible experience... particularly for a young woman, away from home, all alone."

"My daughter has never seen the inside of a jail cell. What the hell are you suggesting anyway?"

"Sir, perhaps you'd prefer that we talk to your daughter elsewhere. We can just as easily do this at our office. We don't need your consent. Your daughter is over twenty-one and therefore an adult. We have reason to suspect that she was a victim of an illegal radar trap...."

"Is that true, Marsha?" Mr. Lane asked his daughter. Worried now that she might be in some sort of trouble for not reporting something.

"Yes," she said softly, not looking at anyone. They had to know the whole story already, or they wouldn't be asking her these questions. She wondered how they had found out.

"So Sheriff Billy Hargis kept you as a guest, behind bars, probably because the fine he mentioned was higher than you could afford. Am I right on that?"

"Yes."

"Honey, why didn't you call us? We would have come to get you and paid the fine. There was no need for you to stay in jail."

"I tried. They said the phone was busy."

"I seriously doubt that. We are always here and hardly ever on the phone more than a minute or so."

"Miss Lane, did anything happen to you while you were being held there?"

"Excuse me one second. What are you suggesting here?" Mr. Lane was almost shouting. Marsha was trembling and fighting back tears. She was glad her mother was upstairs watching TV and not part of this humiliating interrogation.

"We think she might have been drugged and sexually molested. If so, then we need to get a statement so we can file charges against the sheriff. His misconduct is being investigated. We're trying to build a case against him and we need your help." Cody wanted to divert the conversation away from Ralph.

If they could get Marsha Lane to admit she'd been in jail and molested, then they had a motive for the shooting and good reason for going after Ralph, who no doubt knew all about it.

"I'm sorry, I can't help you. They held me there for a few hours, then let me go with a warning, that's all."

"And when was this?"

Marsha told them the date. Mr. Lane showed the agents to the door. Cody knew that he'd get what he wanted when he talked to her alone at the hospital. She wasn't about to tell him the details in front of her father, so he didn't push it.

* * *

"Good morning," Nurse Jenny said brightly taking Billy's temperature and blood pressure. "How are we doing today?"

"I think we're doing just great. I think I dreamt about you last night."

"Oh? You think, but you're not sure?"

"No, I'm sure. Want to know how I'm so sure?" Billy was smiling and hoping she'd notice his morning erection. He had to go to the bathroom, but was willing to endure the pain to watch her expression.

"Does this have anything to do with that bump under the blanket?"

"Yep. I'm glad you noticed. It must have been a real sexy dream I had."

"Well that's really sweet. Sit up while I get you a big glass of water to take this pill." She made him drink all of the water in the glass and saw the pain it was causing him. "Okay, now go pee and let's see if Mr. Happy is still glad to see me when you get back." She laughed and plumped his pillows. She was used to men trying to flirt with her. Most of them were harmless and lonely. A few were pathetic. She didn't think Billy was harmless, but he seemed to be lonely.

Billy was back in bed, sitting up eating breakfast when his first visitor arrived. It was Eulla. She brought flowers, and Nurse Jenny put them in a vase. Jenny wondered if this was the sheriff's girlfriend. She lingered momentarily to see if they kissed each other. When that didn't happen, she left.

"You're really a shit, you know that, Billy? Leaving town the way you did, without saying anything to me. Do you realize how humiliated I've been lately?"

"I'm sorry, I don't remember who you are. I guess we knew each other, but right now everything's a blank."

"Says you. I'm not buying it. You can fool the rest of them if you want to, but you're not fooling me, Billy Hargis. I know you too well. I know all your dark secrets, and don't you forget that." It wasn't meant as a pun.

"Good. Then you can talk to me and maybe it will help bring some things back. I'm sorry if you don't believe me, but I can't remember anything before yesterday."

"Aren't you the lucky one." Eulla thought about making some things up, just for the fun of it to see if she could catch him. "We had a hot date planned, and you ran out on me. It was my birthday and we were going to spend it here in Chattanooga, just you and me... at the Holiday Inn."

"We were?" Billy lost his appetite. Maybe it really was a good thing that he couldn't remember. He kept thinking that perhaps he'd lost his mind some other time. If Nurse Jenny was a 10 on the beauty scale, this woman was a two, maybe a one and a half.

"Don't you remember all those sexy things we did to-gether?" She giggled. She was having fun playing with his empty head. She could tell him anything and he'd have to believe it... for a while at least. She could vent some of her fantasies on him and he'd just have to accept them.

"We did? What did we do? No, wait, don't tell me."

"Oh, you want to guess, do you?"

"No. I want to sleep." Billy closed his eyes. Where did Nurse Jenny go? He hoped this woman would leave soon.

Eulla walked over to the bed and kissed Billy's ban-daged head. She looked over her shoulder to make sure the door was closed and slipped her hand under the covers searching for his penis. As she started to gently stroke him, she saw him smile, eyes still closed.

"Jenny?" Billy asked, enjoying the new sensation.

Eulla was taken by surprise. She withdrew her hand, made a fist and hit him in the jaw as hard as she could, not worrying about his condition.

"I always knew you were a real shit, Billy, I just didn't know how bad you really were until now. All these years I protected you, did special things for you. Listened to all your bullshit, laughed at all your cornball jokes and kept all your secrets. Now I'm seeing the real Billy Hargis for the first time. Too bad it wasn't you in the Bronco when that shot was fired."

The blow hurt. It was the first time Eulla had ever ex-pressed her anger by hitting him. Whatever he'd said must have really pissed her off.

"What shot?"

"Oh bag it, Billy. I'm sorry I came to see you. You really look stupid in that turban you're wearing. I always knew you had a big head. You should see it now." Eulla walked out, bumping into Bobby Lee who was just coming in the doorway.

"Hi, Uncle Billy. You feeling any better today?"

"Where's my fucking money, Bobby Lee?" Eulla's punch jarred his brain and brought it all back.

Chapter 23

Bobby Lee was surprised by his uncle's outburst. "Your money is probably with your clothes in the closet over there." Harvey was still downstairs in the cafeteria having a second cup of coffee.

"I'm talking about the gym bag. It was in the Camero along with my suitcase. What did you do with it?"

"I hid it, so nobody would find it. I guess you got your memory back, huh?"

"Yeah, it came back suddenly, like a shot to the head. I gotta get out of here. Where's Harv?"

"He's downstairs. He'll be here in a few minutes. Do you remember anything about the accident? Looks like the right front tire blew out. You musta been running pretty fast to roll that many times."

"Forget the accident. Where did you hide the money?"

"I've got it hidden under a tarp in the storage yard. I was going to put it in your closet at the house, but…."

Just then Agent Cody walked in and sat down. He nodded to Bobby Lee then turned his attention to Billy.

"Did you sleep well? You didn't eat much of your breakfast." The tray was still beside Billy's bed.

"Mmmm." Billy closed his eyes. He hoped Bobby Lee would keep his mouth shut for a change.

"You want anything? A glass of water?" Agent Cody asked in a friendly tone.

"Tell this young man, I forgot his name, to ask the nurse for some orange juice." Bobby Lee took the hint and left the room smiling.

"Okay, let's cut the crap, Billy. Why is Darius Ott so eager to find you? He was waiting at your house while you were doing rolls in that hayfield. Actually, he was pitching his guts out."

"I'm sorry, I don't know anyone by that name."

"Okay, have it your way. You can't play this game too much longer. We're going to get you indicted for a long list of felonies. Let's see, we've got you for misconduct of an elected official, misappropriation of funds and maybe theft. Assault, battery, and sexual abuse of prisoners while in your custody." Cody was watching closely for a reaction.

"How about impersonating an officer of the law? They tell me I was a sheriff, can you believe that?"

"Actually no. I can't. But anything's possible I guess."

"Look, I don't know why you don't like me. I don't know what it is I did to make you mad at me. And, I don't know this guy you call Darius, or what he wants with me. What did I really do that makes you think you can get me indicted?" This was Billy's one chance to learn how much the TBI guys actually had on him.

"You're not as clever as you think you are, Billy. We're going to get you, and then you'll be the one behind bars when we're done."

* * *

When the TBI agent left, the police officer outside poked his head in to check on Billy. He mentioned that he and another officer were pulling twelve- hour shifts.

"Tell you what, you want to take a snooze, just come on in here and plop down in that chair for a few hours. Nobody will know, and I'm not going anywhere. Somebody comes in you'll hear them, or I'll wake you up. Twelve hours is a long shift when you're not doing anything."

"Tell me about it. Hey I appreciate the offer, and I may take you up on it later, okay?" After a few minutes the officer got up and left.

Billy had a plan. He hadn't swallowed the sleeping pill the nurse gave him last night. He saved it in the nightstand next to his bed.

* * *

Ralph stopped by Marsha's house and took her to work. It was early enough for them to have coffee together in the hospital cafeteria. Ralph didn't have to be at work until 9:00. Marsha was noticeably quiet. She told him about the TBI agents visiting her last night, upsetting her father.

"So what were you doing in Paradise Valley Sunday? The agent said that two people saw you there."

"Yeah, well I was just driving around, looking at houses for sale. I thought I might spot something we'd like…."

"Why is it, I'm just now hearing all this? When were you planning on telling me you were looking for a house?

And why wouldn't you take me with you? And why would I want to live there, after what has happened?"

"Hey, just calm down okay? Actually, it's a nice place. It's the sheriff that's the problem, and I seriously doubt that they'll re-elect him now, after that newspaper article exposed him."

"Were you really just looking at houses for sale?"

"Of course, what else would I be doing there?"

"I don't know, Ralph. I wish I could believe you. You're not thinking about doing something stupid are you? Like trying to get back at the sheriff?"

"What? Did that agent plant that idea in your head? Just because someone saw me there Sunday, then saw me again at the hospital, doesn't make me some sort of criminal. If you don't believe me, fine! Don't. I gotta go to work."

Ralph didn't notice Agent Cody drinking coffee at a table across the room. Cody was watching Ralph's motions, even though he couldn't hear what was being said. It was obvious that Marsha was asking questions and not buying his answers. Good, he thought. He'd try to get a written statement from her today at work. The statement would give them the motive they needed. Then they could arrest Ralph and the sheriff, and start connecting all the dots.

Chapter 24

Billy put on a bathrobe and walked out of his room, surprising the policeman outside.

"I'm just taking a walk down the hall. I need to get some exercise. Laying in that bed all day is killing me."

"Okay, but don't go too far. You expecting visitors?"

"Probably not for a while. You want to take a break, it's okay with me."

Billy walked down to the visitor's lounge. There were a few people sitting around watching TV. Billy waited five minutes then walked back to his room. The policeman wasn't outside his room. Billy planned to do this a few more times to establish a new routine. Four hours later, Billy took his second stroll down to the visitor's lounge.

This time, Bobby Lee was there, waiting for him.

"You're looking a lot better, Uncle Billy." Bobby Lee said. "I left my pickup truck in the indoor parking area on the second level. Here's the parking ticket. Your suitcase and the gym bag are on the passenger side. Here's the key. How are you going to get out of here without being seen?"

"Don't worry about it. All the money still in the gym bag?"

"Yes, Sir. I didn't touch any of it."

"I guess you're disappointed that my memory returned so fast. You might have been thinking about keeping that money."

"No, Sir. I wasn't thinking anything like that, honest."

"Don't say, 'honest'. It just tells me you're lying. Tell Harv I'll keep in touch. I figure he's letting you have the house and furniture, so that's a fair trade for your truck, don't you think?"

"Yes, Sir. That's what Paw said, too. Don't worry, we've got lots of other cars and trucks in the yard. We'll put something together, or I'll snag something out on the by-pass."

"I'd wait a while before I did that. The TBI agents will be watching you for the next year. You tell that to Dent. And don't be getting that girl of his knocked up unless you're planning on marrying her, or Dent will come after you, and I won't be around to protect you. Keep that in mind, hear?"

"Yes, Sir. Me and Robin are thinking about running away to get married, then come back and fix up the house."

"Sounds like a better plan than the one I got. Take care of yourself, Bobby Lee." Billy put the key in his robe pocket and walked slowly back to his room. He nodded to the policeman by his door. "You want to catch a few zees, come on in and use the chair inside. It's a little more comfortable than that one."

"I might take you up on that in a little while. Thanks."

Billy put his clothes and personal items into a pillow case and set it inside the closet. Then he poked his head outside the door and asked the policeman on duty if he wanted something to drink? They discussed who should go down to the cafeteria for the coffee. Billy offered to go, but the officer thought it would be better if he went. Billy gave him a dollar.

It seemed like ages before the door opened and the policeman came in carrying two cups of coffee.

"You mind if I use your toilet?" He asked.

"Go ahead. I don't mind." As soon as the man stepped into the bathroom, Billy opened the nightstand and took out the sleeping pill he'd hidden. He put it into the cup of coffee and started drinking out of the other cup. "Park your dogs," Billy repeated. This was the other policeman, but he knew they both discussed the dull duty and the few cute nurses. Obviously they discussed Billy as well, and had already determined that he didn't pose a problem.

Billy waited a half hour. The nurse who took his temperature and blood pressure had been in two hours earlier, so he wasn't expecting any visits. The policeman was sound asleep with his head leaning to one side, his mouth half open. Billy wrote a brief note and left it for Agent Cody:

> *If someone is trying to kill me, how are you planning to protect me? Or, maybe you're hoping it will happen. I don't think I want to stick around and wait for a surprise bullet.*

It was quiet in the hallway. Billy walked slowly, still in his robe, carrying the pillowcase. Nobody stopped him. Just past the visitor's lounge there was another toilet. He went in, locked the door and quickly dressed, leaving his robe, gown and slippers. As he left the hospital, he became acutely aware of how good the fresh air smelled. Prisoners released from prison must appreciate that nice fresh air smell the same way, he thought.

Billy found Bobby Lee's truck. Everything was exactly as his nephew indicated. Harvey had followed Bobby Lee to the hospital and drove him back, just as Billy instructed on the phone. Billy was pleased to see the tank was almost full of gas. He wouldn't feel really free until he was on Interstate 75, crossing into Georgia. That was only a few miles away and a completely different police jurisdiction.

* * *

Agent Noah Cody waited until Marsha Lane took a break to join her in the cafeteria. They sat at a table away from everyone else and out of hearing range.

"Marsha, we really need your help here. This sheriff doesn't deserve to be free to hurt anyone else, like he did you. I'm sure there are others he hit on as well, but we only need to prove it happened to you. Just give me the facts as you remember them, I'll record everything, have a statement typed and you can sign it before you leave today."

"I suppose it's the right thing to do."

"Yes it is. Your father and mother don't have to know the details. I don't know how much you've told Ralph…."

"He knows everything. I had to tell someone."

"And how did he take it? He isn't blaming you is he?"

"Oh no, he doesn't blame me, but he hates what happened to me. It's affected our relationship somewhat."

"That's understandable. Okay, let's start from the beginning when you were stopped by the deputy."

Marsha told him the entire sequence of events. When she finished, she felt better. Agent Cody patted her hand and thanked her. He had to get the tape transcribed and typed. The information was too sensitive to ask anyone at the hospital to do it, so he drove back to his office, leaving agent Mathews in the lobby to watch for anyone asking for Billy's room. There was a possibility that Darius might return since he was so determined to talk with Billy.

Agent Mathews decided to take a walk and smoke a cigarette outside. He could see the entrance. He was just finishing his cigarette when he spotted Harvey pull into the garage followed by his son, Bobby Lee in another truck. It struck him as odd that they wouldn't be riding together.

He decided to maintain a lookout from his present position until Cody returned. One cigarette later, to his surprise, Harvey's truck was leaving the garage with both of them in the cab. Now that was really strange, since they hadn't been at the hospital more than 10 minutes. It was a very brief visit, he thought.

Ralph stopped by the hospital early, carrying a bouquet of flowers. When he couldn't find Marsha, he gave them to one of the volunteers to put into a vase with water. While he was waiting, he decided to walk past the sheriff's room. When he arrived, he didn't see anyone outside, guarding the door. He thought, maybe they moved the sheriff to another room. When he pushed open the door to take a look, he found the policeman sound asleep, slumped in a chair.

Ralph checked the bathroom, the sheriff wasn't in the there, either. He was gone! As Ralph was leaving, he ran into the Nurse Supervisor coming in. Both were surprised. She too was curious about not seeing a guard posted outside, and decided to check on the patient. She was startled to find the young man coming out of the room.

"What are you doing in this room?" She asked Ralph. Then she spotted the policeman and for a second, she thought something had happened to him. She ran to the bedside call button and pushed it, at the same time yelling at Ralph not to leave. All the commotion woke the policeman from his sound sleep. Panicked, Ralph pushed past the older woman and ran down the hall. The nurse called security and alerted them of a young man probably attempting to leave the facility. The policeman used his cell phone to alert a guard in the lobby area.

Agent Cody was just arriving back at the hospital and saw his associate, Agent Mathews stopping a pickup at the parking garage exit. Billy was behind the wheel.

"Sorry Billy, you forgot to make arrangements to pay the hospital bill. And, you're officially under arrest now, so get out of the truck and turn around." Agent Mathews said.

"I know the drill, spare me, okay?"

"Ah, it seems your memory is returning." Agent Cody said.

Billy was now in handcuffs and being escorted back inside the hospital. There was a flurry of activity in the lobby. A security guard was standing by the entrance. As soon as he explained what was happening, Cody knew it was Ralph they were looking for. He instructed Agent Mathews to hang onto Billy while he went out to the employee parking lot, looking for Ralph's Jeep.

"He's running. We've got to contain him here." Cody yelled. He hopped into the pickup Billy had been driving, and raced for the employee parking area. He spotted the camo-Jeep and blocked it with the pickup. Ralph wasn't there, and he would be unable to leave in his Jeep with it blocked in.

The problem was, there were too many exits to watch and too few security people. The problem was enhanced by the fact that Ralph knew the hospital layout. He was no stranger to the facility and the daily activity.

Ralph was about to leave by a back exit that many of the hospital staff used, when he spotted a security guard coming. He stepped back into a small alcove with vending machines and waited. The security guard opened the door and looked inside, not seeing Ralph. As he turned, Ralph came out of his hiding place and took the guard by surprise, knocking him out then dragging his limp body into the hallway. There was another door leading into a stairwell. Ralph pulled the man inside and immediately started changing clothes.

Agent Mathews knew that Cody needed additional help. He turned Billy over to the Security Guard in the lobby.

"Don't let him out of your sight, for any reason." Mathews explained, heading for Marsha's station on the third floor.

At the same time as Agent Mathews was taking the elevator up to the third floor, Ralph came down the hallway, past the information desk and saw Billy in handcuffs, standing beside a security guard whose nametag said, 'Will'. Ralph looked at the nametag on the shirt he was wearing, it said, 'Hank'. Ralph used the confusion to his advantage. He called to Will as he approached.

"Hey Will, they caught the guy. They need you in the cafeteria. I'll take care of this character." Ralph turned to Billy, so that his back was to Will, hoping the ruse would work. None of the security guards carried weapons, so Ralph still had the advantage of surprise in case he was recognized. Billy did not know Ralph, so he couldn't raise any alarm.

"Let's take a walk," Ralph said to Billy, grabbing his arm and guiding him out the main hospital entrance.

"Well lookie here. If it isn't Billy!" Darius said loudly arriving just as Ralph and Billy were leaving.

"Hey Darius, I heard you were trying to see me. Now might be a good time for that talk…." Billy held up his wrists displaying the handcuffs and nodded toward Ralph who was yelling.

"Get out of the way!" Ralph foolishly attempted to push past Darius.

"What's your hurry, Sport? He's not going anywhere. We've got a few things to talk over. Let's go back inside and sit down." Darius grabbed Billy's other arm.

"Let go of him!" Ralph ordered, pulling on Billy's arm.

"No, Siree. He's not going anywhere just yet." Darius stepped in front of Ralph and grabbed his shirt pulling him forward. "Why don't you just take a five-minute break?"

The two men were struggling with Billy just outside the front entrance when Agent Cody appeared yelling, "Freeze, all of you!"

Agent Cody had his automatic pistol aimed at the group. Suddenly Ralph let go of Billy's arm and started to run. He felt the bullet hit him before he heard the blast, it happened that fast.

He was on the ground, bleeding and going into shock. As he was about to lose consciousness, the last thing he heard was, "So where's my fifty grand, Billy?"

THE END

Epilogue

A Grand Jury was presented with sufficient evidence to indict Billy Hargis on numerous felony charges, including sexual assault on a prisoner. The week before his trial in Harmon County, the wire services were running a follow up to Edgar Ames' earlier piece, entitling it: *Corruption in Paradise.*

A spokesman for TBI explained how they used the sheriff to trap Ralph Goodwin. "It's a technique African natives use when hunting lions. We used a tethered goat. We called it Operation Billy Goat."

Ralph Goodwin survived his gunshot wound and was indicted for the murder of Deputy Terry Wolfe and the attempted murder of former Sheriff, Billy Hargis.

Darius Ott never recovered the $ 50,000 he claimed the sheriff stole from him. Later, the IRS would have a few questions about where the money came from.

Deputy Willoughby Jones was easily elected sheriff of Harmon County with the full support of Bovis Tinch. The celebration was held in his new barn, to be used once again for Saturday night auctions with increased seating capacity.

Eulla Stump became Mrs. Billy Hargis the day before she was scheduled to testify against him in court. Edgar Ames thought of it as a double sentence for Billy and true poetic justice. He sent copies of the newspaper to Nick Alexander, so he could follow all the unfolding events.

About the Author

Richard Standring is retired after a 30- year career in advertising and industrial magazine publishing. During that same period, he maintained a commercial pilot'slicense and owned a variety of aircraft. His father, Edgar, was a professional pilot who taught many people to fly in the Cleveland, Ohio area. Richard's current pastimes are restricted to golf, gardening and writing.

In addition to writing novels, he also writes poetry, short stories and essays. A collection of these is planned for publication at a later date under the title, *Somewhere Along the Way*. Readers can view his poems on the Internet by going to: www.poetry.com.

Richard is originally from Cleveland, OH. He wrote his first novel, **Hustle** about some of the legends in advertising in Cleveland in the '50s and '60s. He currently lives in Cookeville, TN where he plays golf most of the year. Readers who wish to contact him with comments can do so by going to: wordmerchant@cookeville.com